MW01136022

ENTICING DAPHNE

A SASSY ROMANCE

JESSICA PRINCE

Coming Full Circle
A Broken Soul

CIVIL CORRUPTION SERIES

Corrupt
Defile (Declan and Tatum's story – coming 2018)

GIRL TALK SERIES:

Seducing Lola
Tempting Sophia
Enticing Daphne
Charming Fiona

STANDALONE TITLES:

Chance Encounters
Nightmares from Within

DEADLY LOVE SERIES:

Destructive
Addictive

CO-WRITTEN BOOKS:

Hustler – with Meghan Quinn

PROLOGUE

DAPHNE

HAVING two best friends who didn't believe in true love had sometimes been a pain in the ass, especially since I'd been living in monogamous, sex-with-one-person-for-the-rest-of-my-life bliss.

I'd been one of the lucky ones. I found the love of my life early, and was determined to hold on to him with both hands. The day Stefan proposed was the best day of my life. I hadn't thought it possible to be any happier than I already was.

I had the perfect ring, the perfect dress, the perfect flowers. I had the perfect fiancé, and I was going to have the perfect wedding.

Everything was just. Fucking. *Perfect.*

Until it wasn't.

See, that so-called love of my life? Well, it turned out I was the only one in our relationship who felt that way. Unfortunately, the inconsiderate son of a bitch hadn't had the courtesy to give me a heads-up that he'd changed his mind about the whole 'until death do us part' thing.

I could have been spared so much humiliation if he'd just manned up and said, *"Sorry, Daph, darling, but I've had a change of heart. I've decided that loving you through sickness and health is just too much stress to put on one man."*

Oh no. Instead, he decided to take the chickenshit route and keep quiet about the whole ordeal. I don't know what he intended to do once our wedding day finally arrived, but if it hadn't been for the fact that I walked in on him and my mother in bed together, I probably never would have known he'd been cheating.

And yes, I said my *mother*! My own flesh and blood, the loins of my fruit, was sleeping with my fiancé.

I'd been living on cloud nine, totally oblivious that the two people who meant the most to me had turned me into a complete laughingstock. Not only had they been carrying on their affair right under my nose, but, with the exception of Lola and Sophia, most everyone in my social circle already knew about it.

Apparently, unless one of the three of us was around, they hadn't taken great strides in hiding what they were doing.

I grew up knowing my mom was different from all the other mothers I saw dropping their kids off at school. She dressed and acted younger than her age, and after divorcing my father when I was little, my mother had one boyfriend after another, none of them coming even remotely close to her age. She acted more like my best friend than a parent, and for the longest time I thought that was cool. I considered myself lucky that I had a mom who'd let me stay up late, eat junk food, and watch movies most of my classmates weren't allowed to see yet. But the older I got, the more I started to realize that it wasn't just her being laid-back and lenient. No, turned out she just didn't care all that much to be a parent.

Once I hit my late teens, things turned into a competition with her. It was all about who was skinnier, who had the best clothes, the best hair. She even tried turning relationships into a competition, whose boyfriend was hotter. It was absolutely ridiculous, and I tried my hardest not to engage.

Obviously, that didn't matter. Finding her with Stefan made things completely clear—she was going to take what was mine no matter what.

It was fun finding out the man I was planning on spending the rest of my life with had been banging my own flesh and blood for well over a year and that they'd decided to go and fall in love with each other. And by fun, I meant it felt like a million white-hot needles piercing my eyeballs.

Needless to say, I crumbled into a billion pieces. I was inconsolable, a total fucking mess. After locking myself in my apartment and living in the wedding dress I'd never get the chance to wear in public for a solid week, my girls staged an intervention.

It couldn't have come soon enough. I looked like the Bride of Frankenstein by the end of day six. My hair was a greasy, stringy mess. I hadn't washed or moisturized *any* part of my body in far too long. I had pizza sauce and chocolate syrup—that I'd sucked straight from the bottle because I was classy like that —splattered all over my gown.

It was a sight to see. A horrifying one.

Luckily, I had the best friends in the whole entire world, and they were able to kick my ass out of my misery.

It was thanks to them that I was able to get my shit straight and pull my life back together. But the damage from that day had already been done.

I had been forced to learn the ugly truth, that happily-ever-afters were bullshit created by greeting card companies and the Lifetime Movie Network to give women a false sense of hope.

True love didn't exist.

Well, maybe it did, but not without consequences. And I'd

been bitten by that particularly poisonous snake once already. I wasn't about to let it strike again.

I gave up on finding *Mr. Right* and started concentrating on finding *Mr. Right Now.* And I spent the following years teaching other women to do the same. You know, if that was the direction they were already leaning toward.

I wasn't bitter. I was resigned. I built a life that didn't revolve around finding a man, and it was a damn good one.

After my failed first attempt at jumping on the marriage bandwagon, I'd officially joined my friends in the *All Guys Are Assholes* club, and I was totally content to stay there.

After all, once burned, twice shy, right?

No way in hell I was ever going down that road again.

CHAPTER ONE

I LIFTED the mojito the bartender set in front of me and took a long, healthy sip, letting out a relieved sigh after the freshness of the mint and the tang of the lime juice hit my taste buds.

It was exactly what I needed after the week from hell I'd had. I hadn't spoken a word to my mother in damn near seven years. I'd cut both her and Stefan out of my life completely after their betrayal, even going as far as moving and not giving them my new address. But somehow my mom had found me, and for reasons unknown—because there was no fucking way I was going to answer—she'd been blowing up my phone. I had no desire to hear a word she had to say. Two people that despicable deserved each other, and I hoped they made each other miserable. To say I needed a stress reliever was putting it mildly.

I needed to blow off a crazy amount of steam.

And the alcohol was only part of my process. Placing the drink back on the bar top, I turned and scanned the crowd. I'd picked this particular bar for a reason: it was a regular hangout for the thirty-plus business types. I'd gone through my hipster phase, my bad boy phase, and my party boy phase. Now I was all about the sexy thirtysomething professionals who had enough maturity and experience to know how to please a woman in bed.

Unfortunately, it looked like all the good ones were either staying in for the night or hanging somewhere else. I spun my stool back to the bar and picked up my drink, prepared to down the last of it and head home for the evening. Alone. It wasn't ideal, but I wasn't going to settle, even when it came to my one-night stands.

I smiled at the cute bartender—too bad he was too young and too emo for my liking—and slid a couple bills his way before standing and hooking my purse on my shoulder.

"Please tell me the most beautiful woman I've ever seen isn't leaving just as I get here."

I glanced to the right at the man who'd spoken, my interest suddenly piqued despite the lame, clichéd line he used.

His sandy colored hair was styled in a way that said he put in just enough effort to highlight his attractiveness, but not so much that it was obvious he was trying. Golden tanned skin stretched across a jaw and cheekbones that looked like they'd been carved from granite. A strong nose and sky-blue eyes ringed with a thin band of dark gray rounded out his sexy face. My gaze traveled along his impressively tall frame dressed in a designer suit with his jacket slung carelessly over one shoulder.

It was clear he worked out, but he wasn't one of those meat-heads with muscles so thick their heads looked too small for their bodies. He was somewhat lean, but the definition of some impressive biceps showed through his button-down, and his shirtsleeves were rolled up, revealing some lovely forearm porn.

I pasted my most seductive grin on my lips. "Was that your attempt at a pickup line?"

He dropped his jacket onto the empty barstool next to the one I'd been sitting on and leaned his elbows against the bar. The corner of his mouth ticked up in a smirk, revealing two rows of straight white teeth. *Mmm, he's cute.* "Depends. Did it work?"

I shook my head, my voice full of humor as I answered, "No. Not at all."

His chuckle was like melted chocolate— warm, soothing, and sinful. "In that case, it wasn't a line at all. But seeing as you were just picturing me naked two seconds ago, I'm hoping you won't hold my lack of pickup line prowess against me."

"Hmm." I lifted a single brow, toying with him the way I liked to toy with all the guys I picked up. It made things more interesting, fun. "Well, how about you buy me a drink and I'll see what I can do?"

I dropped my purse off my shoulder, hooking it along the back of my stool, and sat back down. He took the one next to mine and lifted his hand to grab the bartender's attention, ordering me another mojito and himself a whiskey on the rocks.

"So," he started once we had our drinks, "what's a gorgeous woman like you doing here all by yourself?"

Swirling the straw around in my glass, I smiled before placing it between my lips and sipping. "For the same reason you are, I'd assume."

He leaned close, his elbow brushing against mine. "Is that right?" he asked in a flirtatious tone. "And what do you think my reason is?"

I turned my whole body in his direction, crossing my legs and sitting up straight. I playfully assessed him from top to toe. "Do I get a prize if I'm right?"

"You're a sassy little thing, aren't you, gorgeous? Tell you what. If you're right, maybe we'll both get a prize at the end of the night."

I tossed my head back with a laugh. "You really are sure of yourself."

His throat worked as he tipped back the amber liquid and

took a healthy swallow, the ice clinking against the cut glass. He set it down with a contented sigh and turned his attention back to me. "I could ply you with more alcohol and pretty words, but where's the honesty in that? I'm a blunt kind of guy. I tell it how it is, and the truth is, if you leave this bar with me I can guaran-damn-tee you'll get off enough times you'll have trouble walking before the night is over."

I almost choked on my mojito. Blunt was an understatement. But I damn sure appreciated him laying it out the way he did. It cut through all the unnecessary bullshit. "And I'm all about honesty." I lifted my drink and clinked it against his. "So I was right, then. You're here to pick up a woman for the night."

"And you're here to pick up a guy. Just my luck."

Okay, this guy checked every one of my boxes when it came to choosing a hookup. Hot? Check. Confident? Check. Able to hold a conversation without talking directly to my tits? Check. Although, I did catch him sneaking a peek once or twice, just long enough for me to know without a doubt that he was interested.

"Cocky or just confident?" I asked, sucking down the last of my mojito.

"Neither. Just stating facts. How about another round?"

Two was my limit on nights I picked up a man. And before you get carried away, it wasn't something I did *all the time*. I wasn't a whore. I just had a healthy sexual appetite. Usually I had a man or two—or sometimes three—who I kept on speed dial. Soph and Lola liked to refer to it as my roster. I typically only had random hookups when a couple of the guys on my 'roster' started getting clingy, wanting more than I was willing to give.

That was why I was out tonight. Aaron and Dylan had both been bitten by the commitment bug and were now gone. Just another example of how the past few days had gone to complete shit.

"Tell you what," I started, picking up my purse once more. "How about we stop delaying the inevitable and get out of here?"

"Can I at least get your name first?"

I uncrossed my legs, planted one foot on the ground, and stood up between the two stools, bringing me even closer to the sexy stranger. "How about you just stick with calling me Gorgeous and I'll call you Blue Eyes? No need in learning the name of someone you're never going to see again, right?"

He tossed two twenties onto the bar and climbed off the stool, grabbing his jacket with one hand and placing the other at the small of my back. "Woman after my own heart. So where to? My place or yours?"

I shot him a wink and started for the door. "Depends on who's closer."

OH. My. God!

He was so much better than I ever would have expected.

My head fell back, my neck unable to support it, as I rode him harder. I was close. So fucking close. His cock hit places inside me that most men couldn't find with a flashlight and a map. "Oh god," I whimpered, digging my nails into his defined pecs as I lifted and slammed down. Over and over.

When we'd gotten back to his place and I got him naked, I almost drooled at the sight of what that suit had been covering up. Firm pecs, chiseled abs, and that damn V carved along his hip bones that dipped into the waistband of his trousers.

Ladies, he had the V! I wanted to lick every single glorious inch of him, but he had other ideas, basically stripping me completely bare and feasting on me like I was Thanksgiving dinner. I came twice from his mouth alone before he flipped us and demanded I ride his cock.

I'll admit, even with my level of experience, the size of it had intimidated me when he first pulled it from his pants. But I'd never been a quitter.

"Fuck yeah, baby. That's it." He squeezed my hips tighter as he forced me to grind against him, rubbing my clit along the base of his dick. "Jesus, *fuck*. You're so goddamn hot."

Stars burst behind my eyelids, my whimpers turning into short, loud cries as my orgasm began washing over me. Just as I was about to come, I felt myself flying through the air—literally.

My back hit the mattress and Blue Eyes began pounding into me at an unrelenting pace. And I exploded. I screamed so loud he had to muffle the sound with his palm.

"Sorry, Gorgeous," he ground out. "Can't have you waking the neighbors."

I panted and mewled against his hand as one orgasm bled into the next. The edges of my vision started to turn black. I feared the lack of oxygen was going to cause me to pass out, but *damn* it was worth it.

Just when I thought I couldn't take it any longer and my eyes were about to roll back in my head, Blue Eyes let out a ferocious growl, followed by "Yes. Yes. *Fuck yes!*" Then he began to roar so loud I had to slap *my* hand over *his* mouth.

"Sorry, Blue Eyes," I mumbled once we'd both started to come down. "Couldn't have you waking the neighbors."

His chest rattled against mine as he laughed. Cool air rushed over me, causing goose bumps to break out across my skin as he exited the bed. He went to the attached bathroom to deal with the condom, and I climbed from the bed and began searching for my clothes that were strewn all around the room.

I'd just slipped my panties back on and was pulling my bra

from where it was draped over the lamp when he spoke, making me jump. "Where do you think you're going?"

I smiled, slipping my arms into the bra straps. "Pretty sure we both got our prizes for the night, wouldn't you say?"

He slowly made his way toward me, not the slightest bit self-conscious with his nakedness—not that he had any reason to be. "Oh, but I'm nowhere near done with that sexy little body of yours."

My eyes nearly bugged out of my head. "*Already?*"

His large hands spanned my waist. "I'm not as young as I used to be, so I'll need a bit more recovery time, but that doesn't mean I can't eat you again." He placed kisses along my neck as he spoke. "And that's." *Kiss.* "Exactly." *Kiss.* "What I plan to do."

I let out a peel of laughter as he lifted me off the ground and threw me to the bed.

By the time I finally dressed and headed back to my house, I'd come three more times. And just like he'd promised, I had trouble walking thanks to my jelly-like legs.

Best. One-night stand. *Ever.*

CHAPTER TWO

DAPHNE

TWO AND A HALF months later

SOMETHING WAS WRONG WITH ME. Like seriously wrong. I couldn't figure out why I'd been in such a slump the past couple of months, but it was like something inside me was broken.

I hated to admit it, but every sexual experience I'd had in the past two and a half months—all *two* of them—had fallen embarrassingly short of the mark. Usually if a dude wasn't up to the task of getting me off, I was able to take control of the situation and get there on my own. But since my night with the man I'd dubbed Mr. Perfect Penis, my orgasms had packed up and disappeared. It was like he'd ruined my va-jay-jay for all other men. *The selfish bastard!*

I hadn't bothered to get his name or number after our hot night together, so I wasn't even able to call him up and demand he fix me. It was starting to mess with my head to the point that I was having trouble focusing at work.

My job as a co-host to Washington's number one talk radio

show, *Girl Talk*, was to offer advice to women with man troubles. Usually I was on point. I'd been doing this show with my two best friends, Lola and Sophia, for the past ten years and loved every aspect about it. But recently I'd been struggling. Case in point: I was barely paying attention to what our current caller was whining about.

"Well... I've been with my boyfriend for about six months now, and lately I've been thinking about breaking up with him," Rose (the caller) droned on.

Lola spoke into her microphone across the studio from me. "And why have you thought about breaking up with him?"

I could hear Rose's breathing through my headset. "The thing is... God, this is so embarrassing."

"Nothing to be embarrassed about," Lola soothed. "We're all friends here. Just let it out."

Typically I was the one offering our listeners comfort. The three of us had our roles when we were on air. Lola was the hard-ass, Sophia was the one to tell it like it was, and I was the soft-spoken shoulder they could lean on.

"Okay," Rose sighed. "Well you see, my boyfriend... he's...."

Something finally registered between all her hemming and hawing, and I found myself blurting out a question. "Is the sex bad?"

"No, no. The sex is good. It's... the stuff leading *up* to the sex that's bad."

Well that certainly got my attention.

"You mean foreplay?" Lola asked.

"Yes. Foreplay. You see... my boyfriend's not very good at... going downtown."

Ding, ding, ding! Ladies and gentlemen, we have a winner!
"Ah," I said knowingly. "We're following."

Lola rolled her eyes, and I knew right then that she was thinking the exact thing I was. "Okay, look," she cut in. "You're not the first woman to call in with this particular complaint, Rose. I've got to ask... have you bothered to try and *teach* your boyfriend what you want him to do down there?"

"Well... no, not really. I mean, he's twenty-five years old. Shouldn't he know what he's doing by now?"

I smacked my forehead. Sometimes I couldn't understand my fellow women.

"See, this is the problem with the younger generation," Lola scolded. "You expect to get whatever you want without having to actually work for it. Here's the hard truth, Rose. Men aren't born with the innate ability to give amazing oral. Just like everything, it's an acquired skill, something taught over time. You can't possibly expect him to just dive in and know what he's doing if you and all the girls before you never bothered to guide him in the right direction.

"You need to pull up your big girl panties and take the bull by the horns—literally. Grab hold of his hair next time he goes downtown and show him what you want. Use your words. When he hits a spot you like, moan, scream, '*Yes*, right there!' Do *something* to let him know what works and what doesn't. Don't be afraid to be vocal. You're in your midtwenties, sweetheart. If you're unhappy with the foreplay in your relationship, there's really no one to blame but yourself."

Right on, sister!

"But... wouldn't he find that offensive?"

"We aren't telling you to give him a bullet-point list of instructions," Sophia said, finally joining the conversation. "There's no need to bruise his ego or insult him. You can do it without him even realizing what's going on. Make it sexy. Compliment him when he does something right. Reward him for a job well done by returning the favor. Trust me, he'll get off on it and keep doing what you like if he sees it's getting results."

"We've said it on this show a hundred times, and we'll say it again," Lola added. "You're just as responsible for your own pleasure as he is... maybe even more so. You can't just sit back and expect to see the results you want. You have to demand them, work for them. You want the best sex of your life? Then teach your man to give it to you."

Rose sounded leery as she asked, "You really think that will work?"

"Oh, most definitely, honey." Lola grinned. "Now you be sure to call us and let us know how it goes."

"Okay, I will. Thanks, you guys! This was exactly what I needed to hear."

"No problem," Lola told her. "We're happy to help out. And we look forward to hearing from you again, Rose."

I let out a relieved sigh when the On Air light clicked off and our producer Jerry spoke through our headphones. "All right, ladies, that's a wrap. Good show."

I slipped my headphones off and set them down, closing my eyes and rubbing at my temples to stave off the nagging headache building in my skull. Thanks to my wandering mind, I wasn't paying attention to what was going on around me until Lola's clipped, agitated tone pulled me back. "What, are you stalking me now?"

My head shot up, my eyelids flying open at the sound of Grayson Lockhart's voice. I'd been on edge for a while now when it came to that man. All three of us had. Ever since the debacle where we'd accidentally humiliated the CEO of our parent company, things had been strained. Unexpectedly, Grayson had turned his sights on Lola almost immediately after that. Not that she wasn't beautiful enough to hold his attention, because she certainly was, but it had been surprising that he'd begun to pursue her right after we inadvertently smeared his name far and wide.

It had been a surprisingly entertaining turn of events,

because even though she acted as soft as a porcupine toward the man, Sophia and I had seen beneath the act. She *liked* him, a lot, whether she was willing to admit it or not.

But as hilarious as it had been to watch her struggle against her attraction to the handsome man these past couple of weeks, that wasn't what had caught my interest at that moment.

Oh no, what had me struck completely speechless was the man who'd walked into the studio *with* Grayson. It was none other than Mr. Perfect Penis himself, almost as if my mind had conjured him out of thin air. Words failed me because *good Lord*, the man was even sexier than I'd remembered. My lady parts cried out with joy at the sight of him even as the rest of my body was frozen in disbelief.

He stuck out his hand for Lola to shake. "Hi. Caleb McMannus. Huge fan of the show. *Huge*," he declared emphatically.

She returned the gesture and quickly made introductions for the rest of us. My heart rate spiked, pounding against my ribs, quick and angry the instant those strange blue eyes of his landed on me. Something flared within them that I thought to be recognition.

But then he spoke. "Hi, I'm Caleb," he repeated, somewhat dazedly. "I'm an Aquarius, thirty-five years old, the CFO of Bandwidth, and I learned the proper way to go down on a woman when I was sixteen."

My eyes nearly bugged out of their sockets. It wasn't recognition I saw in his gaze, not at all. *Holy. Freaking. Shit.* He didn't remember me. He gave me the best sex of my life, effectively breaking my girly bits, and he didn't remember me? Talk about the ultimate humiliation. *That son of a bitch!*

Lola made a strange choking noise in the back of her throat and Sophia snorted with humor, neither of them aware of the raging embarrassment coursing through my blood.

Grayson cursed. "Excuse my friend," he apologized on behalf of Mr. Perfect Penis—now known as Mr. Douche Canoe. "He was dropped on his head as an infant... a lot."

I bit the inside of my cheek nervously. "Uh...." I didn't know what to do, what to say, where to put my hands, how to act. It was like years of confidence had just flitted away with that one rejection. "Good to know, I guess." I shot a look to Lola, pleading with my eyes for her to jump in and save me somehow.

Caleb was looking at me like he wanted to lick me up like an ice cream cone. That look from a man as hot as him usually would have made my belly flutter, but I couldn't get past the fact that the asshole seemed to have forgotten he already did that. More than once!

My ego had taken a serious hit. I needed to get the hell out of there so I could wallow in self-pity and chocolate in an attempt to repair it. I didn't know what I wanted to do more, kick him in the balls or burst into tears. It was looking like a strong tie at the moment.

"Well, it's been a pleasure and all, but we were just heading out to lunch, so...." Lola pointed over her shoulder and started moving backward.

Grayson wasn't having any of it. "Ah, ah, ah. Not so fast. You and I have lunch plans."

"We most certainly do not!"

They started to argue, but I was too busy internally freaking *the fuck* out to care. "Well, we should be going!" I exclaimed, my tone sounding far too chipper in my own ears. "We'll see you later, Lo."

I hooked Sophia's elbow with mine and started pulling her out the door. I heard Caleb shout from behind me just when I thought I'd safely escaped. "I'll walk you out!"

Damn it!

"Dude, slow down." I was practically running down the

hall, dragging Sophia behind me. She stumbled on her heels, forcing me to stop. "What's gotten into you?"

"Nothing. I'm just hungry. Let's go."

But it was too late. The guy formerly known as Mr. Perfect Penis, a.k.a. Mr. Douche Canoe had caught up.

"Hey." Sophia, oblivious to my inner turmoil, looked my way and said, "I'll go grab our purses. Be right back."

Caleb was still looking at me like I was his next meal as he asked, "So where are we heading?"

"*We* aren't heading anywhere," I answered sharply. "My friend and I are going for dumplings. Nice meeting you, *Caleb*." I spit his name like it tasted foul, then turned to stomp off only to have him stop me by grabbing hold of my elbow.

"Whoa, hold on, beautiful."

I swung back around, skewering him with a nasty look. Those intense blue eyes of his scanned every inch of my face. For a second, I thought the jerk might actually lean in and kiss me. Instead he asked the one question that was most likely to turn me homicidal.

"Do I know you?"

Oh *hell* no.

CHAPTER THREE

CALEB

I'D NEVER HAD a woman look at me with such disdain before. I didn't consider myself perfect—far from it, in fact—but I was well aware of my effect on women, and to say her reaction to me just then was surprising was an understatement.

Her mouth opened and closed like a goldfish. "I'm... you... I can't... are you...," she stammered. "Do you *know me*?" she asked in bewilderment. "Do. You. *Know*. Me?"

Hearing her repeat the question, slowly, like she was speaking to a five-year-old, didn't make me understand what was happening any better.

I nodded, racking my brain to try and remember where it was I knew her from. "I swear to god I know you from somewhere. You look so familiar."

She did that open-close thing again with her mouth before barking, "You asshole!" Then she turned on her heels and stormed off.

Minutes ago I'd been in the sound booth with Grayson and the two guys who ran the behind-the-scenes part of the radio show, watching the blonde with the killer rack and a set of legs that went for miles. Now I was standing in an empty hallway with my mouth hanging open like an idiot. "What the hell just happened?" I asked myself.

"Seems to me you just got blown off by the insanely hot Daphne King." I whipped around at the unexpected voice and saw the pimply faced kid who'd been in the booth with us earlier. "What'd you do, bang her and forget to call her the next day or something?"

"What? Of course not! I'd remember someone like h—" Visions of a stunning blonde with a body made for sin and no gag reflex suddenly filled my head. "Oh fuck," I groaned. It had been more than two months since that night, but it was definitely her.

"Holy shit," the kid breathed. "You totally forgot her, didn't you? You forgot having sex with Daphne King? Jeez, man, are you crazy? That woman's like God's gift to the universe!"

She'd rocked my entire fucking world that night. I remembered thinking that I was going to do everything in my power to track her ass down after she left. Then my mother had called in hysterics. She and my father had gotten into one of their epic fights once again and I had to clean up the mess. Unfortunately, after weeks of dealing with their bullshit, the best sex of my life had become a distant memory.

"Wow," the kid kept going. "I mean just... *wow*. I can't—"

"All right!" I snapped, not needing this video-game-playing, basement-dwelling virgin making me feel worse than I already did. "I get it, I get it."

He held his hands out. "Sorry, sorry. It's just... *Daphne King*. I'd give my mint-condition copy of the Batman #7 comic for a night with her, and that's saying a lot. I mean, it has one of the earliest appearances of the Joker." He snorted, like I had the first fucking clue what he was talking about.

"I said I got it! I fucked up."

"Uh, yeah you did." He started laughing uncontrollably as he wandered off, leaving me feeling like an even bigger ass.

I took the elevator back to my floor and headed for my office, racking my brain for a way to fix what I'd done. Sure, blowing off women wasn't something new for me. I made myself perfectly clear that I wasn't looking for more than a couple hours of fun before ever taking a woman to bed, but that didn't mean they always listened. I took what I wanted and left without a backward glance, sometimes upsetting the fairer sex in the process. The way I saw it, it wasn't my fault that women chose not to listen when a man spelled it out for them.

But Daphne had been different. She hadn't wanted any more from me than I'd wanted from her. She was like a sexy, feminine version of myself. And she was smokin' fucking hot in bed. I hated myself for not remembering. If I didn't make it right, there'd be no chance of me getting her back into bed, and now that I knew she was only a few floors away, every single fiber of my body cried out to go caveman on her ass and drag her back to my cave for a repeat performance.

But there wasn't a chance in hell of that happening if she hated me.

I got to my desk and sat down with a heavy sigh. I needed to formulate a plan, something to get back in that woman's good graces, but before I could start the intercom on my phone buzzed.

"Mr. McMannus," my assistant, Stacy, called through the speaker. "There's a call for you on line one."

"Thanks, Stacy. Put them through."

She did as asked and I hit the button to answer the call. "This is Caleb McMannus."

"Hey, dipshit. You sound so professional over the phone. I almost couldn't tell you were a raging asshole."

I rolled my eyes at the sound of Deacon Lockhart's voice.

He was my buddy Grayson's little brother, and I'd grown up around both of them. He was a good guy for the most part, but he loved to give me shit for my reputation as a man-whore just like his brother did.

"Well if that's not the pot calling the kettle black," I returned. "Have you spoken to your big bro lately, or are you still avoiding him for reasons unknown?" It was a touchy subject between the Lockharts, who I considered to be my second family. The three of us had all grown up close, but sometime after college, Deacon and Gray's relationship turned sour. No one really knew why except for Deac, and he wasn't talking about it. It got so bad that he refused to come work for Bandwidth, his father's company, choosing to use his trust fund to open a bar instead of joining the family business.

I'd ended up as CFO, the position Nolan Lockhart had been grooming his youngest son for, when Deacon informed his dad he wasn't coming on board, and it was still a bone of contention between the family to this day.

"As much fun as delving into my family's drama is for you, that's not why I'm calling. I need you to get down to the bar."

My back shot straight. "Why? What's going on?" I had a sick feeling in the pit of my stomach that I knew what he was going to say before he even said it.

"It's your mom, man. I hate to have to call you with this, but she's in a bad way. Figured you'd want to be the first person I called to handle it."

Fuck. I knew it.

"I'll be right there." I disconnected the call before he could say anything else and rushed out of the office, ignoring all the strange looks I was getting from the employees as I passed.

It only took fifteen minutes to get from my office to Deacon's bar, but past experience had already taught me that my mother didn't need even that long to get into trouble. I'd been taking care of her for most of my life.

She'd always been an extremely sensitive woman with a fragile disposition. I'd grown up walking on eggshells, always mindful not to do anything that could send her into one of her alcohol-induced crying jags.

Most of the time it had been all for nothing, considering she'd fallen in love with, and tied herself—for better and for worse—to a coldhearted bastard without an empathetic bone in his body.

My father was an asshole who cheated and manipulated to get his way, not taking into consideration the people he stepped on along the way. He broke my mother's heart over and over, and I was the one left to clean up the mess. I'd spent years trying to convince her to leave his sorry ass, but she always refused, claiming Dad was the love of her life, that she'd be lost without him.

Their dysfunctional shit show of a relationship was why I wouldn't allow myself to be tied down by a woman. I'd seen firsthand what love could do to a person, and I wanted *nothing* to do with it.

I shoved through the thick wooden doors of Deacon's bar, The Black Sheep. It was a name so incredibly telling it was almost laughable. I never said it out loud, choosing to let the Lockharts bury their heads in the sand the way I did about my own flesh and blood, but I often wondered if it would have been subtler for Deacon to name his bar My Parents Loved My Older Brother More Than Me.

I guessed every family had their own dirty little secrets. And mine was currently sitting on a barstool in a dimly lit bar in the middle of the goddamn day sucking back martinis like she was worried there was about to be a global shortage of gin.

Sidling up to the bar, I took a stool next to her. I tilted my chin up at Deacon, getting a similar gesture in return, then looked over at my mom to see she was already good and liquored up.

I placed my hand on her back to get her attention. "Hey, Mom."

Her glassy eyes trailed a few seconds slower than her head as she turned to look at me. "Oh, Caleb," she slurred, rocking precariously on the stool. "Darling, I think your father's having an affair."

I tried my hardest not to roll my eyes as she sniffled and wiped at the lone tear that broke free and trickled down her cheek. It was the exact same song and dance we'd been doing since I was old enough to speak. For the life of me, I couldn't understand why she kept doing this to herself. This wasn't my father's first affair. Hell, it wasn't even his third. He'd delved right into double digits before I graduated college, for Christ's sake. For all intents and purposes, my mother had been his trophy wife, the young, beautiful woman he'd flaunt at events and parties. She was the pretty thing he stored on a shelf while he ran around with his mistresses, pulling her down only when the occasion called for it. And she'd allowed it for as long as I could remember, diving deeper and deeper into the bottle and prescription pills to soothe the ache instead of doing anything about it.

I was sick and fucking tired of having to be the mature one in my relationship with my mother. Most of my life it felt like *I* was the parent, and I resented the hell out of her for putting me in that position. I couldn't understand why she wouldn't stand up for herself, why she didn't demand better. She'd settled for the life my father provided because the money was too good to pass up, and had willingly thrown me into a position no child should've had to endure.

But the fact remained that she was my mother and I loved

her, so I did what I had to do. It was because of situations like this that I hadn't had room in my brain to remember something as outstanding as my night with Daphne.

McMannus skeletons were to remain firmly in the closet, never to come out and risk tarnishing the family name and its legacy. If I wasn't running interference with my parents, drying out my gin-soaked mother after another bender, or being her shoulder to lean on, I was doing damage control to keep her nasty little secret out of the press. That was my life. As far as my father was concerned—and had plainly stated on many occasions—it was the only thing I was good for.

"Come on." I stood, taking her thin elbow in my hand and guiding her from the stool. "Let's get you home."

Just another day in the life of the McMannus family, I thought gloomily as I guided her out of the bar and into a cab.

And people speculated why I was the womanizing playboy depicted in the rags all over the country.

The answer was simple.

Because after spending night after night sobering my mother up and talking her off the ledge, I needed to bury myself inside a nameless, faceless woman so I could forget about my shitty life.

CHAPTER FOUR

GOOGLE WAS QUICKLY BECOMING the bane of my existence.

What had started as curiosity about Caleb McMannus had blossomed into a full-blown obsession. Once you Googled, there was no going back. I was disgusted with myself.

Not only because it seemed I'd banged a guy whose dick had already been in half the female population of the United States, but also because I couldn't stop thinking about the stupid man-whore. It was a sickness. A gross, disappointing sickness that I'd spent weeks trying to cure myself of to no avail.

Each gossip column of his sexcapades, each picture of him in a compromising position—and there were *many*, all of them with a different woman—was cringe-worthy. But I couldn't stop myself from searching them out.

What was worse, I couldn't stop thinking about our night together. It had been the most intense, toe-curling experience of my life. And even though I pretty much hated him for forgetting about me, I wanted it again.

Damn my needy, traitorous vagina!

"Whatcha lookin' at?"

I'd been so ensconced in my online stalk-fest that I hadn't heard Sophia come up behind me. I'd been hunkered down close to the screen because... well, because I thought I could see a hint of abs in one of the pictures of him, and at the sound of her voice I shot up straight, slammed the lid of my laptop down, and spun around in my swivel chair.

"What? No! Nothing! Huh? What are you talking about?" As if my screechy, rapid-fire questions weren't telling enough, I started laughing like a manic hyena.

She looked at me like I'd just lost my mind. "Uh, okay, crazy. Tone it down a bit, would you? You have creepy killer eyes right now."

I unscrewed the loony from my expression and tried to look as normal as possible. "Sorry, you scared me is all. I thought you'd already left for the day."

"I did, but I forgot my cell phone and the number for that Chinese delivery place is in it, so I had to come back. What are you still doing here?" she asked, looking at me with suspicion.

"Oh, uh... I just got distracted doing a little online shopping," I lied. "Lost track of time, I guess."

"Online shopping, huh?" she asked with a knowing smirk. "Wow, I didn't realize that hottie from the hall a few weeks ago was for sale. You should totally buy that."

Son of a bitch! I dropped my head in my hands and groaned. "Ugh. Fine, you caught me. I was... *Googling*." I swallowed the last word down as if it left a terrible taste in my mouth.

Her smirk turned wicked as she propped her hip on the edge of my desk. "Ooh, interesting," she teased, crossing her arms and stroking her chin creepily.

I curled my upper lip. "Will you stop doing that, weirdo? You look like a skinnier, less-bald version of Dr. Evil with boobs."

She laughed and dropped her hand. "Okay, fine. But seriously, why are you scoping pictures of... what's his name again?"

"Caleb McMannus," I answered way too quickly. And it wasn't lost on her.

"Mmhmm." She bit her lip to suppress her smile and I clenched my fists to suppress the urge to smack her. "Anyway, why are you scoping pictures of *Caleb McMannus*? I thought you hated the guy. You came back all rage-y after you talked to him."

"I did... I do. I was just... I mean...." I gave up on my excuses and dropped my forehead to bang it on my desk. When I sat back up, I admitted, "I kind of had sex with him a few months ago."

"You *what*?"

I winced at how shrill her voice got. "I had sex with him," I enunciated. "And you mind not shrieking like that? The glass can't take it."

She pushed back, sitting fully on the desk. "Oh my god," she said quietly. "You slept with him? When did this happen? How did you meet? Was it any good?" she asked in rapid-fire questions.

"Yes. Almost three months ago. I picked him up at a bar when he was trying to pick me up. And...." I hesitated to tell the truth, but finally admitted, "It was the best I've ever had."

She did that high-pitched girly squeal thing and clapped excitedly. "That's so awesome! Wait... if it was the best you ever had, why'd he act like it was the first time he saw you in the studio?" My cheeks flamed with humiliation as realization dawned on her face. Her eyes rounded, her jaw nearly hitting the floor. "Oh. My. God. He *didn't*!"

"He did," I confessed in a hushed voice. "He acted like that because the bastard didn't remember me."

Her mouth opened even wider and her eyes looked like they were at risk of falling out of their sockets. "That *son of a bitch*!"

That time, instead of bitching at her about her screaming, I joined in. "*Right?* I mean, not to toot my own horn or anything, but I'm damn good!"

"I just... I can't believe you had sex with the guy and he didn't *remember* you!"

I shot her a look I hoped would set her hair on fire. "You know, you don't have to keep saying it. I'm already embarrassed enough as it is."

"What an asshole!" she declared. "I hate that guy. We hate that guy, right?"

"Uh, yes!" I replied sarcastically. "We definitely hate the guy."

Sophia quirked an eyebrow. "So if we hate the guy, then why are you cyber-stalking him?"

"Because he's the best I ever had!" I shouted, throwing my hands in the air. "He broke me, Sophia. I haven't been able to have an orgasm since that night!"

She gasped loudly. "Seriously? Not even by yourself?"

I nodded pathetically.

"Holy shit," Sophia breathed, lifting her fist to her mouth. "That's just... I can't...." Then she burst into laughter. I stopped suppressing the urge and slapped the shit out of her arm. "Ow! You bitch!" She rubbed her arm and bit her lip while frowning. I could have sworn she was fighting a smile.

When I tried to kill her with my eyes, she held up her hands in surrender. "Sorry, sorry. I didn't mean to laugh. I'll stop, I promise."

My temples began to throb. "God, Soph," I groaned, massaging at the pain. "I don't know what I'm doing. I mean, the asshole doesn't even remember screwing me, but I can't stop thinking about him! What *is* that? Something is seriously wrong with me."

Her hand rested on my shoulder. "Sweetie, there is *nothing* wrong with you. More than likely, your issues with getting off are all in your head. This guy's gotten under your skin in a serious way. The only way to fix it is to work him out."

"Oh?" I asked with a roll of my eyes. "And how do you suggest I do that?"

Sophia's finger on my shoulder convulsed as a wicked smile stretched across her face. "There's only one way to do it. Bang him like crazy until you've gotten your fill, and then walk away."

I shot out of my chair, letting out a very unladylike snort. "You've officially lost your mind. I'm not sleeping with him again! He's a man-whore! He's screwed so many women he doesn't even remember our faces. I'm never, *ever* having sex with Caleb McMannus again!"

I feigned revulsion at the idea to mask the fact that her theory was actually something I was considering. Truth was, I'd been able to think of little else since that jerk walked into our studio a few weeks earlier. My brain wanted to punch him in the neck while my body wanted to cuff him to my bed and have its naughty, dirty way with him.

"Okay, honey," Sophia said sarcastically, giving my shoulder a condescending pat. "Keep telling yourself that."

She walked away, leaving me all alone with my self-pity. I opened my laptop back up and made a noise of disgust at myself when the image of Caleb I'd been drooling over popped back to life.

"You're pathetic, Daphne," I chided as my desk phone began to ring. I looked at the unfamiliar number flashing across the caller ID and picked up the line. "This is Daphne King."

"Hey, Ducky."

At the sound of the voice, my lungs deflated like two

balloons without helium. A painful, raspy wheeze emitted from my chest through the phone line.

"Daphne? Hello? You there?"

I sputtered for a few seconds before I was finally able to speak. "Stefan?"

"Yeah." I could hear his smile through the handset and imagined what he looked like at that moment, with those stupid capped teeth shining in all their bleached glory. "So good to hear your voice, Ducky."

Christ, that name. When we first got together, he'd playfully shortened my name to Daphy, then thought it would be funny to call me Daphy Duck. That eventually led to Ducky. It was a stupid fucking nickname that I'd hated so much my teeth clenched each time I heard it, but I'd thought I was blissfully in love at the time so, like an idiot, I let it slide. Now it was like hearing nails being scraped down a chalkboard.

"Can't say I return the sentiment, Stefan. Why the hell are you calling me?"

"Look, Ducky—"

I cut him off with a groan. "Please, for the love of god, stop calling me that. You sound like a dumbass."

He cleared his throat, and from years of experience, I knew he was tugging at his earlobe just then. It was something he did any time he was uncomfortable. Any time we fought, he'd make that noise like he was trying to hawk something up and pull at his ear. It was *so* annoying. "Okay, I'm sorry. I-I'm just nervous. I didn't actually expect you to pick up."

"Yeah? Well had I known who was on the other line, I wouldn't have answered, trust me."

"Come on, Duck—er, Daphne. Please don't be like that. I know we left things in a bad place—"

"In a bad place?" I laughed a bit hysterically. "That's what you call it? Really? Because if I remember correctly, where we *left things* was with you buried balls deep *in my mother*!"

"Daph, I'm sorr—"

"Nope," I broke in, officially over the conversation. "Don't you dare apologize to me. I don't give a shit if you're sorry. I don't care how you feel *at all*. I can't for the life of me understand why after seven years either of you would try reaching out to me, but I'll tell you now, it's pointless. I want nothing to do with either of you." He tried to get a word in, but I was done. "Nope. I don't want to hear it. Unless you're calling to inform me that the backstabbing cow gave you a raging case of herpes so bad your dick shriveled up and fell off, you've got nothing to say that I want to hear. Never call me again."

With that, I hung up, slamming the phone back down in the cradle so hard it almost broke.

I grabbed my purse and started toward the elevator bank. My destination was the nearest possible place to get alcohol, because after that conversation, I felt the need to get really, *really* drunk.

CHAPTER FIVE

CALEB

JESUS, I need a fucking drink.

I'd had the day from hell. Work had been a bitch. Grayson had been an unbearable pain in the ass since he started pursuing his girl. She was definitely giving him a run for his money. Usually it was fucking hilarious to watch him turn into a pissy little bitch whenever Lola blew his ass off, but since my father had decided to call this morning and tear me a new one for once again having a rather unflattering picture of myself posted in the gossip rags, I really wasn't in the mood to deal with anyone's shit.

To make matters worse, my mom was calling more frequently, demanding I talk to Dad about ending his affair. She claimed to have a feeling that this time around was different, that it wasn't just another random hookup, and practically begged me to fix it. When I told her there wasn't anything I could do, she sobbed inconsolably, leaving me feeling guilty for not being able to help and bitter because she'd asked me in the first place.

When it came to my folks, I was forever trapped between a

rock and a hard place with no way of escaping. It was a miserable existence.

I ended up at The Black Sheep, sucking back beer while Deacon watched on with a worried expression. Luckily he didn't bother asking what was wrong. Our friendship worked mainly because I didn't stick my nose in his family business and he returned the favor.

"You've got to be shitting me."

I lifted my head and turned to find the woman who'd been plaguing my thoughts for weeks standing a few feet away, glaring at me with her lip curled like the very sight of me offended her delicate sensibilities.

I pasted on my most winning smile at the sight of her. "Well, if it isn't the stunning Daphne King. Please"—I motioned to the empty stool beside me—"have a seat."

She made a noise that sounded an awful lot like a growl deep in her throat, and I had to bite the inside of my cheek to keep from laughing at how freaking adorable she looked when she was mad.

She stared up at the ceiling and declared, "What have I done to deserve this, huh? Is it because I made out with Bobby Gallagher in the confessional booth that one time? I already apologized for that!"

"Seems like she knows you pretty damn well, Caleb," Deacon chided, giving me a shit-eating grin.

I flipped him off and looked back to Daphne. "Come on." I kicked the stool out a bit. "I'm buying."

Her icy demeanor didn't change a bit as she slowly moved closer and finally took the seat next to me. "Well, if you're buying," she stated hesitantly.

I looked at Deacon and lifted my empty beer bottle. "Another for me, and a mojito for the lady."

She let out a surprised gasp. I gave her my full attention

once Deacon started on our drinks. "How did... how did you know I'd order that?"

I lifted my refreshed beer and took a long pull, regarding her closely from over the bottle. "It's what you were drinking the night we met," I finally answered.

She did that cute goldfish thing with her mouth again, the same one she'd done in the hall at work. "But I thought...."

I faced forward and downed half my beer in just a few swallows. "Yeah," I replied, setting the glass bottle back on the round paper coaster. I ran a hand through my hair and let out a heavy sigh. "I'm really fucking sorry about that. I won't make any excuses for how I acted, but if it means anything, I remembered all of it almost as soon as you called me an asshole and stormed off."

I offered a miniscule smile to try and lighten the blow. Surprisingly enough, my confession seemed to thaw her out a bit, so I decided to try my luck.

"You think we could start over?" Her eyebrows dipped together in confusion, so I held my hand out for her to shake. "Hi, I'm Caleb. What's a gorgeous woman like you doing in a shithole like this?"

A bottle cap came flying at me, hitting me in the head. I shot him a look as he mumbled, "Fucker," under his breath before dropping Daphne's mojito off and heading to the other side of the bar.

"Friend of yours?" Daphne asked with a small laugh.

"Something like that," I grumbled, then wiggled my fingers to get her attention back on them. She watched my hand skeptically for several seconds before finally taking it.

"I still don't like you," she muttered, taking her hand back. Her long, thin fingers wrapped elegantly around her drink glass, the nails painted a color so dark it was nearly black, but on her it worked. Watching her hand as she lifted the glass and placed the straw between her plump cherry-colored lips sent me back in time to that night. The image of her fingers and mouth wrapped around my throbbing cock came rushing back, making my dick stir behind my zipper.

I propped an elbow on the bar and turned to lean in to her. "How would you suggest I change that?"

She put her drink down and threw her head back in a bark of laughter that didn't contain a hint of humor. "Wow. You really can't help yourself, can you?"

I shrugged, laying on the charm as I said, "What can I say, I'm helpless against a beautiful woman."

"God, you're unbelievable!" I opened my mouth to reply and her palm slapped over it to stop me. "That was *not* a compliment," she said in a warning tone. "Keep it up and I'll leave, I swear to god. I'm not in the mood for your shit. I just came here to get wasted and forget about the stupid drama in my life. Think you can let me do that?"

I wrapped my fingers around her delicate wrist and removed it from my mouth, but I didn't let it go. "I'm sorry," I said with every ounce of sincerity I felt. "I'm sorry. In all honesty, I came here tonight for the exact same reason." With my free hand, I lifted my beer bottle and extended it toward her. "What do you say we get wasted together and bitch about the people in our lives driving us crazy? Deal?"

She lifted her mojito and clinked the rim of it against my bottle. "Deal."

I SLAMMED my bottle down on the bar with a heavy clunk. I had a pretty decent buzz going from drinking the past couple of hours, but it could have been much worse if I'd gone with my regular drink of scotch instead of beer.

Daphne, however, didn't seem fazed by the alcohol at all. I'd been looking forward to a night with booze as my only company to drown everything out, but the sexy woman next to me turned out to be so much better. And not just because I knew from experience how amazing she was in bed. I'd gotten to know her a bit and discovered that under the hair and legs, the ass and tits, and the stellar smile, she was also the funniest, most interesting person I'd ever met.

And that was without us really talking about anything too in-depth or personal. She just had a way about her, a spirit and light you just wanted to drown in. And the stories she told about her job were too hilarious and detailed to be made up.

"So then she says, 'I understand it was wrong for him to give me chlamydia from that skank he was cheating with, but I really love him.' Can you believe that?" She started laughing at the story she was telling about one of her show's callers. "I mean, the guy was cheating with their nanny while his wife busted her ass at work every day, gives her an STD because the slut he was cheating with was just *all kinds* of nasty, and she *still* wanted to make her marriage work! How insane is that?"

The topic hit a little too close to home for comfort, so the smile I glued to my face was far from sincere. Luckily, she was too far gone to really notice.

"I get loving someone with your whole heart. Believe me, I understand. But have a little pride, right?"

Well that was interesting. From the way she spoke, it sounded suspiciously like there'd been someone very important in her life who was no longer there, but she'd made it clear tonight with her refusal to go too deep that she wasn't going to let me in, so I didn't push.

She sucked back the last of her drink and plunked it down on the counter, letting out a long breath before turning back to me. "Tonight was... actually pretty fun."

I chuckled and scooted to the edge of my barstool, spreading my legs so her crossed knees were sandwiched between them. "Don't sound too surprised about it."

She giggled, her cheeks flushing a tempting pink that turned me on even more. "Sorry, I didn't mean it like that. It's just that I'm kind of surprised."

I placed my hand on my chest in mock pain. "You know, you're really hell on a man's ego, sweetheart."

She smiled so brightly, so beautifully, that I felt the effect of it in my bones. "Oh, and forgetting we'd slept together wasn't a bruise to *my* ego?" she asked, but her tone implied she was teasing instead of angry.

"Wait, you slept with her and *forgot* about it?" I jerked my head in Deacon's direction to see him staring at me incredulously.

"A little privacy, please?" I gritted between clenched teeth, communicating with my eyes that I'd murder him painfully if he didn't shut the hell up and go away. He eventually turned and walked down the bar, but he did it with a mocking grin, the bastard. I looked back at Daphne. "A momentary bout of stupidity on my part," I quipped. "Believe me, once I remembered, there was no forgetting. I haven't been able to think of much else."

Her eyes glazed over, and it had nothing to do with the alcohol. "Me either," she whispered in a soft, breathy voice. "No matter how hard I've tried to stop."

She was driving me out of my mind. The struggle to sit next to her, so close I could smell the seductive scent of lilies and sugar on her skin, and not touch her was becoming almost too agonizing to bear.

"God, you're so damn beautiful," I said quietly. It was supposed to just be a thought, but my brain didn't work properly when I was around her and I found myself blurting words without thinking.

Her eyes rounded as she whispered, "Is that just a line?"

"No," I answered honestly. "It's the goddamn truth. You can walk out of here right now, catch a cab, and leave me here, and I'd still tell you you're the most gorgeous woman I've ever laid eyes on because it's a fucking fact."

Her body swayed closer. "I...." She stopped and swallowed, her throat working visibly. "I don't want to walk out of here right now. At least... at least not by myself."

I moved in closer, barely an inch of space separating our faces. "You need to be sure about what you're saying."

She leaned back, picked up her purse, and slung it over her shoulder. "Take me home with you. Right now."

CHAPTER SIX

DAPHNE

I WOKE up with a dreadful feeling of *Oh my fresh hell, what have I done?* It felt like someone was pounding a bass drum inside my head. My mouth felt like I'd swallowed a handful of cotton balls, and my eyes were gritty and dry from sleeping in my contacts.

But that wasn't why I was currently having an internal mini meltdown. Oh no, that was all due to the long, heavy arm that was wrapped around my waist and attached to a hand that was holding on to my left boob like it was one of those squishy foam stress balls.

I slowly lifted the cover with an impending sense of dread at what I suspected I might find, letting out a whimper when I discovered that a strong and quite naked male body was currently wrapped around my equally naked one.

Worst of all, I knew exactly who all that gorgeous bare flesh belonged to. There were large spans of time from the night before that I couldn't remember, but I *did* remember running into Caleb at The Black Sheep and joining him for a drink that turned into... way too many drinks.

I vaguely recalled the trip back to his apartment, but the one thing that stood out in my mind with perfect clarity was just how loudly I'd screamed each time I orgasmed. All four times. Embarrassingly enough, I was pretty sure I might have cried tears of relief and joy after the first one.

Now, instead of reveling in the knowledge that my girly bits were no longer broken, I was freaking the hell out that I'd slept with the enemy. *Again.*

Damn him and his seductive charm and swimmer's body!

As quietly and smoothly as possible, I started to lift his arm to shift out of his hold. I managed to make it to the very edge of the bed when his arm banded around my stomach once more and I was yanked back into a part of him that was *wide* awake.

"Mmm. Morning." His voice was deliciously thick and raspy with sleep, causing my body to shiver involuntarily.

"Uh... good morning?"

His fingertips started caressing the skin below my belly button as he asked, "Where were you sneaking off to?"

"The bathroom," I lied quickly, needing to escape before I did something incredibly stupid, like have mind-blowing sex with him again. At my response, he let me go and allowed me to scoot away. Holding the sheet firmly across my breasts, I scanned the bedroom floor. "Uh, where are my clothes?"

He pushed up on an elbow and propped his head in his hands, completely comfortable with his nakedness. Not that he didn't have the right to be—his body was the kind of perfection artists dreamed of sculpting, all hard, sinewy muscle beneath impeccable skin tanned a warm golden honey. His chest had the perfect amount of hair that I knew from experience felt *amazing* scraping across my nipples as he moved on top of me.

Focus, Daphne, you dirty whore!

"Pretty sure they're still scattered around the living room."

My head tipped in confusion. "What? Why?"

Even his eyebrows were sexy, which I noticed because the

way they dipped into a frown drew my attention to them. "What do you mean why? Because that's where I tore them off you before we went at each other on the couch."

I rocked back on one foot. "We went at each other *on the couch?*"

Caleb's frown deepened, and he sat up all the way. "You don't remember?" he asked incredulously.

I threw one arm out at my side. "I was drunk!" I cried belligerently.

He shot from the bed, ripping his boxer briefs up his legs as fury radiated off him in waves. "You were *drunk?* Are you fucking kidding me?"

I tried to come off looking as indignant as possible considering all I was wearing was a fucking *sheet.* "I sucked down six mojitos! Of course I was drunk! You think I'd have actually come back here if I were sober?"

He mimicked my stance, slamming his hands down on his hips. "The fuck is that supposed to mean?" he shouted.

"It means you're an asshole who didn't even remember sleeping with me the first time, and if I wasn't boozed the hell up, I never would have touched you!" I shouted in return, letting my anxiety get the best of me and converting it into anger. It was a horrible defense mechanism I'd picked up as a teenager when my mom started making me feel inadequate for being one dress size bigger than her. She'd always been more willowy where I'd been curvier, getting my body shape from my father's side of my family, and she loved to point that out.

It was a nasty habit I needed to break. Starting tomorrow.

Caleb scoffed. "Oh really? Is that why you screamed '*Hallelujah*' when you came? All. Four. Times?"

"You're unbelievable!" I shrieked.

"I know!" he yelled. "You told me over and over and over last night!"

"Ugh!" I stomped my foot. "I hate you!"

"Yeah? Well you seem to love my dick!"

"Asshole!"

"Lush!"

One minute we were screaming at each other, and the very next we were making out like we were trying to suck the air out of each other's lungs.

"Wait, no!" I stumbled backward, clutching the bedsheet. "This is crazy. We can't do this." *God, I really want to do this!*

My body and mind were at war with one another. I knew to my bones that Caleb McMannus was wrong for me in every. Single. Way. But I was drawn to him in a way I had absolutely no control over. The desire I felt whenever I so much as thought of him was foreign and terrifying. I'd loved Stefan deeply before he betrayed me, yet my body didn't sing for his. My skin didn't itch with the need to feel him against me the way it did for Caleb.

I barely knew the man, and what little I knew I didn't really care for, but I still wanted him more than I wanted a pony when I was seven years old. And I'd *really* wanted that damn pony.

He grabbed my face and jerked me back, muttering, "We can. We should," against my lips between searing kisses. "Christ, I can't get enough of you. No matter who I'm with, I'm comparing them to you."

My body froze colder than it had the previous year when Lola, Sophia, and I had done the ALS Ice Bucket Challenge, wearing nothing but teeny tiny bikinis. Those words from his lips were the reminder I needed that he was a despicable man-whore who went around screwing whatever woman handed herself over to him, and I wanted nothing to do with him. I hated myself for being so easily seduced by the prick.

"God, you're such a *pig*," I seethed. Turning on my heels, I bolted into the living room. Sure enough, my clothes were scattered all around the floor.

He followed me, a look of bewilderment on his face. "What the hell did I do wrong now?"

Without a shred of insecurity, I quickly dropped the sheet and started pulling my clothes on, tangling the articles up in my haste to get dressed and get the hell out of there. "I can't believe I slept with you. *Twice!*" My voice had reached an embarrassingly shrill volume as I struggled to untwist my bra and get it into place. "I should have known better. Please god, tell me you at least remembered to wear a condom."

"Of course I wore a condom!"

I looked up at the ceiling, shouting, "Well, thank god for that! Who the hell knows where all your dick has been!"

His face turned red, and I vaguely noticed how he clenched his fists at his side. "You sure as fuck weren't complaining when it was inside *you* a few hours ago."

I slipped my dress over my head as a humorless laugh bubbled from my chest. "A mistake I have no intention of *ever* repeating."

Caleb's arms crossed over his chest, defining the muscles in his biceps. "You sure about that, honey?"

I righted my dress and flung my hair out of my eyes to glare at him. My palm twitched with the urge to slap the smug, condescending look off his face. "What's that supposed to mean?"

The bastard actually had the nerve to smirk. "It means you were the one to climb me like a fucking tree the second my front door clicked shut. You wrapped yourself around me so goddamn tight I was concerned you'd break my ribs."

"Oh please," I scoffed with a roll of my eyes to mask the fact that I was pretty sure he was telling the truth.

Somewhere in the background of our fight, a cell phone

began to ring. I was too wrapped up in the scene unfolding around me to question whether it was his or mine.

"And you're fucking lying to yourself if you think you aren't going to come crawling back."

"You're disgusting!"

The phone stopped ringing only to start back up two seconds later.

"And you're full of shit!"

"Am not!"

"Are too!"

The phone started going for a third time, causing Caleb to snap. He stomped over to the counter separating the kitchen from the living space and snatched his phone off the black granite countertop.

"What!" he barked through the line. He dropped his head a moment later and began rubbing between his eyes. His entire expression went from furious to browbeaten in a heartbeat. "Christ, Mom. Now's not really a good time. Can't you just—" He stopped and pulled in a deep breath. "Yeah. Fine... I said yes. Just give me an hour."

He hung up and threw the phone at the couch across the room before turning his attention back to me. The way his entire demeanor had shifted in that handful of seconds had cooled my temper drastically. The pompous jackass from minutes before now seemed deflated.

"I have shit I have to handle, so I gotta go. But this isn't over." He stressed his point by stepping close and pointing directly at my face. Then he turned and rushed toward the bedroom. I took that as my opportunity and bolted out the door.

My body could be as pissed as it wanted, but whatever twisted shit I had going on with Caleb was *most definitely* over.

Whether he was willing to accept that or not.

CHAPTER SEVEN

CALEB

IT WAS BARELY ten in the morning by the time I pulled into my parents' driveway, but I was already so exhausted I could feel it all the way down to my bones.

The only silver lining was the fact that Mom hadn't been slurring her words when she called earlier to tell me my father hadn't come home the night before. She typically waited until the clock struck noon before starting up.

I pushed the front door of their sprawling mansion open and called out for her. "Mom? I'm here. Where are you?"

"In here, darling."

I followed her voice into the formal family room to the left of the foyer. Walking in there was like walking onto the set of a crappy soap opera. The shades had been drawn, blocking out every bit of sunlight and creating the illusion of nighttime in the morning hours. She was lying on the couch, her head resting on the toss pillows with a chenille blanket wrapped around her. She'd thrown her forearm across her eyes dramatically, ever the picture of the poor, neglected housewife despite having willingly placed herself in that role.

I sighed and reached for the light switch on the wall. "Jesus,

Mom. It's too damn early to be this morose." I made my way to her and pulled the blanket back, revealing her ivory silk dressing gown. "Come on, let's get you up. You'll feel better after you get showered and dressed."

She let out a beleaguered sigh and allowed me to pull her to a sitting position. "I don't possibly see how I'll feel better knowing your father spent the night with *her*."

Between my mother and the bullshit that went down with Daphne earlier, I was dangerously close to losing my shit. That goddamn woman was driving me crazy. She ran so hot for me one second only to turn ice cold the next.

With one hand resting on my hip, I dropped my head and used the other to pinch the bridge of my nose, hoping to lessen the tension building in my skull. "Who's 'her,' Mom?"

"Well I don't know *who* for certain, but what other reason would he have for being gone all night if there wasn't another woman involved?" Her top lip curled into a sneer as she continued, "He said it was because of work, but I know that's a lie."

I didn't need to see proof to know she was right, but my empathy was in really fucking short supply. My father had been exhibiting the same behavior for the past thirty years, and the longer she stayed, knowing he'd never change, the less I was able to tolerate her self-pity.

"Why don't you just fucking leave him already?" I snapped, speaking to my overly delicate mother in a sharper tone than I ever had before.

She put her hand to her chest and sucked in an appalled gasp. "Caleb," she admonished. "Watch your language. And how could you ask me such a thing?"

My mouth dropped open in bewilderment. "How could I ask? Are you kidding me? Because the man's cheated on you *for years*! With god only knows how many women!"

"He's my husband," she returned in a weak voice. "You

don't just turn your back on your vows, Caleb. I love your father, and I know he loves me too. He just... can't help himself."

I let out a loud, booming laugh devoid of all humor. "Wow. You've come up with some creative excuses for his fucked-up behavior over the years, but this one takes the cake!"

"You don't just walk away from your soul mate!" she argued, her tone growing stronger. "You'll understand when you finally meet the love of your life."

I couldn't hide my dumbfounded reaction. "That's a joke, right?" I didn't give her a chance to answer before speaking again. "If there's one thing I've learned from watching you and Dad, it's that love and soul mates are a goddamn joke. If this is what it's going to turn me into, I want nothing to do with it."

She sucked in a stuttered breath. "If that's what you truly believe, then I've completely failed you as a mother."

It was a sucker punch of guilt right to the gut. Despite the resentment I harbored, she was still my mother, and upsetting her sat like stones in the pit of my stomach. "Shit," I hissed, blowing out a puff of air. "Look, Mom, I'm sorry, okay?"

Tears began to well up in her eyes, but I'd had all I could take for one day. I leaned down and placed a kiss on her cheek. "I love you, but I have to go."

"Wait!" she called after me as I headed toward the door, but I didn't stop. "I thought you were going to speak to your father for me."

I paused with my hand on the doorknob. "I will," I seethed through clenched teeth. "Just not today."

My dad, with his impeccable timing, was pulling into the driveway just as I reached my car.

"Caleb? I'm surprised to see you here so early, son."

"Yeah?" Bitterness laced my words. "Well I didn't expect to be here so early, but seeing as Mom called me in a fit of fucking tears because you didn't come home last night"—I threw my arms out at my sides—"here I am."

"Jesus, not this again," he sighed, running a hand through his sandy blond hair, so similar to mine. I got my coloring from my old man. With the exception of the salt and pepper liberally laced in his hair, and the extra wrinkles around his mouth and eyes, we looked freakishly similar.

"Are you surprised? For Christ's sake, Dad, could you make it any more obvious? How about a little discretion? I don't even know why you bother making up lies anymore. Why not just tell her you can't make it home because you're out fucking other women?"

"Watch your goddamn mouth," he snarled at me, stepping so close we were toe-to-toe. I had about an inch and a half in height on him, and a good thirty pounds of muscle, but my father was the kind of man who'd attempt to cow anyone he felt was inferior to him. And he felt *everyone* was inferior to him. "I'm your father and you'll damn well show me the respect I deserve."

My head jerked back as I scoffed. "The respect you *deserve?* Are you kidding me? What the hell have you done to earn my respect?"

Spittle flew from his mouth as he hissed, "I created you, you ungrateful little shit. And don't you dare lecture me on discretion. Do you have any idea how much fucking money I shelled out to remove your name from the papers when you were younger? You humiliated your mother and me. And let's not forget how much your little stunt with the dean of admissions' wife cost me. It's a miracle you weren't kicked out of college!"

"I was a kid, for Christ's sake! And anything I did was because I had *you* to look up to. Such an upstanding role model," I chided sarcastically. "Leaving his poor wife home alone so he can get his dick wet with any available pussy on hand. At least I'm not committed to another woman when I'm screwing around."

The back of his hand came up, smacking me in the face so hard my head jerked to the side and I tasted blood. I stood motionless for a second before facing my father again. I spit the bit of blood on the concrete directly beside his shoe. "That's the last time you lay a hand on me, old man," I warned ominously. "Next time, I'll disregard the fact that you're my father."

With that I climbed into my car and sped off.

"LOOK, man, I'm not one to judge, but isn't it a little early to be sucking back scotch? It's barely past eleven in the morning."

I set the glass back down on the bar top with a loud clank. "I've had approximately three sips. I'd hardly call that sucking it back. And you didn't seem to have a problem pouring it for me when I asked, did you?"

Deacon lifted his arms innocently before smiling. "Well I can't pay for this bar with smiles and hugs, now can I?"

I looked around at the few people who'd come in for lunch. "Not like anyone would want to hug your ugly ass anyway," I returned with a chuckle.

Deacon went back to stacking clean glasses on a few of the shelves behind the bar. "So, what's up with you this morning? I'd have thought you'd be in a better mood considering you left here with that hot chick last night."

"I don't want to talk about it," I grumbled, taking another sip from my glass. "That woman's off her freaking rocker."

"She'd have to be to go home with you."

"God, you're an asshole. Why do I put up with you?"

"Because of my winning personality and access to top-shelf booze," he deadpanned, making me laugh.

"What are you doing here, anyway? I thought Saturdays were your days off?"

He finished stacking the last glass, moved to the whole limes and lemons set up along the bar, and began slicing as he talked. "Got some family thing tomorrow at my folks' house."

He sounded as excited about a family dinner as he would a root canal. "You don't seem too happy about it."

"I'm not." His knife banged harder against the cutting board. "Grayson's bringing his new girl over to meet the whole family, so my presence is mandatory."

"You talking about Lola? I've met her. She's a good woman. Seems to have your brother twisted into knots."

"About time someone finally did."

I slid my glass back and forth between my hands as I studied his blank expression. "You finally want to tell me what the hell happened between you and your brother?"

He stared daggers at me. "You want to tell me what's got you day-drinking in my bar?"

I knew he expected me to back down. Maybe it was my agitation. Maybe it was the scotch. Or maybe it was just the fact that I'd had my fill of bullshit for one day, but I decided to call his bluff. "I'm in here having a drink because my fucking father's fucking around on my mother *again*. And she's still got her head so far up her ass that she refuses to leave him, so she expects me to somehow fix it for her *again*. On top of all that, the one woman I can't get out of my head, who just so happens to be the best lay I've had in my fucking life, is certifiable!"

He stood stiff for several seconds before muttering, "Shit, man. That's harsh." Then he grabbed two shot glasses, filled each with tequila, and slid one to me. We downed the shots, slamming the glasses back on the bar.

"Your turn," I hissed past the burn of the alcohol.

Deacon's hands rested on the bar top as he let out a heavy breath. "Remember Fiona Prentice?"

My brows dipped in confusion. "Of course I do, we grew up with her. Not to mention she's Gray's ex."

His knuckles turned white with the pressure he exerted pressing them into the scarred wood of the bar. "Yeah, well, she never should've been his ex. She never should have been his fucking anything."

My eyes went round and I pushed the shot glass back in his direction for a refill. "I think it's safe to say you and I are going to need a few more of these."

CHAPTER EIGHT

DAPHNE

THE PAST SEVERAL days had been unbelievably stressful. I was worried about my friends. Sophia was pretending like she hadn't had a bomb dropped on her when Lola informed us that her brother Dominic, who just so happened to be Soph's ex-boyfriend, was in town for an indefinite period of time. I tried to get her to open up, but she insisted that she was totally fine. I wasn't buying it, seeing as the man had completely demolished her heart ten years earlier, but I let it go.

Lola, on the other hand, was quickly spiraling out of control. After a meeting with Grayson's family had ended in catastrophe, she'd slowly started slipping. But when pictures of him out with his ex-girlfriend, a stunning redhead named Fiona, hit the papers, Lola had officially lost it. She'd gone from moping around like someone had run over her beloved puppy to on-air tangents with our callers during our radio show. Sophia and I tried our hardest to get through to her. It was obvious she wasn't handling her split with Grayson well—I'd never seen her so lost in all the years I'd known her—but trying to convince her to talk to him was like beating our heads against a brick wall.

The final straw had been when she punched our station

director, Sam, in the nose. Granted, the asshole had it coming with his chauvinistic remarks about Lola and Grayson, but the situation could have been handled much more professionally. It led to yet another meeting with HR and the higher-ups. If we kept going down the road we were currently on, I had no doubt that the station would can *Girl Talk* without so much as a backward glance.

The only plus side to all the drama happening around me was the fact that I hadn't had much time to think about Caleb and how my body still yearned for him.

I let out a heavy sigh as I made my way from the conference room. To say Lola had gotten off lucky with just a mandatory three days off for breaking our boss's nose was putting it mildly.

"Well this is really going to make the gala interesting, isn't it?" Sophia asked.

I looked at her, confused for a second. Then it dawned on me. "Ah hell, is that this weekend?"

I couldn't believe I'd forgotten about that. The charity gala at the Seattle Art Museum for the Wave Foundation was something Bandwidth hosted every year. And as hosts of KTSW's most successful talk radio show, Lola, Sophia, and I were always a big part. This year we decided to up the stakes and auction ourselves off for dates to the highest bidders in the hopes of raising even more money.

"You forgot?" Sophia asked in shock. "How could you forget? It's your favorite event of the year!"

She was right. I loved the gala more than Christmas, New Year, and Oscar season combined. It was the one time a year I got to dress up like a movie star walking the red carpet and not feel guilty for spending *way* too much money on designer gowns and shoes. The expensive dresses I wore for the event each year were the closest I was *ever* getting to a wedding gown again, so I basked in it.

"Can you blame me for being a little distracted? You and I have been kind of consumed with helping Lola to not self-destruct. And look how well that's gone. She broke Sam's nose, for Christ's sake."

Sophia gave me a lopsided grin full of mischief. "You sure your distraction doesn't have anything to do with a certain sexy blond dude with a skill at giving orgasms?"

I nearly choked on my tongue. I hadn't confessed to her that I'd fallen off the Caleb McMannus wagon again, and had no intention of ever admitting it to anyone, but it was almost as if she was reading my mind. I laughed maniacally. "What? No! Of course not!"

She looked at me with narrow-eyed suspicion. "I don't know who you're trying harder to convince, me or yourself."

I released a very loud snort, like every word out of her mouth was utterly ridiculous. "I don't even know what you're talking about. I'm totally over the whole Caleb thing. I'm going to grab a latte from the cart in the lobby. You want one?"

She crossed her arms over her chest, grinning knowingly. "No, thanks, but nice effort to change the subject."

I shrugged and started for the elevators. "It's just one of my many gifts."

"You know, you can't avoid talking to me forever," she called at my back as I jabbed the button to take me down.

"But I can sure as hell try," I murmured to myself as I watched the floor numbers light up above the elevator. I gave the Down button a few more good stabs with my manicured finger, letting out a sigh of relief when I heard the ding and a set of doors slid open.

Closing my eyes, I rested against the back wall of the car and dropped my head back against the mirrored panel with a frustrated sigh. I'd have given anything to be back at home with a bottle of wine and my recorded episodes of *Outlander*. Jamie was the only man I could count on to never let me down. Unfortunately, my beloved ginger was a fictional character. And I'd already discovered the brutal truth that real-life men could never live up to the ones in books.

I opened my eyes as the elevator slowed to a stop and opened to the ground floor. The smell of fresh pastries and ground espresso beans coming from my favorite little cart made my mouth water as I stepped out onto the shiny marble floor. I stood in the ever-present line, hoping they hadn't already run out of my favorite cheese Danish, when a voice from behind me made goose bumps break out across my arms.

"Looks like it's my lucky day."

I bit my lip to suppress a groan, ignoring the way my nipples tightened into aroused peaks beneath the lace of my bra as I slowly turned to face the man standing directly behind me.

The faint spiciness of his cologne overwhelmed one of my senses while the sight of him totally affected another. Three of my five senses had already gone into shock over this infuriatingly perfect man. All that was left was touch and taste, and you could bet your ass my body wanted to do both.

God, I hated him.

"So you're stalking me now?"

"Bumping into you was just a happy little coincidence, but it does remind me." He stepped closer, lowering his voice to a whisper. "You and I have some unfinished business."

I somehow managed to stop from shivering as his warm, minty breath slithered deliciously across my skin.

Not wanting him to see the longing I was sure radiated in my eyes, I faced the front of the line, sending up a silent thank-you to God that it had moved. There were only two people in front of me now. I was that much closer to my blessed Danish and a soothing latte. But more importantly, I was that much closer to escaping Caleb.

"I don't know what you're talking about," I said flatly, refusing to look back at him as I spoke. "Anything between you and me is so finished it's already dead and buried."

"Yeah? Then I guess that means your rock-hard nipples are just because you're cold and have nothing to do with the fact that you want me." He was so dangerously close his words blew a few tendrils of my hair across my shoulder.

I quickly crossed my arms over my chest and spun around with fire in my eyes. "You're such an egotistical asshole!" I hissed under my breath. "Just to make things *perfectly* clear: I. Do. Not. Want. You."

I was sure we were quite a sight to the people around us. They were probably wondering whether we were about to rip each other's throats out or rip each other's clothes off. If I were being honest, I wasn't too sure of the answer myself.

"Your pupils dilate and you bite your lip every time you look at me. When I get close, you get goose bumps, and don't think I haven't seen the way you shiver when I whisper in your ear. I've got enough experience to know when a woman wants me, Daphne, and your body's practically fucking screaming for it."

Damn him and his uncanny powers of perception!

I opened my mouth to spew a denial, but the lie just wouldn't form. The best I could come up with was "I hate you!"

"You may hate me, sweetheart, but you still want to fuck me."

I threw my hands in the air with a loud "Gah! You're unbelievable!" My heels clicked loudly as I stormed back toward the elevators empty-handed. Just another reason to hate Caleb—he was coming between me and my necessary midday sustenance.

"You running away isn't going to change anything," he continued as he followed me.

"Will you just leave me the hell alone," I snapped, pushing the Up button so hard my finger ached.

"Not until you admit the truth."

I let out a garbled yelp of agitation, not just at Caleb but also at the elevator for being so damn slow. "Screw it! I'll take the freaking stairs."

It most definitely hadn't been my brightest idea.

"You know, I can do this all day long if I have to." Caleb's voice carried up the flight and a half I'd just ascended, and the bastard didn't even sound the slightest bit out of breath.

Meanwhile, my lungs felt like they were on fire, as though I'd just run a full marathon at a sprint. "Oh god," I panted, grasping the railing like it was the only thing keeping me standing—because it really was. "So. Many. Stairs." I inhaled and exhaled through my mouth as a painful stitch twisted my side.

"Jesus, really?" Caleb stopped two steps below mine. "You've barely gone up fifteen steps. How are you this winded?"

"Shut up." I massaged my side, hoping to rub the singe away. "This is all your fault, making me do cardio."

"How the hell is it my fault? I didn't tell you to take the stairs!"

I lifted the hair off the back of my sweaty neck and fanned at my burning face with the other. It was embarrassing how out of shape I was. "Well I wouldn't have had to if you weren't following me!"

"For Christ's sake!" he barked, yanking his hands through his hair. "Why does everything have to turn into an argument with you?"

"Because you drive me crazy!"

"Feeling's mutual, sweetheart!"

And just like that, I launched myself at him. He caught me like I weighed nothing, spinning me around until my back was pinned against the cool cinderblock wall. Our mouths battled against each other's for dominance in a kiss that heated my blood. Our teeth clashed together, our tongues tangled. Caleb's hands roamed feverishly over every inch of my body he could reach.

A groan slipped past my lips as his muscular thigh forced mine apart, making room for his trim hips. I rubbed myself against him like a cat in heat, desperate for more of his touch.

"Fuck," he gritted, trailing a heated path from my jaw to my neck with his tongue. "Why does fighting with you turn me on so goddamn much?"

I arched my back, giving his lips more room while pressing my breasts harder against his chest. "There's something seriously wrong with us," I panted, out of breath and crazy with desire. Caleb's fingers dug into my hips, forcing me to grind on his leg. I whimpered as arousal flooded through me.

"Half the time I don't know if I want to strangle you or kiss you," he grunted, pressing his thigh higher.

I moaned wantonly. "I want to strangle you all the time," I said while riding his leg like a total hussy.

One of his hands left my hip and fisted in my hair, angling my head so he could see my eyes. "Admit you want me."

I couldn't force the word out, not when my body was so close to detonating. All I could do was shake my head in denial.

"Why are you being so goddamn stubborn? I can feel how wet you are for me. You've soaked right through my fucking pants. Just admit it."

I tangled my fingers in his hair, trying to pull his mouth closer to mine. "Stop talking and kiss me."

An annoyed growl worked its way up his throat. "Three little words, Daph. That's it. I. Want. You. Just say it."

I was close. So freaking close I wanted to cry. My lips parted of their own accord, but before I could get the words out, a door a few floors up opened and the sound of voices echoed through the stairwell.

Caleb and I both stood frozen, completely silent as the voices grew fainter before finally disappearing behind another door. Despite thwarting my impending release, the interruption really was a blessing in disguise. It gave me the time I needed for reality to set in.

Placing my hands on Caleb's chest, I pushed until there was enough space for me to slip from between him and that wall. With a trembling hand, I brushed the hair out of my face. "This has to stop, Caleb. We can't keep doing this."

His face hardened like stone. "Give me one reason why."

"Because you're completely wrong for me!" I cried in frustration. I began to pace the small landing as I ranted. "I've done the whole man-whore playboy thing before. I didn't like it then and I don't like it now. You're not the kind of guy a woman gets invested in, Caleb. You're the fling, the fun one-night stand. You're the guy who screws so many women he can't recognize them a few months later!" I shouted, feeling the bitterness course through my blood.

He prowled toward me, a menacing glare plastered on his face. "Don't make the mistake of thinking you know everything about me, sweetheart." His words were spoken softly, quietly, but there was no missing the warning in them. "If you think all there is to me is the number of women I've fucked, then you're sadly mistaken."

With that parting shot, he stomped down the stairs and disappeared through the door to the lobby, leaving me standing on unsteady legs, suddenly feeling very unsure about everything.

CHAPTER NINE

CALEB

"I FUCKING HATE THESE BLACK-TIE EVENTS," I grumbled, tugging at my collar. It was like my bow tie was trying to strangle me.

"Welcome to the lifestyle of the rich and famous," Deacon muttered as he sidled up to the bar. I ordered a scotch on the rocks while Deac got whatever was on tap. "Speaking of rich, where's dear old dad?"

I sucked back my drink and motioned for the bartender to pour me another as I rested my elbows on the bar. "I don't know, but I'll need at least three more of these before he shows up."

"Well you might not want to get too drunk," Deacon said in a tone that piqued my curiosity.

"Yeah? And why's that?"

"Because that hookup you claim is nuts is currently checking you out. And we both know what an ass you can be when you're drunk."

I shot up straight and twirled around, spotting her in an instant. She was by far the most beautiful woman in the room. Her glossy blonde hair fell down her back in soft waves that shone beneath the ballroom lights. One smooth alabaster shoulder was bared by her sinful dress. She was an absolute vision. A picture of pure sex and beauty, unapologetically feminine. She was fucking exquisite.

And she was staring right at me.

The moment our eyes met, I saw her cheeks turn a pink a few shades darker than her dress from all the way across the room. Her chest rose with a deep inhale, her pouty lips puckering into a seductive O as she blew the air out.

Oh yeah, she still wants me.

"Thank god you guys are here. I needed to see a few familiar faces." I turned my attention from Daphne to Fiona as she made a stop before Deacon and me.

"Fiona," Deacon greeted in a bland tone. We hadn't discussed his feelings for her any further after his confession to me a few nights before. I understood his need to keep it to himself, considering she and his brother had been in a serious relationship years before that we all thought was going to eventually lead to marriage. But the fact was it hadn't worked out between them. Gray had moved on to Lola, and Fiona was fair game. He needed to get his thumb out of his ass and make a move already.

Despite her and Grayson not working out, Fiona had grown up right alongside the three of us and was firmly entrenched in our circle of friends. She'd been working in Paris the last few years but had recently returned after her company transferred her back to the States. I knew there'd been drama with her when Gray took Lola to meet his parents, but I hadn't gotten the full story. From the jittery look on Fiona's face, I sensed that whatever had happened between the three of them was still unfinished.

"Hey, Fee. How's it going?" I opened my arms and pulled her into an embrace. I caught the way Deacon's jaw ticked at the sight of my hands on her and quickly ended the hug. Christ, he had it bad. He knew damn good and well I wasn't a threat, but that green-eyed bitch named Jealousy had still reared her ugly head.

"Good. It's going good."

My attention skirted to where I'd last seen Daphne, only to discover that she was no longer there. Fiona and Deacon were talking next to me, but I was too busy scanning the faces in the crowd, searching for the one in particular that I wanted to pay attention to what they were saying.

It wasn't until I spotted a flash of coral in a corner of the huge room that I breathed a sigh of relief. Until I saw who she was talking to.

"Excuse me," I said in way of an apology before leaving Deacon and Fiona and making a beeline to the woman who had been making me insane for over a freaking month.

The man she was locked in a conversation with reached up to tuck a strand of that blonde hair behind her ear, and I suddenly understood the jealousy that Deacon had been dealing with. I wanted to rip the jackass's arm off at the shoulder for touching any part of her.

When I finally got close enough to see her expression, the rage boiling inside me dropped to a simmer. Her beautiful face was pinched and white as a sheet as she jerked her head away from his fingertips. She took a step back and jabbed an angry finger into his chest. Whoever this man was, he wasn't someone Daphne was happy to see, that was for sure.

The guy moved closer, lowering his head in a way that indicated privacy and a hint of intimacy I did *not* like. He said something that made Daphne throw her hands up and gesture wildly as she spoke.

I picked up the pace, the instinct to protect racing through my blood.

"Baby, there you are. I've been looking everywhere for

you." I slipped my arm around her waist and pulled her flush against my side, hoping she could read the message I was trying to communicate with my eyes. *Just go with it*, they said as I leaned in and placed a gentle kiss against her lips. Her mouth parted in surprise as I pulled away to look at the stranger now glaring at my hand that was resting precariously on her hip.

I didn't bother with a polite introduction. "And you are?"

That seemed to snap Daphne out of her daze. "Oh, uh... Stefan, this is Caleb. He's—"

"Her boyfriend," I piped up. "Nice to meet you."

I extended my free hand for him to shake. He stood momentarily stunned before returning the gesture. I squeezed the prick's hand tighter than necessary to relay my point: Hands off, motherfucker.

"So, Steven—"

"It's Stefan," he said with a frown.

"Whatever," I replied with a casual shrug. "How do you know my girl here?"

"I'm—"

"He's no one," Daphne interrupted in a clipped voice. She turned hate-filled eyes his way. "And he was just leaving."

"Ducky, we need—"

She cut him off once again as she looked up at me. "Dinner's about to be served. We should probably get to our table."

I nodded, knowing she wanted out of her current situation. With my hand resting firmly on her back, I led her through the throng of partygoers toward our assigned seats.

"You want to tell me what that was all about?" I asked below my breath as we walked.

"Not even a little bit" was her quiet answer. "But I will say thank you for saving me. I can't believe that asshole showed up here. I really appreciate you swooping in when you did."

And that was all she said. Once we hit the table, she pulled away and tried her best to avoid me.

Unfortunately for her, I wasn't going to let that happen.

DAPHNE

THE EVENING WAS TURNING into a freaking nightmare. After having spent days stressing over how my last conversation with Caleb had ended, I'd finally realized that he'd been right. I'd judged him without really getting to know him. I'd decided to find him during the gala and apologize. I'd hyped myself up to the point that I was searching him out once I got there, but when I saw that stunning redhead come up and hug him, all my courage had fled the building. My throat burned like I'd just swallowed acid at the familiarity of their embrace.

It was obvious by the affection on his face that he knew the woman, but I just didn't know *how well*. And I hated how the thought of them having been together made me feel.

I had been making my rounds through the guests, trying to drum up interest in the upcoming auction, but once I'd seen the two of them together, I needed to escape. I'd been on my way to the ladies' room for a bit of privacy when the last person I ever wanted to lay eyes on cornered me.

I searched for my girls as I rounded the table, needing the support and security I felt whenever I was around them. I spotted Sophia first and breathed a sigh of relief.

"Looks like all is right in paradise," she whispered. I followed her gaze and smiled at the sight of Lola and Grayson cuddled up together as they headed to our table.

The chair next to mine pulled out, and I didn't need to look to see who'd just taken a seat beside me. The familiar spice and musk filled my nostrils, and if that hadn't been enough, my body automatically reacted to his presence before my mind even became aware.

"You know you can't avoid me forever, right?"

"I can try," I mumbled into my wineglass, taking a fortifying sip.

He leaned in closer. "There are those goose bumps again." I looked down and silently cursed the betraying bumps on my arms. "I just saved your ass. I'd think you'd be just a little bit grateful."

The table filled up around us, but all I could see was Caleb. "I am. I already thanked you for that."

"Then how about you stop trying to run away from me like I've got leprosy?"

I opened my mouth to speak when the servers appeared and started setting out the first course, interrupting the moment. Thankfully, Caleb and I were engaged in conversations with other people throughout dinner. It gave me an excuse for avoiding him without making it too obvious that it was exactly what I was doing.

I watched curiously throughout the meal as Lola and the redhead I'd spotted with Caleb earlier kept leaning in to each other, laughing at whatever they were whispering about. That pang of jealousy was still there at the sight of her, but I was more curious as to who she was at the moment.

I got my answer shortly after the dessert course. Lola found a second to gather Sophia and me and made introductions. "Guys, this is Fiona Prentice."

My eyes bugged out at her name. Not missing my and Soph's flabbergasted expressions, Lola quickly prattled on. "Long story short, I had it wrong. She's not trying to steal Grayson from me. The pictures were totally taken out of context. We had a good talk about it earlier and decided we were going to be friends."

And that was it. It was just that simple with Lola. She might have liked to act all tough and hard, but at the center of it, she was as soft and forgiving as anyone I'd ever known. If she said Fiona was a friend, then Sophia and I both understood what that meant. Fiona was now a part of our circle. I still felt a twinge whenever I thought about her and Caleb hugging, but Lola had a gift at reading people, and if she thought Fiona was a good person, then I knew I needed to give her a chance.

The four of us chatted for a bit, getting to know the newest member of our circle, and I was remiss to admit that she was actually pretty cool. Lola explained that she was going to have Fiona take her place in the auction since she planned to get up on stage and profess her love to Grayson.

The whole thing was terribly romantic, and despite my aversion to relationships, I was insanely happy that my best friend had found someone who made her smile in a way I'd never seen before. She deserved it.

CHAPTER TEN

CALEB

I WATCHED the stage with my jaw clenched so tight it began to ache. When the MC announced that an auction was about to begin, I'd been momentarily confused. I hadn't heard anything about an auction.

Then Lola, Daphne, and Sophia had taken the stage and it all started to make sense.

Daphne, along with her friends, was offering herself up on a silver platter for all these bastards with padded pockets. It was charity, for a good cause, blah, blah, blah. Lola rattled on into the mic about offering dates to the highest bidders to raise more money for the Wave Foundation, but all I could think about was some other asshole throwing in enough money to win an evening with Daphne. *My* Daphne.

I did a mental calculation of my funds in my head. I had my checking account, which, thanks to my salary at Bandwidth, was nothing to sneeze at. There was the savings account I'd set up, the lucrative investment accounts, and the trust fund I'd received at twenty-five and never touched.

I had more than enough, and I was willing to bid it all to keep her out of the clutches of some other fucker.

"Sucks for you, man," Deacon chuckled. He was way too happy to rub my discomfort in my face. Then karma smiled down on me, and Lola announced that she was pulling herself from the auction because of Grayson and her love for him, yadda, yadda, romantic bullshit, yadda. When she announced that Fiona would be taking her place, it was all I could do not to laugh at the sudden change in Deacon's demeanor.

"Welcome to the boat," I mumbled sarcastically. "We're currently heading up a shit creek and are all out of paddles."

"For fuck's sake. I didn't bring my checkbook. You think they'll take plastic?" He looked frantic as he pulled out his wallet and started checking all means of payment.

"For our sakes, I really fucking hope so."

By the time my attention returned to the stage, Sophia had just gone for an impressive hundred grand. She exited the stage, her face white as a ghost beneath her fake smile. She met the man who'd just paid a small fortune for her at the base of the stairs, looking none too happy to see him. They wandered off, but my focus returned to the stage when I heard the dude with the microphone say Daphne's name.

"Now, gentlemen, don't be disheartened for losing out on the lovely Sophia, because up next is the equally ravishing Daphne King! She loves rainy days, romance novels, and DIY TV shows." Jesus, the guy sounded like a shitty game show host. The bidding started at five grand and rose at an unfathomable pace.

"Thirty!" I shouted loud enough for everyone to hear. Daphne's eyes jerked to mine and she gaped in shock.

"Forty thousand!"

I turned from her to the jackass who'd tried to outbid me. The sight of that dickhead Stefan caused me to bite the inside of my cheek so hard I tasted blood. "Forty-five," I returned.

His glower landed on me as he countered with another ten

thousand. Bastard wanted to get in a bidding war? Fine by me. I had more money than most small countries. I could do this all fucking night.

"Sixty thousand," I boomed in a confident tone.

He began to fidget, and I knew he was starting to grow concerned. I offered him a cocky smirk. *That's right, asshole. I've got more money* and *a bigger dick. Bring it.*

"Sixty-two."

I chanced a peek at Daphne to see her chewing on her lip anxiously. She hated the idea of Stefan winning just as much as I did.

"Seventy thousand."

He swallowed hard, and I could see the perspiration building on his brow from three tables away. "Seventy-one."

Really? Why wouldn't he just give up? "Eighty."

"Sold!" Daphne's shout pulled me from the staring match with that doorknob Stefan. She'd rushed the makeshift auctioneer and was battling for his mic so she could close out the bidding at my last number.

"Well, uh...." The MC laughed awkwardly into the microphone as he struggled with Daphne to get control over it. "Congratulations to the gentleman with the highest bid at eighty thousand dollars!"

Daphne's release of her death grip on the microphone was unexpected, and the MC stumbled back a few feet before catching himself. Seeing as she was already clearing the stairs and heading in my direction, he turned to the next item up for bid: Fiona.

"Can I talk to you?" Daphne asked once she reached me. She looked at the few remaining people left at our table since Grayson, Lola, Sophia, and the guy who'd won her had all disappeared. "In private?"

I took her elbow and guided her through one of the exits into the massive empty hall just outside the ballroom.

She was twisting her fingers together and biting her lower lip again when she spun around to face me. "I'll pay you back the money, I swear," she blurted, leaving me thoroughly confused.

"What?"

"The eighty thousand dollars you bid. I have it. I'll give it to you."

I moved closer to her, untangling her hands so I could slip my fingers between hers. Her gaze turned down to them like my touch was unexpected. "Daph, I don't give a shit about the money."

Her eyes jerked back up to mine. "That's a lot of money, Caleb."

"Yeah, and I'm good for it if that's what you're worried about," I replied shortly, more than a little offended that she'd think I'd bid money I didn't have.

She gave her head a fierce shake. "No, that's not... I didn't mean it like that. I know you have it. You're not the kind of guy who'd lie like that just to get his way." That worked wonders in easing some of my ire. "It's just... you did it for me, because you knew Stefan was bidding. You didn't have to, but you rescued me again. Paying you back is the least I can do."

I used her grip on my hand to pull her closer, twining an arm around her tiny waist to hold her against my chest. "Don't worry about the money, sweetheart. I'd have outbid any of those bastards in there. It was just a coincidence that it turned out to be that guy."

Her eyes rounded in such a sexy, adorable way that I felt myself growing hard at the sight of it. "Y-you would have?"

A rumble of pure, unadulterated desire vibrated from my chest. "I've made it pretty clear how much I want you, Daphne.

Do you really think I'd have let any of those pricks get even a second with you if I had the chance to stop it?"

I felt her sway into me. I saw the goose bumps form on her arms, watched as her pupils grew so wide the black nearly swallowed all their color. "I thought you hated me," she said in a breathy whisper.

"You drive me out of my goddamn head, baby, but I don't hate you."

She closed her eyes and pulled in a strong breath before looking at me again, having regained her composure. "I'm sorry. I've been meaning to tell you that all night. After you left me in the stairwell... well, I thought about what you said, and you were right. I judged you without knowing much of anything about you, and for that I apologize."

I couldn't stand it anymore, being so close to her, smelling her sweet, floral perfume. That scent made it impossible not to want to taste her, and I lowered my head to do just that when an unwelcome voice burst our cozy little bubble.

"Is that really something you should be doing out here in the open for anyone to see?"

The growl I emitted right then had nothing to do with desire and everything to do with fury. Daphne jerked back so quick I had to grab hold of her waist to keep her upright. Only once she was steady did I bother turning to face the bane of my existence.

My mother hung on my father's arm like being paraded around at the gala was the highlight of her life. Her appearance was flawless, from her hair, to her makeup, to her tastefully chosen gown. If I hadn't already known better, I never would have suspected that the woman before me was fond of all her meals in liquid or pill form. "Father," I grunted unhappily. Then, ever the doting son, I leaned forward to place a kiss on my mother's cheek and greeted, "Mom. You look beautiful."

Thanks to recent Botox, her lips barely formed a smile.

"Thank you, darling. You as well." She patted my arm and resumed her clutch on her husband.

My father's eyes were firmly on Daphne standing just behind me. The predatory gleam in them made my skin crawl. "Since my son isn't polite enough to introduce me to his new... friend, I'll do it myself. I'm Christopher McMannus."

I had to rein in the beast that roared to life within me when she stuck out her hand to shake his. "Daphne King. Nice to meet you."

His grip on her fingers visibly tightened, bringing them to his lips to place a kiss on her knuckles. I wanted to shove my fist so far through his face that he swallowed his teeth. "The pleasure is all mine, dear. You're quite lovely."

Two things happened in that very moment that were both fascinating and worrisome. The fascinating thing was the way Daphne's mouth tightened in displeasure as she tried to hide the fact that my father's touch made her uncomfortable. The worrisome part was the way my mother glared daggers in her direction, like Daphne was the one to blame for my father's inappropriate behavior.

"So how do you know my son, Miss King?" Mom asked in a falsely cheerful tone.

"Oh, well...." Daphne struggled to string her words together, looking up at me as if asking for guidance. "We're friends."

My father made a noise in the back of his throat. "My son has many *friends*. He's quite notorious for it. I do hope a woman of your caliber won't allow herself to be misled by his charms."

I was about to lose my fucking mind, but before I could rip into the hypocritical motherfucker, Daphne spoke, rendering anything I'd have to say moot.

"Yes, well, you know what they say about taking stock in what those magazines print. I've always been one to form my own opinion about a person. Listening to other people's gossip leaves a bad taste in my mouth. I think it speaks more to the person's character who's spreading the foul rumors than it does the subject of the gossip, wouldn't you say?"

It was classy and cutting all at the same time. The strength behind her words made their meaning clear: she didn't give a single shit what my father had to say about me, and held his opinion in low regard.

Christ, she was magnificent. My cock got even harder at the effortless way she'd just flayed the powerful man in front of her like he was absolutely nothing.

She turned and gave me a smile that held a hint of compassion before turning back to my parents. "It was nice to meet you both, but I feel a headache coming on. I think it's time for me to go home."

I jumped at the opportunity presented to me. "I'll drive you."

She stutter-stepped in her sky-high heels at the pressure I put on the small of her back. "Oh, you don't—"

"Of course I do," I interrupted. "If you're not feeling well, it would be irresponsible of me to let you drive yourself, or get in the back of a stranger's car." I looked over my shoulder at my folks, not bothering to examine their expressions as I said, "Enjoy your evening."

I grasped her hand in mine, holding so tight she had no choice but to follow as I led her far away from the toxic atmosphere that surrounded my parents no matter where they went.

I was taking her home. Once there, I intended to find out just how *sorry* she really was, and then use that to my full advantage.

CHAPTER ELEVEN

DAPHNE

I WATCHED the city lights pass by outside my window as Caleb guided his car through the quiet streets. The only words I'd spoken since climbing into his passenger seat were directions to my house. Since then we'd both remained silent.

I was still rattled from the events of the entire night.

Finally, Caleb broke through the strained quiet that filled the small space. "I'm sorry about my father."

I looked over at him, his profile illuminated by the faint glow of the lights coming from the dashboard. "He was...." I couldn't think of a PC term to use when describing Caleb's dad. I didn't have the first clue what their relationship was like, and I didn't want to offend him by telling him his dad was creepy as fuck.

"He's a bastard," he finished for me. I let out a small sigh of relief that I wasn't alone in that opinion.

He glanced in my direction just long enough for me to give him a slight grin. "Well, I wasn't going to say anything."

That knot in my belly tightened even more when his expression remained set in stone. "The man's a world-class jackass. When he touched you, I just about lost my shit."

"Is he always like that?"

His voice was monotone as he answered, "Has been for as long as I can remember. The son of a bitch has treated my mom like a doormat their entire marriage, and she just lies there and takes it. Won't even consider leaving him even though he cheats on her with any willing woman. What he did tonight"—his jaw ticked furiously—"hitting on you like that in front of her, degrading me? That's his M.O."

I'd come across more than my fair share of women just like that in my line of work, and to this day I couldn't understand that kind of mindset. It made me sick to my stomach when women allowed themselves to be walked on. And sadly, those kinds of women always blamed the other woman, leaving the man completely blameless. They gave our gender a bad name.

Growing up, I'd discovered that women fell into categories. Most of those categories were harmless, but I had learned from experience that there were two types that I couldn't stand. These types of women were clingers. Men were the most important things in their lives, no matter the consequences. They didn't have the first clue how to function as single ladies.

The first category was what I called The Dependent Clinger. Caleb's mother fell into that group. It was where the woman gave every single ounce of power to the man in her life, so scared of losing him that she catered to the man's every whim. The man could do no wrong; what he said was law.

The second category was The Entitled Clinger. This was where my mother fell. Instead of working to earn the lifestyle they felt they deserved, they glommed onto men with money. They used sex and all other forms of feminine wiles as a manipulation method, making those guys feel like the center of their universe so they'd feel inclined to give the woman whatever her heart desired.

I turned my attention to the windshield and said quietly, "I'm sorry."

The sudden feel of his hand on mine caused me to jolt in my seat. "Don't apologize," he commanded in a strong, intimidating voice. "You didn't do anything wrong, you hear me? He's the asshole for making you uncomfortable. It was his fault, not yours."

My heart actually began to ache for him. "I wasn't apologizing for that. I was apologizing because you've had to deal with this shit your whole life. It's not fair to you. And for that I'm sorry."

Without thinking, I turned my hand over beneath his so we were palm to palm, lacing our fingers together.

"This is me," I said a few minutes later, pointing at the huge, rambling Victorian I'd bought for a song about six months earlier.

Several seconds of silence encompassed us after Caleb put the car into Park. Then he declared vehemently, "No. No way. You can *not* live here."

I twisted to the side to face him. "What? Why not?"

"It's a fucking pit, Daphne!"

"It is not!" I objected, feeling defensive of my amazing home. Sure, from the outside things might not look all that great thanks to the boards covering some of the broken windows, the busted outside lights I hadn't yet fixed, and the rotted shingles, but there was a reason I got it so cheap. And I'd slowly been working to get her back to her former glory. My house was going to be magnificent once I was finished with it. "It's got character."

"It looks like it's got termites," he grumbled. "One wrong step and it's going to fall down on your head."

With a roll of my eyes, I pushed the car door open and stepped out. "Come on," I said, leaning back down to catch his eyes. "Come inside and I'll show you why this house is so awesome."

Considering our track record, I knew inviting him into my

home, my own personal sanctuary, wasn't smart. I just couldn't help myself when it came to showing off my baby.

He looked no less skeptical as he climbed out of the car after me, but I knew I'd win him over the moment he walked inside. I unlocked the front door and pushed it open before flipping on my entryway lights. Stepping to the side, I waved him in with a flourish, crying, "Ta da!" as he walked past.

I could see the change of heart written all over his face the instant he walked through the threshold. "Wow," he mumbled in wonder. "This place is amazing."

"Told you. It's not a pit," I informed him happily.

The foyer was my absolute favorite part of the house. I'd started my renovation there, wanting to restore it so everyone who entered my home was hit with the magnificent wow factor. The ceiling was completely open to the second floor, with a gorgeous crystal chandelier hanging above that I'd painstakingly cleaned piece by piece. A beautiful staircase with wrought iron balusters between the oak handrail and outer string split the entire room in two, with the parlor to the left and the formal dining area to the right.

The lower parts of the walls were covered in a gleaming oak wainscoting, and I'd painted the areas above a soft ivory to help warm and brighten the space.

"It took me forever to strip all the paint from the woodwork and remove the hideous wallpaper the previous owners put up, but it was totally worth it."

Excitement coursed through my veins as I took his hand and pulled him into the parlor. "See all this awesome crown molding?" I waved my hand above me. "Can you believe someone would paint that? It's ridiculous, right?" I was getting lost in describing all the work I'd done on the room so far. "And they laid down wall-to-wall carpet over these hardwood floors. A travesty! I ripped it all out and sanded it down. There were some boards here and there that needed replacing, but I was able to maintain the original flooring for the most part."

Caleb's hold on my hand tightened, forcing me to stay in place and calling my attention back to him.

"You're saying you did all of this yourself?"

"Well, not all of it," I answered. "I mean, I had to bring someone in to do the insulation, and I don't know the first thing about wiring, so I had to hire an electrician—"

"But all of this, all the cosmetic stuff"—he waved his hand, encompassing the room—"you did all of this?"

The way he said it, the pride in his voice as he looked from the room to me, filled me with a warmth I'd never felt before. I couldn't have stopped the smile that stretched across my face if I'd wanted to. "Well, I'm not done with the whole place yet. I have to take my time and work room by room, but yeah. I'm kind of a do-it-yourself nut. When I first saw this place, I knew it would be magnificent, and I wanted to be the one to bring it back to life."

He turned me to face him completely and ran the backs of his fingers along my cheekbone in a gentle caress. "You're pretty magnificent yourself, you know that?"

His words coupled with the sincerity in his voice made my stomach swoop in an all-too-familiar way. My body swayed closer, my face pressing into his touch. "You think so?" I asked on a breathless whisper.

"I know so. I already knew you were amazing, but what you've done with this place so far just proves I was right."

My gaze traveled down to his lips, and I was instantly bombarded with the desire to feel them against my own. "Stop being sweet. It makes me want to kiss you."

A seductive growl rumbled up his throat as he took a step closer. "Ask me to stay."

"Huh?" I was so consumed by my need to feel every part of

him against every part of me that I didn't comprehend what he'd just said.

His fingers pressed beneath my chin, tilting my head up so I was looking into those fascinating blue eyes. "Ask me to stay the night and I promise I'll spend hours kissing every single inch of you."

Once again, my body and my brain went to war with each other. "I don't know if that's smart," I said, letting my brain take control for a moment.

"Fuck being smart," he ground out. "You want me just as much as I want you, so why fight it?"

"We drive each other crazy, Caleb. We argue constantly. Half the time we can't even stand each other."

"Admit it, that just makes the sex even better."

He certainly wasn't wrong about that. I was prepared to put up more of an argument when he closed the remaining few inches between us and pulled me against him. His hard cock pressed into my belly, instantly making me wet. "You can put up as much of a fight as you want, but I won't give up until I have my fill. And gorgeous, with how hard you make me come every time I fuck you, I seriously doubt I'll have my fill any time this century."

My body officially won the battle with my brain.

"Caleb?"

"Yeah, sweetheart?"

"Stay the night with me."

CHAPTER TWELVE

CALEB

I WASN'T GIVING her a chance to change her mind. No fucking way. The second the invitation left her mouth, I slammed my lips against hers in a kiss that did nothing but fuel my need for Daphne.

She went completely pliant under my touch, letting me take the lead just like every other time we came together. "Bedroom," I growled against her mouth while pawing at her ass through the silky material of her gown.

"Too far," she panted, ripping at my bow tie. "Need you now."

I was all too happy to accommodate, seeing as my cock was moments away from bursting through my pants. I fisted her dress in my hands and yanked it up to her hips, exposing my eyes to the sinful thigh-highs she was wearing beneath. Only thigh-highs and nothing else.

"Fuck me," I groaned. "This is what you've been sporting under that dress all goddamn night?"

Her head fell into the crook of my neck where she planted a trail of fiery kisses. "I couldn't wear panties with this dress. Now stop talking and fuck me."

I moved until her back hit the wall just inside the parlor. Wrapping her hair around my fist, I pulled until her lips were at a perfect angle for me to feast on. It was just as hot, just as frenzied and demanding as it always was. Precum spilled from my dick at the thought of sinking inside her, but there was something else I just *had* to do first.

Dropping to my knees, I threw one of her legs over my shoulder and dove in, feasting on her like she was my last meal. I'd never tasted anything so fucking intoxicating in my whole life. Her head fell back against the wall with a loud thunk as her nails dug into my scalp on a sharp, keening cry. My cock got even harder at how responsive she was every time I touched her. It was the hottest thing I'd ever experienced.

"Oh god. Caleb!" she whimpered, thrusting her hips closer to my face. She was so close, I could tell just by the sounds she was making. But I needed her to get there *now* or I was likely to come in my pants.

I circled her clit with my tongue at the same time I shoved two fingers deep inside her heat. Curling them, I found that spot that would set her off. Daphne's whimpers turned to moans for a second before becoming full-on cries of release as I rubbed and thrust and licked. I didn't let up, prolonging her pleasure until her knee buckled.

I quickly slid her leg from my shoulder and shot up, gripping her waist to spin her until her chest hit the wall. "Tell me you're protected," I demanded, pulling her dress up over her ass before freeing my dick from my pants.

"What?"

"You on the pill?" I asked as I lined the head of my cock up with her slick entrance.

"I... yes, I'm on the pi—"

I drove into her bare before she had a chance to finish her sentence. Being skin to skin like that, feeling her clench around me without any barrier between us, was almost too much to bear.

"Ah, *Christ!*" I grunted, pulling almost all the way out. I slammed back in so hard Daphne shouted at the invasion.

"Don't stop! Oh my god, Caleb. Harder!"

I fucked her as hard as I could. "Now try telling me this is a bad idea." I gripped her wrists and lifted them above her head, caging them in place with one hand. With my free one, I brushed the hair off her shoulder and dropped my forehead there. Beads of sweat trailed down the back of my neck as I plowed in and out of her. Both of us were grunting and moaning with exertion.

"Let me touch you," she pleaded, her pussy clenching me so tight I knew she was about to go off.

I lifted my head. "Next time, baby," I breathed into her ear as I snaked my hand down her body until I could rub at her clit. "I've been dying to feel this ass pressed against me as I fucked you."

She made a sound deep in her throat before throwing her head back against my shoulder and coming so violently she nearly screamed the house down.

There was no way I'd have been able to last, not when she clamped down around me like a vice. Two seconds after she came, I planted myself to the root and roared out my own release.

Starbursts exploded behind my eyelids, and I had to work to pull air into my deflated lungs as we both trembled against each other. Her arms dropped limp to her sides when I finally released her hands, and I wrapped both of mine around her in an embrace, placing one of my palms flat against her chest right above her heart.

The beat of her heart eventually slowed to match mine.

"Next time you try to talk yourself out of being with me just remember how that felt."

Her back shook against my chest as a light giggle broke free. "I won't be forgetting that any time soon. I don't think I'm going to be able to walk after that."

I pulled out, loving the thought of my cum still being inside her even though I no longer was. After tucking my dick back into my pants, I zipped up my fly and spun her around before scooping her up in my arms. She let out a startled yelp at the sudden motion and wrapped her arms around my neck. "What are you doing?"

"Carrying you to bed," I answered as I moved toward the stairs. "It's the least I could do after fucking you so good you aren't able to walk."

She smacked me on the chest with a laugh, and the sound did wonders in lifting the heavy weight of stress that had been resting on my shoulders since the run-in with my parents earlier that night. Being with her just did that for me; whether we were having sex or not, just her company was enough to beat the demons back.

"Such a gentleman," she said in a fake deadpan.

I looked down at her and winked as I started to climb the stairs. "I'm nothing if not chivalrous, gorgeous. And to prove it, I'll even let you have a short nap before I attack you again."

CHAPTER THIRTEEN

I WOKE with a jolt thanks to the clap of thunder outside that shook my entire house. A quick peek at my bedside clock showed it was barely after five in the morning. The sun wouldn't be up for hours.

The rain beat against the windowpanes in my bedroom. I'd forgotten to draw the curtains the night before, so I had a front row seat to the storm raging just outside, but it wasn't wind or the lightning that cut through the black sky that had me unsettled. It was the heavy arm wrapped around my waist.

Caleb had stayed the night. And despite knowing I probably should've woken him up and kicked him to the curb, I couldn't bring myself to do it. The truth was I actually *liked* seeing him in my bed.

And that was the most frightening part about the whole thing. I could easily see myself falling for Caleb. And that was nothing more than a one-way ticket to another broken heart. He might not cheat on me like Stefan did, but he'd certainly hurt me in the long run. It was just in his nature. He wasn't a guy who stuck around.

After meeting his parents the night before, I couldn't very

well blame him for that, seeing as he grew up like me, without a single person to show us what a healthy relationship looked like. But that didn't change the fact that he was the type of guy who didn't want to stick around. And I was the kind of girl who fell easily if I let myself get attached. That was the very reason I'd sworn off committed relationships after Stefan. I couldn't go down that road again.

Been there, done that, and got the shitty T-shirt as a reminder of how bad it sucked.

Trying to fall back asleep—especially with Caleb's temptingly warm body next to me—was going to be impossible, so instead of spending the next few hours tossing and turning, I decided to do something more meaningful with my time.

Climbing out of my cozy bed, I padded across the room to my dresser, pulling out a pair of underwear and a bra from the top drawer before digging through the one below it of old, tattered clothes I kept to wear when renovating. I grabbed a pair of paint-splattered overalls and a threadbare tank, then moved into the bathroom to get dressed.

I'd bought the house six months earlier and started fixing it up right away. Through a lot of sweat, a ton of tears, and the occasional bit of blood, I'd managed to get the entire downstairs completed, but with the exception of my own bedroom and bathroom—for practical purposes—the upstairs was still a construction zone. I treated it just like the downstairs, completing one room before starting the next, so when I left my bedroom I went straight to the one I'd designated as my office.

It was my second favorite room in the house, and for damn good reason. If it'd had an adjoining bathroom, I would've made it into my master suite. The entire back wall was nothing but built-in bookshelves that went from floor to ceiling. Across from that were huge, beautiful bay windows that gave me a stunning view of nothing but forest as far as I could see. I stuffed my earbuds in my ears, queued up my DIY playlist, and shoved my phone in the front pocket of my overalls. Then I got to work on sanding my kickass wall of shelves so I could stain them a beautiful cherry.

It was going to take me forever, but once I had them finished and could move on to the flooring, the room was going to be breathtaking.

I'd completely lost track of time, sanding while singing and dancing along to "Feel it Still" by Portugal, The Man, when two arms wrapped around me from behind, causing me to shriek and spin around, knocking the earbuds out in the process.

"Holy shit, Caleb!" I placed my hand on my chest to calm my racing heart, using the other one to smack his. "You almost gave me a heart attack, you jerk!"

He grinned down at me, pulling me even closer. His hair was rumpled, and his face was still adorably sleepy. Once I got over my fright, I was able to notice he was in nothing but his tuxedo pants from the night before. They were only zipped, left unbuttoned at the waist, so the tantalizing view of that deeply ridged V was peeking at me.

Beneath the arousal that came every time I looked at him, there was the discomfort thanks to that longing I'd woken up feeling. I needed space to clear my head and shake off the unsettled tension coiling in my gut.

"Sorry, sweetheart. I said your name, but I guess you didn't hear me over the one-woman show you had going on in here."

I flinched, suddenly embarrassed that he'd heard me sing. I was bad. Like the first few episodes of *American Idol* bad. You know, the ones where they show the worst of the worst before finally getting to the singers who would actually make it into the competition? Yeah, I was William Hung.

"Crap, I'm sorry. Was I too loud? I didn't mean to wake you."

"You didn't. I woke on my own and came searching when I found you already gone. How long have you been up?"

"Uh, I'm not sure." I took a step back and he thankfully let me go. I picked up the sanding block I'd been using and pretended to examine it. "I woke up a little after five."

"You've been up for three hours already?"

My eyes got big. I looked back at the bay windows, but because of the storm rattling against the glass, the sun was nowhere to be seen. It still looked like it was nighttime outside. "Wow. It's already after eight?"

"Yeah. You really get into this whole renovation thing, huh?"

I tucked the earbuds into the pocket with my phone and moved to the shelf I'd been working on before he showed up. I needed something to do with my hands, some way to keep my attention off his impeccable form, or I'd crumble. "Yeah, I guess. I get in the zone and lose track."

I scrubbed furiously at one area on the wood until I'd stripped the spot of years of stains and paint.

His voice was directly behind me when he asked, "Why won't you look at me?"

I blew out a breath and dropped the block before turning guilty eyes to Caleb. "I—" He made a face, the warning clear: *Lie and pay the price.* I amended what I was about to say. "What are we doing?"

His forehead wrinkled in bewilderment. "You mean right now?"

It was my turn to give him a look. It clearly stated, *You know what I mean, asshole.*

"I don't know, Daph, we're... having fun?" At the unhappy face I made, he quickly backpedaled. "I didn't mean it like that. But do you really need a label on this? Why can't we just enjoy it for however long it lasts without putting any pressure on ourselves? We like spending time with each other." His face went lazy with arousal, his eyelids going half-mast as he moved closer, placing his hands on my hips. "We *really* fucking like having sex with each other. Can't that be enough, at least for right now?"

Could it? If we went into whatever this was with full disclosure and eyes wide open, with no strings attached, could it possibly work? It's basically what I did with the other men I saw somewhat steadily. The only reason I hadn't considered the same kind of arrangement with Caleb was because *I* felt things with him I hadn't felt with any of those others. But if we made it clear from the very start....

Finally, after thinking, rethinking, and overthinking the situation, I answered, "Yeah. That can be enough."

Caleb leaned back at the waist so he could get a better look at my face. "You sure?" he asked hesitantly, almost as if he was afraid I'd change my mind.

"I'm sure. If we both agree to just have fun and ride this out, then you're right, there's no pressure."

He kept watching me, staying quiet for so long that I actually started to get concerned that *he'd* change his mind. "Are you for real?"

I tilted my head, not understanding the question. "How do you mean?"

"You're hot as shit, you fuck like a dream, and you're cool without any labels. You aren't like any woman I've ever met before. So I have to ask, are you for real?"

I smiled seductively and rested my palms on his muscular chest, relishing the feel of the light smattering of chest hair beneath my fingers. "Oh, I assure you I'm very, *very* real. Pretty sure I proved that to you last night."

He hummed appreciatively, sliding his hands down to the swell of my ass. "I wouldn't be opposed to a little refresher."

I felt him growing hard against my abdomen. Heat pooled in my belly, but I had other ideas. "Well," I started teasingly. "I did have something in mind that requires a bit of... exertion."

His deep "Tell me" came out like a growl.

I pulled from his grasp and slowly started backing up. "It'll take a while. It'll be hard. You'll definitely build up a sweat...."

"Christ, gorgeous. You're killing me. I'm hard as a fucking rock."

I giggled wantonly, then reached behind me and grabbed the extra sanding block off the shelf, tossing it his way. "Get started on that shelf over there. And really put some muscle into it. I want these bookcases stripped by the end of the day."

Caleb's face fell and he let out a string of curses as I burst into laughter. Once I got myself under control, I told him, "Do a good job and maybe I'll let you buff my floors."

"Oh, I'll be buffing something, all right. But it won't be your fucking floors."

I started laughing again, and both of us eventually got to work. We'd fallen into an easy, companionable silence when a question began nagging at me, leaving me no choice but to ask it.

"We agreed we wouldn't put any pressure on this, right?"

"Yeah?"

"So, what if we don't tell anyone we're... doing whatever it is we're doing?"

I kept sanding even though I heard him stop. I couldn't bring myself to make eye contact. Not just then.

"You don't want to tell anybody?"

The tone of his voice dripped with disapproval, leaving me with a painful, twisted stomach. I felt like I'd just asked him to be my dirty little secret. And I never wanted him to feel like that.

I dropped the block and turned around to face him. He was standing with his hands firmly on his hips, looking as pissed as he sounded. "If Lola or Sophia found out we were sleeping together, it would be a disaster. You could kiss any hope of no pressure goodbye, because those two are the very definition of meddlesome. Especially Lola now that she's all sickeningly in love with Grayson and stuff. And if you were to tell Grayson, do you really think he'd keep it from her?"

He looked to be giving that question some thought, so I decided to drive my point home. "We want this to be easy, right? Fun. I love my best friends, but they'd ruin that by trying to turn us into something we aren't. I'm not trying to keep you a secret because I'm ashamed. I want what you do. I want us to enjoy what we have while we have it, and that can't happen if our friends start sticking their noses in our business."

His chest rose on a long inhale, showcasing that delicious six-pack he was sporting. Finally, he put me out of my misery with one simple word. "Okay."

It took a second for what he'd just said to register in my brain. "Okay?" It was too easy. I'd gotten used to everything being a fight between us, so I guess I'd been gearing up for the worst. "Just like that?"

"I see your point, Daphne. And as long as you and I know exactly where we stand, then I agree with you. There's no reason to let anyone else in our business."

"I... wow. Well that was simple. I was expecting you to argue or start yelling or something."

"Why would I do that?" he asked incredulously.

"Because it's what we do!" I declared, like what I was saying made all the sense in the world. "We fight. We yell. We shout and call each other names. Then we rip each other's clothes off and go at it like animals. It's kind of our thing." And why the hell did I sound so disappointed that we weren't going to have a blowout that would lead to mind-numbing sex?

He offered me one of those grins that made me weak in the

knees. "Sweetheart, we don't have to fight in order to go at it like animals. You want it like that, all you have to do is say so."

My pussy quivered, and I clenched my thighs against the sudden desire building in my core. "Really?" I asked breathily.

His expression turned positively wicked as he slowly started advancing like a lion about to pounce. "Is that what you want? You want me to tear at your clothes and fuck you hard and fast? Make you scream so loud the walls shake?"

Oh god yes. I wanted *all* of that.

I didn't need to verbalize my answer; I knew he saw it written all over my face when he smiled. "I'll give you a head start. But when I catch you, you better be naked, or there will be consequences."

He started counting and I bolted out of the room the instant he said, "One." By the time he got to three, I was totally ready for him.

CHAPTER FOURTEEN

DAPHNE

THREE MONTHS. Caleb and I had somehow managed to keep our friends in the dark for three whole months. And they'd been the most exciting, most *exhausting* few months of my life.

It was as though we were in a race with time, trying to cram in as much sex as humanly possible before the clock ran out—whenever that may be. Some days, just walking proved to be difficult. I hadn't thought I'd ever meet a man I couldn't keep up with sexually—I had a pretty healthy appetite—but I was actually starting to worry that Caleb might turn out to be more than I could handle.

My cell phone vibrated on my desk. After a few close calls, I'd quickly learned to start placing it facedown so my girls didn't see the dirty things Caleb liked to text me in the middle of the day.

I picked up the phone and glanced at the notification, seeing it wasn't from Caleb this time. It was actually from Fiona. I'd gotten to know her pretty well since the night of the auction, and we'd become good friends.

Fiona: S.O.S. *I need your ear and a shitload of wine. Please tell me you're free tonight.*

I quickly responded.

Me: *I'm all yours. My place at 7?*

Fiona: *Sounds good. And I hate to ask, but can we keep it just us?*

Fiona had managed to infiltrate my girl circle with an ease no other woman we'd ever met had been able to do. But even though she was close to all three of us, I'd formed a bond with her that was even tighter than the one she shared with Lola and Soph, so I knew that whatever she had to discuss was pretty serious if she didn't want the two of them to find out.

I couldn't judge her for wanting to keep them out of the loop considering I was basically doing the exact same thing with Caleb.

Me: *You got it. See you then.*

Before I had a chance to exit out of my texts, I got another notification.

Caleb: *Listened to the show this morning. I found your topic of discussion quite entertaining.*

I giggled as I stared down at the message. We'd had a woman call into the show that morning because she was worried there was something wrong with her. It took us a while to talk her off the ledge and explain that the fact that she'd never experienced multiple orgasms wasn't something she needed to seek medical treatment for. I'd given her a list of some of my favorite sex toys and suggested she mention using them with her partner.

Me: *I'm sure you did, you pervert.*

Caleb: *You love my perverted side. I'm hard as a fucking rock after listening to you. Meet me in our spot.*

I clenched my thighs as my clit began to pulse and throb with desire. A few weeks earlier, after a business trip had taken Caleb out of town for several days, both of us were more than a little desperate to see each other. We'd snuck off to the stairwell for a midday romp between our two floors, and ever since, that place had been referred to as our spot.

Me: *I can't. It's the middle of the workday!*

His message came instantly, like he'd been expecting me to argue.

Caleb: *It's been over twelve hours since I was inside your sweet pussy. If you don't meet me in the stairwell, I'll have no choice but to come down there and GET YOU.*

I let out a laugh, knowing his threat was anything but empty. We'd just been together the night before, but every time the man touched me I got the distinct impression that it still wasn't enough for him. That feeling of being desired was the most euphoric thing I'd ever experienced. I was quickly growing addicted to it.

"What's so funny?"

I let out a startled yelp and spun around in my chair, clutching my phone to my chest. Lola and Sophia walked into our shared office, studying me peculiarly like I was a specimen under a microscope that they couldn't quite figure out.

"Oh, uh... I was just watching some of those cat videos on YouTube that Lola likes so much." The lie slipped easily past my lips. Too easily. I'd gotten so good at deceiving my friends these past two months that the guilt was beginning to wear on me. I was just having too much fun with Caleb to stop.

"Funny, right?" Lola asked, moving to her desk to grab her purse. "Those damn videos get me every time."

"Yeah, they're great."

"We're heading out to lunch," Sophia said. "You in?"

"Actually, I got a dress at Nordstrom's a while back that doesn't really fit right. I was going to use my lunch to return it." See what I meant? The lies just came easily. I *did* have a new dress from Nordstrom's, but I totally rocked the hell out of it.

Sophia studied my face like she was searching for the meaning of life or something. "You okay? You've been a little weird lately."

"Weird? How have I been weird?" I asked in a suspiciously high voice.

"Yeah, I've noticed too," Lola chimed in. "You've just seemed a little distant. Is everything all right?"

Talk about the mother load of guilt being hurled at me. I felt like the world's worst friend. I was going to lose my woman card for sure, and probably my lifetime membership to the sisterhood. I was lying to my best friends because of a *guy*. The penis-wielding enemy. Okay, so that was slightly dramatic, but when all three of us had gotten our hearts stomped on, that was how we started referring to men.

But I couldn't help it. The sex was just *that good*. And if I were being honest with myself—which I totally wasn't—it wasn't just the sex. It was *him*. My feelings for Caleb were growing even though I'd told them to knock it the hell off.

Stupid feelings. I hated feelings. They were such jerks.

"I'm sorry. I haven't meant to be distant."

"Aw, don't apologize, honey." Lola came up and wrapped an arm around my shoulders. "I'll admit that I've been a little too preoccupied with Grayson lately. I guess we've all been a little busy with our own lives. Let's just make a deal right now that we'll get some quality girl time in this weekend."

And just when I thought I couldn't feel any worse, Lola took some of the blame for me being an asshole. "It's a deal."

"Ooh, girls' night!" Sophia cheered.

"Perfect," Lola declared, backing toward the door. "We'll look at our schedules for a night when we're all free and get everything set."

"Okay. Enjoy lunch, guys."

They headed out with waves in my direction, none the wiser, and I quickly shot off a text to Caleb.

Me: *Five minutes.*

"AH, fuck! Yeah, that's it, baby. Take it deep. Jesus Christ, you've got the perfect mouth."

His whispered words were such a turn-on. I had one hand wrapped around the base of his cock as I sucked him with abandon, and I slid the other up my skirt and into my panties, hoping to alleviate the ache building in my core.

I moaned when my fingertips hit the right spot, causing Caleb's dick to twitch in my mouth.

"Fuck, sweetheart. You have to stop. I'm about to come."

So was I. And I was too drunk on the feeling to stop. I took him as deep into my throat as I possibly could, sucking hard as I bobbed up and down. The closer I got, the faster I moved. I was seconds away from detonating when I was suddenly airborne.

Before I could make a sound, my back was against the wall. Caleb's mouth came down on mine as his hands pulled at my skirt until it bunched around my waist. He tugged at my panties until they pooled around my heels. "Hop up," he ordered against my lips. I did as instructed, wrapping my legs around his waist.

Caleb entered me in one hard, brutal thrust. I moaned at the sensation of being filled and stretched so wonderfully.

"Christ. Blew me so good I'm not going to last, gorgeous."

I bit my lip on a whimper, trying my hardest to silence the cries that wanted to escape from my chest. It was impossible to remain quiet when Caleb fucked me.

"I'm close," I panted on a whisper. I was already so primed from sucking him that it took no time at all.

He began driving into me faster, harder. "Touch yourself."

One of my hands slid down between my legs, and the instant my fingers brushed my clit, I exploded. Caleb muffled my moans with his palm as he buried his face in my neck and emptied himself inside me, covering his own sounds of release in the blanket of my hair.

He held on tight until we'd both come down and he was sure my knees would hold. "How is it that every time with you is better than the last?" he asked as he tucked himself back into his slacks.

I looked up at him with a grin as I righted my own clothes. "I don't know, but the feeling's mutual." I looked around the floor for my underwear, not seeing them anywhere. "Where are my panties?"

Caleb shot me a devilish wink and held my lacy thong from his index finger. I reached for them only to have him snatch them away before stuffing them in his pants pocket.

"I felt the need for a little memento."

"You can't keep my underwear," I demanded on a whisper. "They're part of a set. And they're La Perla. Give them back."

"Sorry, sweetheart." He grinned. "Finders keepers. But don't worry, I plan on getting the second piece of the set *very* soon."

I scowled. "You are *not* stealing my bra."

He shrugged and finished straightening his shirt and tie. "We'll see about that. So whose place tonight, yours or mine?"

I finger-combed my hair so it wasn't so obvious what I'd just been up to. "Tonight's no good. I have plans with Fiona."

Caleb placed his hands on my hips and pulled me into him. "So you're telling me I have to wait until tomorrow to have you again?"

I let out a baffled giggle. "You *literally* just came!"

"Doesn't matter. I'm already thinking of the next time I can have you before I've even gotten off. That's how crazy you make me."

Dear Lord, I was losing it over this guy if him saying that flattered me the way it did.

I patted his chest and pulled from his hold. "Something tells me you'll survive." I stood on my tiptoes and pressed a quick kiss to his lips. "Enjoy the rest of your day."

Then I made my way back up the stairs to my floor before anyone could see.

CHAPTER FIFTEEN

DAPHNE

I HANDED Fiona a glass of wine and took a seat on my plush, cushy sofa opposite her. "Okay, so what's going on?" I took a sip of my wine and waited for her to answer.

Chinese takeout containers were spread out all over the coffee table in front of us from our gorge-fest when she'd first arrived. I'd given her the time she needed to broach the subject she wanted to discuss, but it had already been an hour and all we'd talked about was how creepy the previous week's episode of *American Horror Story* was.

"It's... well... it's Deacon."

My ears instantly perked up. According to Lola, Deacon'd had a crush on Fiona since they were kids. Actually, from the sound of it, it had been a lot more than a crush. The guy was head over heels for her, but he never made a move or told anyone, so she and his brother eventually started dating. It got pretty serious, and Deacon reacted like a typical guy with a broken heart and gave Grayson the cold shoulder for years.

It wasn't until he saw just how serious Lola and Gray were that he finally started to thaw.

Unfortunately, I'd been told all of that under the strictest of confidences, so I wasn't allowed to scream at Fiona to get her head out of her ass and see what was standing right in front of her.

"What about Deacon?"

"He...." She chugged down her wine before finishing. "He kissed me."

"*Eeeep!*" I screeched excitedly. "He *did*? That's awesome!"

"That's terrible!" she declared, shooting up from the couch.

My head jerked back. "What? Why?"

"He's... he's *Deacon*. He's not supposed to kiss me, Daph! He's my ex-boyfriend's brother. I grew up with him, for crying out loud! He's one of my best friends."

I set my glass on the coffee table and held up my hands. "Okay, okay. Just slow down. Tell me what happened from the beginning."

She sucked back the last of her wine and headed for the kitchen for a refill. "Well, you know he bid on me at the auction, right?" I nodded. A few weeks after the event, she disclosed that Deacon had spent ninety grand to secure a date with her. She wasn't sure what she felt more, flattered or freaked. "And I told you how we'd started hanging out after that?"

She'd spilled the beans on that as well, so I nodded again.

"It's been great. Really great. I felt like I finally had my friend back after all these years, you know? I missed him. Anyway, he came over last night, just showed up out of the blue in the middle of the night. He started going on about a bunch of stuff that wasn't making any sense, like how he should have acted sooner, or that he should have told Grayson the truth, and then these last several years wouldn't have happened. I asked him what he was talking about and instead of answering, he just... kissed me. Right there on my front porch."

I bit the inside of my cheek to keep from laughing at her flabbergasted expression. "Well, how was it?"

She resumed her spot on the couch. "How was what?"

"The kiss, you jerk! How was the kiss?"

"It was...." She got a dreamy, faraway look on her face.

I grinned knowingly. "That good, huh?"

Her expression grew serious and her eyes refocused on me. "I can't even begin to describe it."

I knew all about kisses like that. Caleb was exceptional at them. "So what happened next?"

She looked down into her glass, crestfallen. "Then I freaked out, pulled away, and asked him what the hell he thought he was doing." I couldn't control my flinch at hearing that. "I know!" she shouted. "I totally reacted badly, but what was I supposed to do? I mean, this is a guy I always thought of as a brother!"

I couldn't flat-out tell her what I knew, but maybe I could help guide her in the right direction; at least then I couldn't be blamed for being the one who let the cat out of the bag.

I started carefully. "Fiona, think back to when you were growing up. What was your relationship like with Deacon?"

"Well, he was pretty much my best friend. We did every-thing together." She smiled happily, recalling memories from her childhood. "When we were ten, we built our own tree house in the woods behind his house. The thing was a death trap, but we didn't care. You know how fearless kids are. Anyway, no one knew about it but us. We were scared that if our parents found out, they'd never let us use it, or worse, they'd tear it down. I remember being really upset one day because Katy Pierson had made fun of my red hair in front of the whole class. As soon as school got out, I ran straight to that damn tree house. I was all alone, crying my eyes out because everyone had been laughing at me, when Deacon showed up all of a sudden.

"He climbed in there with me and held me while I cried, telling me that Katy was just jealous because she'd never be as pretty as me, and that the rest of those kids were just stupid and their opinions didn't matter."

I smiled fondly, feeling a whole new sense of respect for a man I hardly knew. "He sounds like he was an awesome kid."

"Oh he was," Fiona replied adamantly, almost as though calling him awesome was an understatement.

"So what happened next?"

She burst into laughter before answering. "Well, he convinced me to come out of my hiding place and go back to his house since his mom was making after-school snacks. I was halfway down the ladder when one of the boards snapped, and I broke my arm when I hit the ground. I'd never seen Deacon so scared in all my life." I couldn't quite decipher the look on her face; it was as if she was coming to an important realization. I wanted to prod, but interrupting would have been counterproductive. "But it wasn't because he was worried he'd get in trouble. He was just scared that I was hurt. He practically carried me back to his house and took full responsibility for building the tree house. Said it was his idea, and that I'd gotten hurt when he tried to talk me into going inside. He was upset for weeks after that, blaming himself for what happened to me. He was... he was always taking care of me any way he could."

I scooted closer, nudging her knee. "Like how?"

"Like our senior prom. He was all set to go with Marcy Danowitz when he found out my boyfriend had broken up with me for another girl. Deacon beat the shit out of him for upsetting me, and when prom night rolled around, he showed up at my door in his tux. He even had a corsage that matched the dress I'd bought and everything. He totally bailed on Marcy to be my date so I wouldn't miss my prom."

Her story was actually making me a little weepy. It was so

sweet and romantic. I couldn't understand how she didn't see what had been happening all that time. From the sound of it, Deacon had been in love with her since they were ten years old. "When do you think he started pulling away from you, Fee?"

Her brows pinched together in a confused frown. "I don't know. I guess...." She paused to give it some thought. "I guess it was around the time I started dating Grayson. He'd just graduated college, and Deacon and I were in our second year. The two of them had spent most of their lives competing with each other, but it had always been in a friendly way, you know? It got worse when Gray and I got together. The competitions got ugly. Then one day he just stopped talking to us altogether."

It was time for her lightbulb moment. If she didn't put two and two together soon, I was afraid I was going to smack the hell out of her. I hadn't been a believer of true love in a very, *very* long time. Don't get me wrong, I was thrilled that Lola had found someone who adored her, but if there had ever been a story about unrequited true love that needed to get its own happily ever after, it was Deacon and Fiona's. The more she talked, the more that ice Stefan had helped build around my heart began to thaw. The woman was actually making me soft!

I spoke in slow, concise sentences, praying she finally *got it*. "Okay, so consider how he was with you all your lives up until you started dating his older brother. He was your best friend. He'd do anything for you. He took care of you. Then he just disappeared. Why do you think he'd do that?"

"I don't—" Her eyes bulged out of their sockets. "*No!* You don't think...?"

I nodded. "Oh, I totally think. In fact, I'm confident enough, after everything you told me, to claim I *know*. He's ass over elbow for you, honey."

"But he's... he can't... that's not... omigod! And I dated his brother! No wonder he hates me. I'm such an idiot!" She dropped her head in her hands.

I moved in closer and wrapped an arm around her shoulder. "You're not an idiot—well, I mean, maybe you are." Her head snapped up and she glared fire at me. I smiled and gave her a little shake. "Hey, you're in the inner circle now. Sisters by choice don't sugarcoat things. It might have taken you a while to see the truth staring you in the face, but at least you finally saw it. That's what matters. And Deacon doesn't hate you. He wouldn't have shown up on your doorstep like that if he did."

Her head fell into her hands again, muffling her voice as she lamented, "God, this is all so messed up. What am I supposed to do now?"

I gave her a squeeze, turning her attention back to me. "I can't answer that for you, babe. That's something you have to come up with on your own. But I will tell you this: you need to think long and hard about everything you discovered tonight. It's obvious that what he feels for you goes so much deeper than just a childhood crush. He deserves to have a woman who feels the same way about him as he does her. If you can't give him that, then you need to let him go. But if you *can*, then the ball is in your court. You need to make the next move and show him you're all in."

Fiona left a little while after having that bomb dropped on her. After hugging her goodbye and telling her I was there if she needed me for anything, I started shutting off all the lights, preparing to go to sleep by myself for the first time in a long time. And as I climbed into my big bed, I was feeling hopeful for the future of my friend and the guy who'd loved her for so long.

Maybe it was all the phenomenal sex I'd been having, maybe it was simply the fact that Caleb had made these past few months the most fun I'd had in a really long time, but as I fell asleep, I actually found myself wishing for a fairy-tale ending for Deacon and Fiona.

Who'd have thought that a woman who gave up on fairy-tale type love so long ago would discover she still had a romantic side deep down?

CHAPTER SIXTEEN

CALEB

IT HAD BEEN over a week since I last saw Daphne. Between juggling our day jobs and finding time to spend with our friends, we hadn't been able to sync our schedules up.

The weekend had finally rolled around, and I'd been looking forward to getting more than just a passing text or phone call here and there. But after Lola and Sophia had gotten suspicious about a month earlier, they had implemented a mandatory weekly girls' night, leaving me all alone one designated night every week.

I thought that maybe the break was a good idea. We'd agreed on no-strings-attached fun, and spending every available minute with each other for the past few months had kind of blurred that line.

I decided to use the time apart to catch up with my own friends. Deacon hadn't wanted to spend his night out at the same bar he worked at sixty hours a week, so I'd decided to take him and Grayson to a pub I used to frequent before The Black Sheep became my home away from home. Lola's brother, Dominic Abbatelli, had recently started working at Bandwidth after making the move from New York to Seattle, so we'd invited him to tag along.

Deacon took a sip of his drink and winced. "This place fucking blows," he grumbled, setting the drink on the table. "What kind of bar doesn't know how to make a proper Old Fashioned?" He'd been in a piss-poor mood for weeks now. I tried to talk to him about it but had eventually given up when he threatened bodily injury if I didn't leave him alone about his shitty attitude.

"What kind of man in his early thirties orders an Old Fashioned in the first place?" I countered, sucking back more of my scotch. "Contrary to your behavior lately, you aren't actually seventy years old."

Dominic laughed while Deacon flipped me off. Grayson's head was too buried in his cell phone to notice anything going on around him.

"Jesus Christ," I grunted, snapping in Gray's face to get his attention. "Will you get your goddamn nose out of your phone already?

He looked up apologetically, setting his phone on the table next to his untouched beer. "Sorry. I just worry about those four together."

I chuckled, picturing all the different kinds of trouble those women could get into. "I bet they've fully corrupted poor Fee by now." At the mention of her name, Deacon grew tense but didn't say a word.

"Lola's not replying to any of my messages. I can't help but imagine the worst."

Dominic tipped his beer bottle at Gray. "If by 'the worst' you mean them being stuck in holding for a drunk and disorderly, then you're probably not far off the mark. Wouldn't be the first time."

"Son of a bitch," Grayson hissed, standing from his chair.

"Excuse me for a minute. I need to make a couple calls." His phone was already to his ear by the time he hit the front door.

Dominic chuckled. "Might as well get another round while he tries to track down my sister. Anyone need a refill?"

I shook my head while Deacon indicated he wanted another in spite of bitching that it wasn't made right just minutes before. When Dominic walked off, I took that as my opportunity. "Okay, look. You've been in a shitty mood for damn near a month. I'm not an idiot. I know whatever's got you pissed has something to do with Fiona. Any time her name's mentioned, you lock up so tight I'm surprised you haven't pulled a fucking muscle. You finally going to say what's bugging you, or you just want to keep acting like a dick until no one wants to hang around your miserable ass?"

Deacon blew out a sigh, raking a hand through his hair. "I made a huge fucking mistake a while back. I took a shot and told Fee how I felt."

I couldn't contain my wince. "And how'd that go?"

He shot me a look that spoke volumes. "You said it yourself, I've been a miserable prick for weeks. How do you think it went? She shot me down."

"Shit, man. I don't know what to say."

A bitter smile tilted his lips. "Nothing to say. At least now I know for sure that it's time to move the hell on, right? I wasted too much time hung up on a chick who didn't feel the same way. Turned out not to be worth it in the long run, but at least I learned my lesson. I won't be making that same mistake again."

"Jesus Christ, man, when did you become so cynical?"

His voice was completely flat as he answered, "When the woman I've spent the better part of my life pining over blew me off without so much as a fucking backward glance. And if you're smart, you'd check the shit you've got going on with Daphne before you're in the same boat as me."

I looked around to make sure the other guys hadn't come back yet. Leaning forward, I dropped my voice so only he could hear. "First of all, keep your voice down. You're the only asshole who knows about that. Secondly, it isn't like that with Daph and me. There are no strings attached, we're just having fun."

He let loose a humorless laugh. "You sure about that? Because I don't know about Gray, but I sure as hell haven't seen much of you these past four months. Seems to me like you've got yourself pretty tied up in her already."

A cold, clammy sweat broke out across my skin at his insinuation. Was he right? Were we getting so tangled up in each other that we'd started down a path I never had any intention of traveling?

No, not a chance. Daphne wasn't like other women. She'd made it clear from the start that she had no interest in more than I was capable of giving.

Unbeknownst to the swirling vortex of anxiety and concern he'd just created, Deacon turned his gaze toward the bar to a sexy woman in a skimpy dress who was giving him the all-too-familiar *fuck me* eyes. I'd had that look directed at me on far more than one occasion, and had taken full advantage of it more than I cared to admit. Because that's who I was. I was the good-time guy. The one-night stand—or more recently, the steady fuck buddy. Nothing more. I wasn't the type of guy to get serious or take a woman home to meet my folks. I saw firsthand the kind of train wreck a committed relationship caused thanks to my parents, and I wanted no part of that.

"Now if you'll excuse me, I'm gonna go start the healing process. And that blonde at the bar looks more than willing to lend a helping hand."

My head spun as I stood from the table, an intense pressure suddenly resting on my chest. My lungs couldn't suck in enough air. Pulling my phone out of my jacket pocket, I headed for the quiet of the back hallway. I needed to call Daphne and clear things up ASAP if I had any hope of breathing normally again tonight.

The call was on its third ring when I caught sight of something that made my brain short-circuit and forget everything I was doing.

I quickly disconnected the call. My arm holding the phone to my ear dropped, right along with my jaw. "You've got to be fucking kidding me," I growled at the table that had caught my attention.

My dad's head came out of the unknown woman's neck in order to twist in my direction. "Caleb." He stood from his chair, looking between me and the woman who most certainly *wasn't* my mother. "Wh-what are you doing here?"

My jaw was so tense it made a strange cracking noise as I spoke through gritted teeth. "I could ask you the same question, *Dad*. But then I'm pretty sure I already have the answer, don't I?"

I stared down at the woman my father was clearly having an affair with. There was something familiar about her, something I couldn't quite put my finger on as I glared into her unrepentant eyes. Whoever she was, she obviously didn't give a shit about being caught with a married man, or the fact that the person who busted them was the man's own son.

"Look, this doesn't concern you—"

"Doesn't *concern* me?" I threw my head back on a sharp laugh. "That's a joke, right? 'Cause I'm pretty sure I'll be the one who has to clean up this fucking mess when Mom finds out. You're getting lazy, Dad. Either that or you just don't give a shit if the whole world knows you've got a whore on the side anymore."

He was in my face faster than I could blink. "You'll watch

how you fucking speak around Connie. You understand me, boy?"

I squared my shoulders, standing tall with my chest puffed out just to show the miserable son of a bitch that I was bigger than him. "I haven't been a boy in a long fucking time, *old man*. And you'd be wise to remember that warning I gave you the last time we were in this position."

His face paled, but he didn't make a move.

"This has all been one big misunderstanding," my father's latest skank said. "There's nothing going on here. Your dad and I are just good friends, that's all."

I looked at her, all the animosity I was feeling painted across my face. "Just good friends, huh? I must be doing something wrong, because the only time I sucked on a woman's neck like that was when I was screwing her. Guess I missed the memo on how *friends* are supposed to act."

"Everything okay here?" I turned at the sound of Deacon's voice to discover him, Grayson, and Dominic had just gotten a front row seat to my fucked-up family dynamic.

The pity and concern reflected at me from my friends only added to the tension I'd started to feel moments before stumbling across my bastard of a father.

"Everything's fine," I lied, my tone full of sarcastic derision. "Just another glorious fucking day for the McMannuses."

I started toward the exit but stopped when I was shoulder to shoulder with Deacon. "You're right about it all being a waste of time, brother," I told him ominously. "It's not worth it when the end result means turning into a piece of shit like him." I threw my thumb over my shoulder at my father before storming out of the pub, wanting nothing more than to get away from everyone and every fucked-up thing swirling around in my head.

I was halfway down the block when I heard Grayson's voice. "Caleb, hold up. Will you just slow down for a second?"

He finally caught up with me, keeping stride with each one of my wide steps. "Seriously, man, just stop for a second. Tell me what's going on."

I kept going. "Nothing to talk about."

"Jesus, Caleb." His hand landed on my elbow, effectively pulling me to a halt. "Talk to me. What just happened back there?"

I grabbed my hair with both hands and yanked, needing the pins-and-needles sensation on my scalp to drown out all the other shit coursing through my veins.

"What just happened was that I got a face-to-face meeting with my father's current fuck. Not that he hasn't had plenty of them over the years, but this is the first one I've actually met in the flesh. And the fucked-up thing about it all is that my mom knows. She knows! And she won't do a goddamn thing about it. It's always *their* fault, never his. She makes excuses for him being a cheating son of a bitch, but when it gets to be too much for her, she expects me to clean it up."

"Shit, man. I didn't realize it was as bad as all of that. Is that what your parting comment to Deacon was all about?"

"I don't expect you to get it. You grew up with Cybil and Nolan. They're like the goddamn Cleavers. But I had *that*"—I point in the direction of the pub—"as an example growing up. So yeah, that's what my comment to Deac was all about. Far as I'm concerned, monogamous relationships are a fucking joke."

Grayson looked uncomfortable all of a sudden, his skin turning a sickly gray color. "Then I guess it's not a good time to ask you to be my best man?"

I heard the sound of tires squealing to a stop in my head. "I... *what*?"

"The best man... in my wedding."

My brain exploded. "You're getting *married*?"

He offered a tentative smile. "Well, I hope so. I mean, I

haven't actually asked her yet, and there's a chance she could say no. And I'll admit I'm a little freaked after everything you just said—"

"Shit, brother. I didn't... Fuck, I'm sorry. You know I think Lola's great, right? And I don't have a single doubt she'll say yes. I was just taking my shit out on you. I'm really happy for you."

The skepticism didn't fade from his expression as he asked, "You mean that?"

I felt like absolute shit for taking my drama out on my best friend. "Hell yeah! And I'd be fucking honored to stand up there with you when you get married."

He breathed a sigh of relief, his shoulders visibly drooping. "Thanks, man. I really appreciate that. And you know, if you ever need to talk, I'm he—"

"I know. And no offense, but after what just went down, I need to get the hell out of here."

Grayson clapped me on the shoulder commiseratively. "I get it. I just wanted you to know."

We said our goodbyes and I was finally on my way home. It wasn't until much later that evening that I remembered I'd been in the middle of calling Daphne before the shit had hit the fan.

CHAPTER SEVENTEEN

DAPHNE

I WAS STARTING to get worried. Caleb had called a while ago, hanging up the second I answered the phone. But every time I tried to call him back since, all I got was voice mail.

I couldn't explain why, but my gut was telling me that something was seriously wrong.

"What's up with you? That's like the seventh time you've checked your phone."

My head jerked up from the screen at the sound of Lola's voice. Girls' night had taken place at my house that week, and we were all currently gathered around my kitchen island, drinking wine and munching on the yummy little appetizers I'd made.

I set it facedown on my refurbished butcher-block countertop. "Sorry. Just trolling Facebook. I'll stop." Fiona gave me a curious look while Lola and Sophia seemed to buy my answer easily enough. I took a large sip of my wine. "So, what were we talking about?"

Sophia looked over at Fiona with a wicked smile. "We were talking about the fact that half the women in this room right now have slept with Grayson Lockhart."

"We were *not* talking about that!" Lola shouted while the rest of us burst into laughter.

"Oh god," Fiona cried dramatically, dropping her head onto the counter. "When you say it like that, you make it sound so gross."

I fell into the spirit of the evening, letting myself forget about the stress over Caleb, and teased, "When you think about it, it kind of is."

Lola threw a wonton across the counter at me. "Stop it. Don't make it weirder than it already is."

"Ohmigod!" Sophia squealed. "You've both totally seen Grayson's O face! Aw, it's like a special bond between you guys."

Lola clapped her hands over her ears and chanted, "I'm not listening! I'm not listening."

The laughter was still ringing loudly from the others as I lifted my phone as discreetly as possible and checked the screen once more. Still nothing. I couldn't take it any longer. "Hey, guys, I'll be right back. I need to go to the bathroom."

I hurried into the powder-blue half bath on the first floor and quickly dialed Caleb's number again.

"Hey, you've reached Caleb. I'm either in a meeting or screening my calls, so leave a message and I'll get back to you."

Damn it. "Hey, Caleb. It's me. Again. I... well, I don't really know. I just... will you call me back when you get a chance? I saw you called earlier and I'm starting to get a little worried."

God, I sounded like an obsessed stalker or something. I disconnected the call and pretended to wash my hands in the bathroom sink, stuffing my phone in my back jeans pocket.

I went back out and tried my best to act like everything was business as usual, that I was just a normal woman having a typical girls' night. But by the time my friends headed home a while later, I still didn't feel any better.

Luckily I hadn't had much wine, so I was fine to drive. I rushed out of my house only five minutes after they all left.

I was a ball of nerves by the time I got to his door, second-guessing my decision to show up at his apartment unannounced. But I couldn't bring myself to leave until I made absolutely sure he was okay. It was like there was a sixth sense that just wouldn't let me.

I knocked on his door and waited for an answer. And waited. And waited. I lifted my hand to knock again when the sound of the elevator dinging behind me made me turn around.

Caleb stepped out of the car, his head down with his hands shoved in his pockets.

"Caleb?"

His head shot up at my voice. "Daphne? What are you doing here?"

I tangled my fingers together and chewed on my bottom lip. "I... um... I'm sorry. This is weird. I shouldn't have just shown up like this."

He came closer, placing his hands on my shoulders in a soothing gesture. "Hey, hey. What's wrong?"

"Nothing. I just...." I chewed my lip so hard I actually tasted blood. "It'll sound stupid, but I just had a feeling something was wrong, and I wanted to make sure you were okay."

His head tilted to the side while he studied me in complete silence for several agonizing seconds. "You were worried about me?"

"Yeah," I admitted hesitantly. "But now that I've said it out loud, I realize it sounds a lot creepy, so I'm just going to go. You're obviously okay, and I've embarrassed myself enough for one ni—"

I sidestepped him in an attempt to get to the elevator, but my words and movements were cut off when he grabbed my arm and yanked me back. Threading his fingers in my hair, his lips came down in a hungry kiss that I was all too happy to return. I hadn't realized until right then that I'd felt like something was missing these past several days.

I'd purposefully ignored the tiny black hole that had formed in my chest when Caleb wasn't around. After three months of nearly constant companionship, it was like I was missing a limb. The moment he kissed me, I was whole again. The concept was worrisome, but I was so consumed with *him* that I couldn't bring myself to care. Not about the fact that I was starting to feel more for him than I should, or that I had put Caleb McMannus in a place in my heart he had no business being.

I was content to love in the moment. So when he finally broke the kiss, leaving me breathless and weak kneed, and softly spoke, "Stay with me tonight," I was more than happy to oblige.

I SLOWLY WOKE, my limbs deliciously languid from a night of sex that was more intense and demanding than I'd ever experienced.

I stretched my naked body and reached across the bed only to discover that I was all alone.

I climbed off the mattress and grabbed one of Caleb's T-shirts from the bedroom floor, slipping it over me before following the sound of running water into the bathroom. I peered through the glass of the shower, finding him standing beneath the showerhead letting the spray rush over him. I licked my lips at the sight of the water trickling around each rippled muscle.

"Hey."

He spun around at the sound of my voice, and an odd sense of foreboding twisted my stomach at the look on his face. It was almost as if he'd forgotten I was even there. My smile fell as I asked, "You okay?"

He swiped the water off his face with one hand as he twisted the knob to shut off the shower with the other. "Yeah. Everything's fine," he answered as he stepped out of the glass-and-tile enclosure. I had to step back quickly to get out of his way as he pulled a towel off the rod and slung it around his hips. "What makes you ask that?"

There was something about his demeanor that was just... *off*. I couldn't explain it or put my finger on it, but I felt it to my bones. "I don't know. You just seem a little different, I guess." I slipped my arms over his damp shoulders, not caring that pressing against him made the shirt wet. "If you'd woken me up, I could've showered with you," I said in a low, sultry voice.

Caleb's smile looked forced, not meeting his eyes as he placed his hands on my hips and nudged me back. "Sorry. I just remembered I have some stuff at the office I need to finish up before Monday."

I watched his reflection in the mirror as he squeezed a bit of toothpaste on his toothbrush and went to work. That knot in my gut tightened to an almost painful point. "Oh. Okay. Well, if you have time, how about I bring you some lunch? Or maybe you could come by when you're done and help me finish stripping the wallpaper in the guest room."

He spit and rinsed, turning to face me once again. "I'll just order something to be delivered. It's probably going to be a pretty late night for me."

I got the distinct impression that he was blowing me off, but I didn't want to be one of those women who made a big deal out of something that was all in her head. "Did something happen last night?"

His face softened a bit at my question, and he leaned in to place a quick kiss on my lips. "Nope, I'm all good. Just busy."

He left me standing in the bathroom by myself. I waited for a few seconds, trying to get my bearings before following him into the bedroom. He already had a pair of jeans on and was working on the buttons of his shirt.

I could have reverted back to the unsure, insecure woman I'd been back when I was with Stefan, letting my anxieties fester until I finally exploded in a mess of accusations. Or I could be the woman I'd turned into afterward who was self-assured and confident. One who refused to be a doormat for anyone and demanded answers. I chose the latter, knowing full well what the former had led to in the past.

"You're avoiding me," I said with a confidence I most certainly wasn't feeling. That nagging doubt in the back of my head began to grow into anger. Anger at myself for becoming too attached to Caleb. Anger at him for rehashing old feelings within me that I'd buried years before.

"Sweetheart, I'm not. I swear. I just have a lot of shit going on at work. If I don't take care of it this weekend, it's going to bury me come next week." He moved into me, wrapping his arms around my waist as he gave me that lazy, carefree smile I'd seen him wear countless times in all the gossip magazines. It wasn't a smile that had been directed at me, at least not since our relationship had changed.

I hated that smile and the cocky confidence it held.

"Besides," he continued, "there's nothing to avoid, right? I mean, we're just having fun. No strings. It's not like we're really together or anything."

It was like a knife had been plunged straight into my gut. And I had no one to blame for the searing pain I was experiencing right then but myself. He was only echoing the very words I'd said four months before. It was my own damn fault that I'd gotten carried away and complicated things with useless emotions.

I swallowed down the golf ball–sized lump that had suddenly formed in my throat and did my best not to let my sorrow seep into my words. "Y-yeah. Sure. Exactly. Just fun."

That black hole in my chest grew until it took up every inch of space.

He winked at me. The jerk actually *winked*. "Then we're all good. I have to go, but feel free to hang around here as long as you want. Just be sure to lock the doorknob before you leave."

And just like that, with a peck on the tip of my nose, he left, taking a piece of me with him.

CHAPTER EIGHTEEN

CALEB

I HADN'T SPOKEN to Daphne since I walked out of my apartment three days earlier, and I hadn't been able to shake the feeling that something was missing. I knew exactly what was causing my discontent, but I couldn't bring myself to do anything about it. The one-two punch I'd received at the hands of Deacon and my own father a few days earlier was still fucking with my head in a serious way.

The intercom on my phone chirped just a moment before my assistant's voice came through the speaker. "Mr. McMannus, you have a visitor to see you."

I quickly pulled up the calendar on my laptop and saw that I didn't have any meetings scheduled, but it wasn't unusual for someone to stop by unannounced. Thinking it might have been Daphne, I hit the button that rang back. "Thanks, Stacy. You can send her in."

A blonde walked through the door, but definitely not the one I'd expected or secretly hoped for. I shot up from my chair, propping my hands on my desk to keep me upright since I felt like my legs were about to give out. "What the fuck are you doing here?"

Connie, the woman I'd seen with my dad a few nights back, shut the door behind her and sauntered into my office looking entitled and snooty as she took it upon herself to have a seat in one of the two chairs in front of my desk.

"Pleasure to see you too, Caleb. I thought maybe it was time we had a chat about your father."

A loud burst of bewildered laughter escaped my throat. "Is this a joke? Are you off your meds? What in the ever-loving hell would make you think I'd have any desire to sit with my father's latest whore and have a conversation?"

Her blasé expression morphed into the best facsimile of a glare she could make considering the bitch had been botoxed to within an inch of her life. "I'd suggest you stop with the insults. Christopher won't be pleased to hear that you've continuously insulted me."

I let out a derisive snort and took my seat, pressing my fingertips together in a steeple beneath my chin. "Lady, I don't know what delusion you're currently living in, but if you think my old man gives two shits about you, you're seriously fucked in the head. You're just his current fuck. Not the first and, sadly, won't be the last."

The woman had to be well into her fifties, but she'd had so much work done she looked at least ten years younger. However, no amount of surgery could mask the cold vindictiveness on her plastic face. "I wouldn't be so sure about that." She smiled callously. "Christopher's quite taken with me. You'd do well to treat me with some respect. There's a possibility that I'll soon be your stepmother. I can make life very, *very* difficult for you."

My fists clenched against my desktop so hard my knuckles cracked. "You crazy bi—"

"No! Ms. King, you can't just walk into—"

My office door swung open and Daphne, followed by my

beleaguered-looking assistant, came rushing in. "I'm sorry," Daph directed over her shoulder at Stacy. "I know I shouldn't barge in, but I really need to talk to him."

"Mr. McMannus, I'm so sorry," Stacy sputtered. "She wouldn't take no for an ans—"

Daphne's eyes landed on Connie a second later and a frigid chill suddenly enveloped the entire room. "*Mom?*"

"Daphne?"

I shot up again. "You two *know* each other?"

DAPHNE

I WAS SO DAMN thankful the stalls were empty as I rinsed my mouth in the sink, swishing and spitting the water around to get rid of the nasty taste from being sick. My stomach had been a mess for days. I attributed it to my stress over Caleb. It had thrown my entire body off. It was either stress or a stomach bug, but whatever it was, I couldn't shake it.

I rested my hands on the basin and looked up into the mirror above the sink. My complexion was pale and clammy, my makeup streaked from throwing up.

The bathroom door creaked open and Sophia's voice came through. "Daph, honey? You in here?"

I blew out a breath through my mouth, hoping to stave off the nausea that still lingered. "Yeah," I answered.

She and Lola moved inside, staring at me with matching expressions of concern. Not that I could blame them. Ten minutes before, as soon as the On Air light had gone off, I'd bolted from the studio with my hand clamped over my mouth.

"You still feeling sick?"

Stupid Caleb. Stupid feelings. Stupid non-relationships with no stupid fucking strings attached! "Yeah. I think I've got a bug or something."

Lola came up to me, a frown marring her pretty face as she lifted a hand to feel my forehead. It was a motherly gesture that I'd never experienced from my own mom; she was too busy with whichever man she was trying to scam to worry about her daughter being sick. I might have struck out in the parent department, but I'd seriously lucked out with my friends. "Aw, honey, I'm sorry. You think you should maybe eat something?"

My stomach revolted at the mention of food. I gagged and placed my hand on my traitorous belly to calm it down. "Uh, no. Think it's safe to say I'll be skipping lunch today. But you two go. I'm heading home shortly. I'll see you guys tomorrow."

They each gave me a hug, Sophia adding a kiss to my fore-head, and headed out. I stayed in the restroom a while longer, running cold water over the inside of my wrists before feeling well enough to go back to the office. I'd just finished packing up my stuff when I was hit with an idea.

For someone who claimed not to be avoiding me, Caleb was doing a freaking *awesome* job at it. I wasn't going to feel better until I confronted him, and I couldn't go another day feeling this sick.

That was it. Whether or not the conversation ended badly, it was going to give me the closure I needed to hopefully be able to hold down a damn meal.

I took the elevator down to Bandwidth's floor, working on my deep breathing the whole way. I was terrifyingly close to losing my nerve the closer I came to his office. Then I reached the pretty brunette sitting at the desk right outside the door.

"Hi. I'm Daphne King. I just need to speak with Caleb for a second if that's okay." I didn't stop walking as I blurted that all out.

The woman stood from her chair and scuttled around her desk after me. "Oh, wait. No. I'm sorry, Mr. McMannus is in a meeting."

"That's okay. I'll just be a second."

The woman kept going. "No! Ms. King, you can't just walk into—"

I shoved the office door open, looking over my shoulder at the poor frantic woman as I spoke. "I'm sorry. I know I shouldn't barge in, but I really need to talk to him."

She looked past me, addressing Caleb. "Mr. McMannus, I'm so sorry. She wouldn't take no for an ans—"

But I had already turned around, my gaze landing on the woman sitting across from the man who was basically destroying my health. "*Mom?*"

She looked as surprised to see me as I was her. "Daphne?"

Caleb bolted out of his chair, his face completely flabbergasted. "You two *know* each other?"

My head pretty much exploded right then. I spun to look at him. "What are you doing talking to *my mother*?" I shrieked.

"Calm down, darling girl."

My attention jerked to the devil woman who birthed me. I jabbed my finger in her direction. "You don't talk! Especially to me!"

She uncrossed her legs and rose on her expensive heels, moving in my direction all regal and bitchy as always. "Honey, I've been calling you for months."

"I know!" I shouted. "It hasn't just been a coincidence that each of those calls has gone unanswered! Why the fresh hell are you here?"

"Well, I originally came to Seattle for you—"

"Not here!" I waved my arms wide. "I mean *here*. In Caleb's office. Why are you in. Caleb's. Office?"

"Well—"

"Enough!" Caleb boomed, his voice so loud it practically shook the windows. "Stacy, please, go back to your desk." The brunette now known as Stacy scurried out of the office like her ass was on fire. "And you!" He jabbed his finger in my mother's direction. "Get the fuck out and do *not* come back, or I swear to Christ, you'll regret it."

Mom slung her purse strap over her shoulder and flipped her hair before sauntering out like the queen of everything.

My head whipped back in Caleb's direction. "Why was she here?" I demanded the instant the door shut behind the she-monster.

"Funny little coincidence," Caleb said in a tone that didn't hold a single ounce of humor. "Turns out your slut of a mother is fucking my dad behind my mother's back."

My jaw dropped to the floor. Then the thought of my mom and Christopher McMannus bumping uglies made my stomach drop. I lunged for his trash can, barely making it before I emptied the contents of my stomach. "Oh my god," I gasped once I was finally able to breathe again. "I can't believe this. She's doing it again. She's destroying my fucking life!"

"Jesus Christ." His hand landed on my back, rubbing in a soothing gesture as I hunkered over the trash can. "Are you okay, sweetheart?"

I snatched a few tissues from the box on his desk and wiped my mouth before standing up and facing him. "No. No, I'm not okay." That was all it took for my rant to come pouring out. "I've been so stressed over what the hell is happening with you that it's been making me sick, so I decided to come up here and confront you and finally get some answers, only to find the bitch mother from hell sitting in your chair! So no, I'm not okay, Caleb!"

He took a step away with a sigh and raked his hands through

his hair. "What are you talking about? There's nothing happening with me."

"Really?" God, my emotions were so off the charts that I actually felt tears burn behind my eyes. "So you aren't avoiding me?"

"Of course I'm not. I've just been busy, like I told you. Where's all this coming from? You're the one who wanted this to be easy. I'm just giving you what you asked for. I thought maybe we were spending a little too much time together and complicating things, so I took a little step back, but that doesn't mean anything has to change between us." He reached out and pulled me against him. "We can still have mind-blowing sex."

"You...." I closed my eyes and pulled in a long breath. I wanted to reach out and slap him, or scream and curse him name. But I couldn't. Because he was right. Well... about everything but the sex at least, because no way in *hell* was I going there again. But he was right about everything else. I'd pushed for easy. That wasn't on him. I couldn't blame him for not developing feelings for me the way I had him. So instead of raging like I wanted, I opened my eyes and exhaled. "You're right. I'm sorry. I think... I think whatever's been making me sick lately just has me feeling overly emotional. Maybe I need to go to a doctor or something."

He caressed my forearms, watching me carefully. "You sure?"

I faked a smile as best I could. "Yeah, I'm sure. I mean, I did just hurl in your wastebasket after all. And I don't think my mother was fully to blame for that." I paused, running my fingers through my hair. "I can't believe she's sleeping with your dad. I'm just... I'm sorry. I don't even know what to say about that."

His eyebrow quirked up as he studied my face. "So you

didn't know about any of this?" I didn't miss the accusation dripping from his words.

"What? No! Of course not! I haven't even talked to the woman in seven years. I had no idea."

He moved around his desk and started pacing. "Okay. If you say so—"

"I *do* say so," I interrupted, anger surging up inside me. "I do fucking say so." I let out an emotionless laugh. "You know what? I think I should go. I'm suddenly feeling sick again," I said bitterly.

"Hey, wait." He darted toward me and grabbed my arm as I headed for the door. "I'm sorry. I didn't mean it like that. I'm just... this whole-fucked up thing with my folks has me on edge. I took it out on you and I'm sorry."

I pulled out of his grasp and reached for the knob. "It's fine. I'll talk to you later."

Then I left, feeling no better than when I'd arrived.

CHAPTER NINETEEN

DAPHNE

I DIDN'T HAVE the first clue what Mommy Dearest was playing at, but if I were being honest, I really didn't give a shit. Caleb and his whole family could go straight to hell.

Okay, well that might not necessarily have been true. The fact that the woman whose DNA ran through me was screwing with people attached to me in any way made me sick. She didn't care who she hurt—even if it was me—as long as she got what she wanted. She'd always been like that.

The anxiety from knowing she was in town, along with the throbbing ache in my chest thanks to Caleb, had worn me thin. The second I got home from work, I changed into my most comfy jammies with unicorns and rainbows, and fuzzy socks. I'd sat down in front of the TV and passed out in the middle of some crappy daytime television show.

I was woken up by someone banging on my front door. I sat up groggily, noticing that the sun had set some time while I was sleeping, and night had officially fallen. The banging recommenced and I stood from the couch, shuffling on my socked feet. "I'm coming, I'm coming!"

The second I pulled the door open Lola lunged. "I'M

GETTING MARRIED!" she screamed so loud I winced at the assault on my ears. Then what she'd just said registered.

"*What?*" She wiggled her left hand in front of my face, flashing a brilliant diamond engagement ring. "Oh my god!" I screeched, pulling her into my arms for a hug. "Oh my god! You're getting married!" We bounced around in a circle for several seconds before I finally got my shit together and pulled her inside. "Tell me everything," I demanded. "When did it happen? How? When's the wedding?"

I led us to the couch as she answered. "He asked over dinner tonight. He made a special meal at the house and popped the question right there. You should have seen it, he was so nervous. It was adorable. I climbed him like a tree the second he slid the ring on my finger. Wore him out so good he was still passed out when I left to come here."

I shot up. "We need to celebrate! This calls for all the wine. I'll open a bottle, you call Sophia and Fee. Tell them to get their asses over here for an impromptu girls' night."

I hustled into the kitchen, pulling out one of my most expensive red blends. I listened to her talk on her phone as I uncorked the bottle, feeling unbridled excitement for my best friend that thankfully outshined the bit of envy that simmered just beneath the surface.

I refused to let Lola or anyone see that I was anything but ecstatic. She'd had just as bad luck when it came to relationships as I did. And her father was only slightly less of a piece of shit than my mother. Despite all the crap swirling around in my life, I wanted what was best for my friends.

"They're on their way. Shouldn't be more than twenty minutes or so."

I left two empty glasses on the counter next to the open bottle and brought the two I'd filled back to the living room. It was then that she noticed my haggard appearance.

"Oh, honey. I didn't think. I'm so sorry. I just barged in here without taking into consideration that you're sick."

I curled my legs beneath me and took a sip. "Don't even think like that," I said. "I'm fine. I just needed to sleep it off. I'm just fine now, and I'd have been pissed if I'd been left out of this."

Her face got soft with a look of love just a second before she set her glass down and pulled me into a bear hug. "I love you."

"I love you too," I replied, suddenly choked up.

I SPENT three hours happily celebrating the fantastic news with Lola, Sophia, and Fiona, but by the time they headed home I felt like I hadn't slept in a week. It was an exhaustion heavier than any I'd ever felt before. Even back in college when I'd spend days cramming for finals it hadn't been this bad. I wasn't sure if it was the few glasses of wine I had, or simply the fact that I was getting older, but I was completely and utterly spent. Bone freaking tired.

My head had just hit the pillow when my phone chimed with an incoming text.

Caleb: *You hear the news?*

Jeez, the guy was killing me. I hit Reply and quickly typed out a message.

Me: *Yep. Girls just left.*

To my surprise, he kept texting. After what he'd said earlier that afternoon, I'd expected not to hear from him for a while.

Caleb: *How are you feeling? Any better?*

I kept my response short and sweet, needing—more than hoping—for the conversation to come to an end.

Me: *Just tired. Actually about to go to bed.*

Caleb: *Okay. Well, good night, sweetheart. Sleep well. And I'm sorry for all the shit that landed on you today. We can talk about all that later when you're feeling better.*

I exited the messages and blacked the screen, placing it on my bedside table.

Then I did something I hadn't done in longer than I could remember. I wasn't even sure *why* I was doing it, but that night, I cried myself to sleep.

CHAPTER TWENTY

CALEB

I WAS AN EPIC PRICK.

I kept telling myself that I was only giving her what she wanted, that our arrangement was exactly what she'd asked for, but there was no convincing myself that it was true. I couldn't help but feel like I'd fucked up royally, in a way that would be practically impossible to fix if I didn't figure something out soon.

Unfortunately, I didn't have the first fucking clue how to do that.

And it seemed like every time I tried to come up with a solution, some other bullshit in my life reared its ugly head and blew me off course.

Case in point: my father's sudden appearance in my office doorway.

"Jesus Christ," I groaned to the heavens. "I'm not doing this again."

"I got word that Connie paid you a visit a few days ago," he said, disregarding my declaration without so much as blinking.

"You got *word*?" I asked incredulously. "You make it sound like you're a connected man."

He sat in the same chair Connie had been in just three days

prior. "When you have as much money as our family does, you have connections everywhere. So answer my question."

"Oh, I'm sorry," I scoffed. "Was there a question in there somewhere?"

"Always such a fucking smartass," he grumbled unhappily. "What did Connie come here to talk about?"

I leaned back in my chair, giving the impression that I didn't have a care in the world, which couldn't have been further from the truth. "Such a charming woman," I said drolly. "Definitely one of your more ambitious gold diggers. She seems to think she's in the running to be the next Mrs. McMannus."

He shoved a hand through his hair. "Christ." I didn't think I'd ever seen him rattled before. He was a man who thrived on appearances. Always the most expensive, well-pressed suits, never a hair out of place. He was known for putting on airs, and made no apologies for it. Growing up under his critical, assessing eye had been a pain in the ass. As a child it wasn't uncommon for me to be punished for something as trivial as leaving the house without putting in the effort to look my absolute best. Seeing him so disheveled and shaken up would have been a goddamn joy had dread over what he was about to say not put a damper on the situation.

"What the hell going on?" I asked, prepared to hear the worst.

"I... I made a mistake. I thought... *Shit.*"

My palms grew sweaty, but it wasn't concern for myself that had me agitated. It was because of my mother. I had a feeling that whatever bomb was about to be dropped on me would have an even greater impact on Mom. And there was no way she'd be able to handle it.

"What the fuck did you do?"

"Connie's blackmailing me. She... there's a video—"

I told myself I was prepared for the worst and God laughed.

I was going to be sick. I held my hands up, my face twisting in disgust. "Fuck, stop! Just stop. I don't want to hear any more." I shook my head furiously in the hopes of clearing the images that filled my head. I was only two seconds from puking my guts up. "Just fucking pay her off. You've got enough money, you could use cash to wipe your own ass and still not take a hit."

"It's not as simple as that. She doesn't want a payoff."

Oh fuck. "What does she want?"

He scraped his palm along the stubble covering his jawline. "She wants me to leave your mother and marry her."

I leaned forward, slamming my forearms down on my desk as my brain exploded. "Are you *shitting me*?" I bellowed.

"Keep your voice down," he hissed angrily.

I chose to ignore his command and continued talking. "So let me get this straight. You, the man who hasn't been able to keep his dick in his pants *ever*, turned out to be a nasty perv who hooked up with a con artist bitch who videotaped you having kinky sex and is now threatening to release said video if you don't divorce my mom and... what? Marry her?"

"More or less."

I collapsed backward, causing my chair to let out a loud creak as the weight of everything he'd just dropped on me set in. "Jesus fucking Christ."

"I need your help, son."

And the hits just kept coming. I couldn't believe he had the nerve to ask for my help, especially right then. "I'm sorry, come again? Because I obviously didn't hear you right. It sounded like you just said you want me to clean up *another* of your goddamn messes. Please tell me I heard you wrong."

He actually had the common decency to look contrite, but that didn't stop him from being a world-class dickhead. "I wouldn't ask if I had any other choice."

"Bullshit," I snapped. "I've been covering your ass my whole fucking life, so don't sit there and pretend like you feel bad for coming to me."

"Son—"

"No," I interrupted. "I'm done. I'm not doing shit for you this time. You've finally dug yourself a hole I won't help you out of. You're on your own."

Gone was the remorse, quickly replaced by the bitter hatred I was so used to seeing on his face. "And just let your mother deal with the fallout? Please," he snorted disdainfully, the arrogant prick. "Like I'd buy that for one goddamn second. You'd never let your sweet, sensitive *mommy* take that kind of hit. So here's what's going to happen. You're going to help me clean this shit up, and then we're never speaking of it again. Do you understand me?"

I was going to snap in a way that would lead to some serious jail time if this happy little father/son moment didn't end soon. Standing, I dug my fingertips into the wood of my desk until my knuckles popped and turned white. "Get out. Get the fuck out of my office right now, or I swear to god you'll regret ever stepping foot in here." I waited a few seconds for him to move, but he didn't. "Do *not* make me repeat myself. And don't ever come back."

Finally, showing he was at least a little smart, he stood and walked out without another word.

THE LAST THING I wanted to do after the shit I'd dealt with earlier was go to some fancy-ass private room in an expensive-as-hell restaurant, celebrating the engagement of my best friend and his new smoking-hot fiancée, even if I *was* happy as hell for them both. I just wasn't in the mood to party.

I was leaning against the bar, looking out at all the partygoers, living in their own happy little bubbles, totally oblivious to the shit life could rain down on a person. *Ah, to be that naïve.* It must have been nice.

A flash of blonde passed in my peripheral vision, drawing my attention from my miserable thoughts. Bad mood aside, my body instantly responded to the sight of her. My blood heated, my chest tightened. Hell, my *pants* tightened. I felt myself getting hard just watching her walk across the room in the sexy little cocktail dress she was wearing.

I stared in fascination as one moment she was smiling at the people she passed, offering friendly words, and then the next she froze. Her back went straight and her head turned in my direction, as though she could feel my gaze on her.

She turned away just as fast and started in the other direction, and I had a lightbulb moment. Pulling my cell from the pocket of my slacks, I shot off a quick text.

Me: *You keep pretending not to notice me and I'll be forced to make a scene.*

I turned my eyes from my phone back to her. She lifted the tiny little purse in her hands and pulled out her phone. Those gorgeous eyes of hers bugged out as she read my message.

Daphne: *This coming from Mr. Avoidance himself? What a joke.*

Feisty little minx. I smiled down at my screen as I typed.

Me: *I need to talk to you. Either you come to me or I'll come to you. And I won't be subtle about it.*

After the way I'd treated her, it was a risk, pushing her even further like that. But I had to get her attention some way. Her head shot up in my direction, her gaze practically burning me from across the room. Her cheeks, still slightly pale from being sick, pinked with an angry blush that only made my dick harder, but at least she was now moving in my direction.

I pointed discreetly to my left, toward a short hall that led to the coatroom, and headed that way without looking back, my gut telling me she wasn't too far behind.

I made it to the small alcove at the very end before turning around.

"Well?" she asked agitatedly, her heels clicking furiously on the marble as she stomped the last few feet between us. "What do you want?"

She crossed her arms over her chest and cocked a hip out. Christ, she was cute as hell when she was pissed. It was so much better than the sadness that had filled her beautiful face a few days before when she walked out of my office.

God, I miss her. And I hated myself for being the one who'd upset her. I just wanted to get us back to the way we were before shit got so complicated. I'd never felt so comfortable or had so much fun with a woman in my life. I wanted that back.

"You look beautiful tonight." It definitely wasn't what I'd planned to open with, but the words just rolled off my tongue.

"Oh my god. Really?" she snarked.

My head jerked back in surprise at her tone. It was as if I'd offended her somehow. "What?"

"Are you seriously trying to hit on me right now?"

What the hell is happening? "I was just telling you the truth, that you look beautiful. What's so wrong with that?"

My sincerity must have been evident, because she uncrossed her arms, resting her hands on her lush, curvy hips. But she didn't thaw completely. "Fine. Thank you. But I know that's not what you called me back here for, so why don't you tell me what's going on?"

I should have prepared better, written a speech or something. I'd never been good at flying by the seat of my pants. Unfortunately, life had gotten in the way. All I knew for sure was that there was no way I was telling her anything about what

I'd learned today. From how she'd been with her mother, I knew they more than likely had a worse relationship than I did with my father. And the pallor of her skin indicated she was still on the mend from that nasty stomach bug. She didn't need the stress, and I'd do whatever I had to in order to shield her from it.

"Look, I...." I exhaled heavily, running a hand through my hair. "I don't like how we left things before. I got the feeling you were upset. And you've been sick, so I guess... well, I guess I was worried."

Her face went soft, the same way it did just seconds before I sank into her. I knew that look well, and it fueled that fire inside me to have her again. For as long as I possibly could.

"I need to see you tonight."

Her silky blonde hair cascaded down one shoulder as she tipped her head in confusion. "I'm not following. You see me right now."

"Not like that," I said on a growl, stepping close so I could touch her creamy skin. "Later. It's been too long. If I don't fuck you soon, I'm going to lose my goddamn mind.

That softness in her expression went hard as granite. "Unbelievable," she gritted out. "You know what, Caleb? Go fuck yourself."

She whipped around so fast her hair smacked me in the face, leaving a lingering scent of lilies and sugar in her wake as she stormed off.

I stood in the empty hallway by myself, watching her walk away, once again pissed off, only this time it wasn't nearly as cute as it had been a few minutes before.

"What the fuck just happened?"

Dear Lord, I really don't understand women.

CHAPTER TWENTY-ONE

DAPHNE

GOD, he was such a *pig*. I couldn't believe I actually thought he was being sincere. He just wanted to get laid again, that was all.

And I fell for it. Only for a second, but still. I was an idiot.

I heard the sound of his footsteps rushing up behind me. I contemplated making a run for it for a millisecond, but knew I'd eat it if I tried running in five-inch heels. That was added humiliation I just didn't need.

"Hey, wait. Will you just wait for a fucking second?" Caleb grabbed my arm and pulled me to a stop, spinning me around to face him. "What did I say?"

My skin prickled with the desire to smack some sense into the jackass. "Seriously? How are men so freaking clueless?" I declared to the ceiling before looking back at him. "No wonder your gender dies first. It's baffling that some of you even make it to old age."

He gave me a funny look, like he was waiting for me to grow fangs and rip his throat out. "I feel like something important just went down, but I'm not sure what it was."

I narrowed my eyes in a steely glare. "Why am I not surprised? Well let me spell it out for you. If you're looking to get your dick wet tonight, you're going to have to find someone else, because this booty call is officially off the market." Exasperation enveloped me as I threw my arms out to the sides.

"Leave it to a woman to totally misconstrue the meaning of something a man says."

I was going to kill him. Like seriously murder his ass *dead*. "I didn't misconstrue anything!"

"If you think I was instigating a booty call back there, then you sure as hell did."

And for the billionth time in just a handful of days, I felt like crying again. *Sweet merciful Mary, what the hell is wrong with me?* "You're an asshole!"

"And you're a neurotic pain in my ass!" he shot back.

I turned and stomped off before I did something like scream bloody murder in the middle of the party before clawing his eyes out.

Screw Caleb McMannus.

No... wait. That was what I was supposed to be avoiding. *Caleb McMannus can go screw himself.* There, that was better.

I pasted on a fake happy face as I joined Sophia and Lola just as one of the waiters set a whole tray of full champagne glasses on the table beside them and took off.

"Ooh, a whole tray!" I picked up a glass and began sipping as Lola and Sophia chugged theirs down like they were competing with each other. My eyes bugged out. "Wow. I see it's going to be one of those nights."

"I love Grayson, I really do," Lola started. "But what was he thinking, putting everyone we know in the same room together?"

I understood exactly what she meant. The Abbatellis were a different bunch, prone to drama wherever they went. And Grayson's family had a few nutters too. More specifically his hilarious, slightly scary Nana. But I lied to try and make her feel better. "It's not that bad."

Lola gave me a droll look. "Between Soph and Dominic, Gray's cane-wielding nana, *my mother*, and the best man trying to bone every woman in the room under the age of forty, tonight is bound to be a bigger bloodbath than The Red Wedding."

My stomach clenched and my heart tore a bit at the comment about Caleb, but I somehow managed to hide my reaction. But then I turned in the direction my friends were staring. We watched as the waitress he'd been whispering to reared back and slapped him right across the face.

"Ooh!" All three of us winced on his behalf as the girl stormed off.

Sophia giggled while a little piece of me died on the inside. "That looked like it hurt."

"Serves him right," I hissed bitterly. "It's about time someone shot him down." I wish the woman would have kneed him in the nuts, or worse.

CALEB

SON OF A BITCH. That fucking woman was going to drive me into a goddamn loony bin. But for whatever sick, twisted reason, I couldn't stop going back for more. She was my addiction.

"I'll show her," I mumbled to myself as I entered the throws of the party. I scanned the crowd looking for an unsuspecting victim and smiled wickedly when my eyes landed on one of the blonde servers. She was exactly the kind of woman I used to go for before Daphne. Now that I'd had her, other women did nothing for me, but that didn't mean I couldn't use them to drive Daphne as crazy as she was making me.

"Excuse me." The server turned. Once she got a good look at me, she gave me one of those suggestive smiles I was so used to seeing. *Not a chance in hell.*

I leaned into her in a way that would look slightly salacious to those who couldn't hear what I was saying.

"I need you to do me a favor," I whispered into her ear. "There's a woman over there that I'd like to make jealous. Could you feel me up for a second and maybe pretend like you're going in for a kiss?"

The chick jerked back and slapped me right in the face as hard as she could. "You're a disgusting pig!" she seethed before taking off.

My cheek burned like fire.

I seriously didn't fucking understand women.

DAPHNE

I WANTED TO RANT, but I couldn't seeing as I stupidly kept our little... tryst or whatever a secret from my friends.

Fortunately, or unfortunately for Sophia, Lola's brother, Dominic Abbatelli, chose that moment to interrupt my inner rage. "Evening, ladies."

My eyes darted to Sophia instantly, trying to gauge her reaction to his appearance. He'd been living in Seattle for a while now, and even though she claimed she was totally over their past, I still couldn't help but worry about her.

"Dominic," Lola greeted, but he only had eyes for Sophia.

"Hello, Dominic," she offered in a somewhat stale tone.

"Butterfly. You look beautiful."

Ugh! Guys and that line!

Mine and Lola's attention bounced between the two of them like a ping-pong ball. I wasn't sure about Lo, but I was hesitantly waiting for the impending explosion that was sure to come when those two were within spitting distance of each other. So you could have knocked me over with a feather when she politely replied, "Thanks. You look nice too."

"What's happening?" I asked Lola in a none-too-subtle, panicked whisper. Before she could answer, someone announced that dinner was being served, so we all moved to take our seats.

I did my best to keep an eye on the situation with Sophia, but the second I sat down, Caleb pounced, taking the chair next to me. "Mmm. Dinner looks delicious. Almost as delicious as you."

I snorted in offense into my champagne glass. "You are beyond belief," I hissed.

He smiled self-assuredly, making my palm tingle with the need to slap him. "Why thank you."

"That wasn't a compliment, you jerk."

I turned back to the table, doing everything I could to ignore the man next to me. My plan was to engage in other conversations around me. However, everyone at our table seemed to already be engrossed in ones of their own. To keep my attention forward, I watched Deacon Lockhart like it was my job, curious as to what had taken place between him and Fiona since I'd last talked to her.

Man, I really hope those two have gotten their shit together.

"You know, this isn't going to work," he whispered into my ear.

"What isn't?" I asked, pointlessly cutting the lettuce in my salad with the precision of a neurosurgeon. Anything to not look into those strange, beautiful eyes of his.

"Pretending you aren't affected by me sitting right next to you." He moved impossibly closer, his palm resting softly on my thigh beneath the table. "You've got goose bumps again, gorgeous." I was turned on and disgusted all at the same time. Leaning away from him, I carefully moved my fork toward my lap so as not to draw attention, and jabbed the sharp prongs into the top of his hand. "Ow! Son of a bitch!" He yanked his hand back, shaking out the pain.

"Have you already managed to forget that you were *just* hitting on a waitress not even ten minutes ago?"

He winked, one corner of his mouth quirking up. "Jealous?"

I was just about to stab him again when the blonde server he'd been getting cozy with walked up, dropping Caleb's dinner on the table in front of him with a loud clatter. "Be careful with this one," she told me warningly. "He's only using you to make a woman here jealous. He tried his shit on me a little while ago. Don't waste your breath on this asshole."

Oh. My. Gah! My eyes went as big as saucers, and I spun in my chair, letting out a giggle of disbelief as I faced an embarrassed-looking Caleb. "Oh, that's *great!*" My giggle turned into a full-blown laugh as the waitress wandered off. "Are you using me to make another woman jealous?" I teased.

He faced forward, lifting a glass of scotch to his pouty lips. "Shut up."

I worried that I wouldn't be able to get control of my laughter, but just then I was hit with the smell of Caleb's dinner, and the Veal Piccata, a meal I typically loved made my stomach lurch so violently I had to clamp my hand over my mouth to keep from throwing up right then.

"Excuse me," I mumbled, stumbling from my chair. Luckily Lola and Grayson were too consumed with each other, and

Sophia looked to be quietly arguing with Dominic, to notice me as I hurried from the table.

I'd only made it as far as the hall outside the banquet room when it happened. Thankfully, there was a potted ficus not too far from the door. That was going to have to do.

How humiliating.

CHAPTER TWENTY-TWO

CALEB

THE WAY her entire body went white as a ghost and a sweat broke out across her forehead just one moment before she took off worried the hell out of me. I quickly got to my feet and followed her. The instant I cleared the room I found her, leaning over a potted plant just outside the door, hurling her guts up.

"Fuck, sweetheart." I went to her, gathering her hair at the back of her head with one hand while I rubbed soothing circles on her back with the other.

The sound of her retching made me gag once or twice, but I was somehow miraculously able to hold it back. I had a nasty habit of puking when I saw or heard others puke. Daphne certainly didn't need that.

Blessedly, it didn't last long, and she eventually stood. I released her hair and handed her the handkerchief I had stashed in my pocket so she could wipe her mouth. "Thank you," she breathed, closing her eyes and resting against the wall while pulling in a few deep breaths.

"Are you all right?"

Her eyes remained closed as she answered, "I'm fine. I just...

the smell of the food got to me. I guess I'm not over this stupid stomach bug."

I moved closer, concern for her overriding every single instinct to back away from the puke breath. I guess you could say I was worried sick. "Maybe you should go to a doctor. This can't be good for you."

Her eyelids finally lifted, but it was like there'd been a weight tied to them and she was struggling to keep them open. "Yeah, maybe you're right."

Just then, Fiona came rushing from the room, her head turning one way and the other before she finally spotted us. "Daph, are you okay? I saw you run out like you were on fire."

"The smell of the food made her sick," I answered, looping my arm around her waist to take most of her weight. "I think it's best I take her home."

"What? No!" Daphne argued. "I'm fine. I feel totally fine now. Let's just go back in—"

"Poor thing. You're still sick?" Fiona asked with an intense frown as she studied the way I held on to Daphne, and how Daph let me, leaning farther into me for support.

"It comes and goes. It's weird. The strangest things set it off. But I'm fine now, seriously."

"I don't want to risk it," I told her. "What if something else sets you off, huh? I'm taking you home. And tomorrow I'm getting you in with a doctor."

Coming to her senses, she started to struggle against me, but I tightened my arm, keeping her in place. "That's a complete overreaction. I don't need you to do any of that."

"I think he's right," Fiona chimed in. I could have kissed her right then for taking my side. "Just let him take you home." She turned to me then. "But I'll swing by her place tomorrow to check on her.

"You don't have to do that."

"I don't mind."

"Works for me," Daphne chirped, causing me to frown down at her. "What if... it's lady problems or something? I'd just feel more comfortable with Fee."

I wasn't going to lie, hearing that last bit stung like a mother-fucker, but what the hell did I know about periods or uteruses and shit? "Fine," I relented with an unhappy grunt. "But we're leaving now. Fee, would you mind grabbing Daphne's stuff and letting Lola know she wasn't feeling well?"

"On it." She disappeared back into the room, leaving Daph and me alone once more.

"God, I'm so tired all the time." She curled into my side and closed her eyes again. "I just want to get home, curl up in bed, and go to sleep."

"Hopefully not before you brush your teeth," I joked, earning a glare. And even that looked pretty on her.

"HEY, sweetheart. We're here, time to wake up." She looked so peaceful asleep in my passenger seat that I hated waking her.

"Hmm?" Her head came up and her eyelids blinked, but stayed half-mast with sleep.

I undid my seat belt and pushed my door open. "Hold tight. I'll come around."

I rounded the hood and pulled her door open. Leaning in to unfasten her belt, I lifted her into my arms and started for the house.

"I can walk, you know," she argued. But the words were slurred because of how tired she was, and there wasn't an ounce of fight in her body.

"I know that. I just like carrying you. Makes me feel all

chivalrous and stuff." She snorted, resting her head on my shoulder. "Need you to get out your keys, gorgeous."

Daphne rummaged through her tiny purse and pulled out a set of keys, slipping one into the lock once I reached the door. "Okay. I'm all safe and sound inside. You can put me down now."

I ignored her and started up the stairs. She let out a sigh of defeat and settled in for the climb. It was only when I reached her bedroom that I placed her on her feet. Before she could take a step away, my hands were on her waist. Reaching behind her, I found the small zipper at her spine and slid it down.

"What...." She swallowed thickly. "What do you think you're doing."

I shot her a tiny grin. "Relax, Daph. I'm not trying to cop a feel, just getting you out of this so you can put on something more comfortable."

She wriggled and squirmed until I had no choice but to let her go. "I can do that, thank you."

"Okay, well get changed and ready for bed. I'll get you a glass of water from the kitchen. Be right back."

"Caleb, you don't—" But I was already moving down the stairs.

I filled a glass with water from the fridge and rummaged through the cabinets until I located the medicine. Daphne had a box of dissolvable anti-nausea tablets, so I popped two of those out and carried them and the water back to the room. When I stepped past the threshold, she was just coming from her bathroom, face freshly washed of makeup and in a cute pair of PJs with what looked like Care Bears decorating them.

I extended the hand with the tablets. "Here, take these. They should help."

She popped the meds without objection and sucked back

half of the water before climbing into the bed like her limbs had cinderblocks tied to them. "Thanks."

The rustling of my clothes seemed to shake her from her near-slumber. She shot up on one elbow and looked at me with big eyes. "What are you doing? Why are you talking your clothes off?" she squeaked.

"Because I can't sleep in a suit," I answered in a tone that said *duh*.

Daphne sat up fully. "You're not sleeping here!"

I dropped my pants, letting them fall to the floor where I'd just thrown my shirt, shoes, socks. "You're even crazier than you act if you think I'm leaving you alone after how sick you've been." I moved to the bed, throwing the covers back and climbing in wearing nothing but my boxer briefs. "I told you I wasn't going to cop a feel and I meant it. But you just emptied the entire contents of your stomach a little while ago. I'm not leaving you alone. Now scoot."

Cursing me to hell and back beneath her breath, she moved to the other side of the bed... *all* the way to the other side of the bed, and curled up on her side in a tight ball, taking up as little surface area as humanly possible.

If there was anything I'd learned in my months with Daphne, it was that she slept sprawled out on her stomach, not afraid to cuddle or spoon. What she *didn't* do was sleep on her side in a tiny little ball. With an annoyed huff, I reached across the expansive bed, hooked Daphne around her waist, and jerked until she was in the middle, right beside me, uncurled and lying flat on her stomach.

"There. Better. Now sleep."

"I hate you," she grumbled under her breath.

I'd let her believe that for the time being if that was what she needed. As long as she kept letting me spoon her in this kickass bed.

CHAPTER TWENTY-THREE

DAPHNE

I WOKE TO AN EMPTY BED, telling myself that I was relieved Caleb was gone when the truth was it made me sad. I climbed out of bed with the singular thought of coffee on my mind, grateful that it was the first morning in a long time that I didn't wake up having to shove my head in the toilet.

The smell of freshly brewed coffee greeted me as I padded down the stairs toward the kitchen. The sight of Caleb in nothing but his dress pants from the night before, standing at my stove with a spatula in hand, was the last thing I expected to see. I froze in the middle of the living room and stared as he flipped a pancake with a flourish.

The floor creaked beneath my feet, alerting him to my presence. The smile he graced me with was the very one that made me fall for him in the first place. *Damn it.* "Morning." He moved away from the stove and came to give me a kiss on the forehead. I was nowhere near awake enough to shore up my defenses against Caleb's charm. "How are you feeling?"

"I'm, uh, okay."

"Good." He turned and headed back for the kitchen. "You

think you can eat something? The pancakes are done, and I just threw the bacon on."

Uh-oh. It was like fate was laughing in my face. *Ha! You think you got away without puking this morning? Well I'll show you!* The smell of the sizzling bacon hit my nose like a sharp jab, traveling all the way to my stomach.

"Son of a bitch," I muttered before running for the powder room. I dry heaved into the toilet, the retching so painful thanks to the fact that there was nothing in my belly.

"Okay, that's it," Caleb declared sharply. "You're going to the doctor. This has gone on long enough."

I would have argued had I been able to talk past all the heaving. My doorbell chimed just then, and he turned and disappeared out of the bathroom doorway. Seconds later Fiona appeared, hunkering down next to me to brush the hair off my forehead. "Oh no. Again?"

"The bacon," I panted between breaths. "The smell."

She looked over her shoulder at Caleb. "Put the bacon down the disposal and open a window. I'll take care of her."

From the brief peek I took, I saw that Caleb didn't look happy to leave me be *at all*, but quickly moved to do as ordered. Fiona closed the door, locking us in the privacy of my tiny powder room.

"Ugh, what the hell is wrong with me?" I grumbled, flushing the toilet as I stood. I grabbed for the spare toothbrush I kept by the sink and headed for the vanity to brush the taste from my mouth. "Maybe I really do need to go to the doctor," I muttered around the toothpaste foam filling my mouth.

"Oh, you'll need to go to the doctor, all right. Just not right at this moment."

I spit and rinsed, looking at her curiously in the mirror. "What are you talking about?"

She stood, and that was when I noticed the paper bag in her

hand. "I'm pretty sure I know what's wrong with you. I have to say, I'm a little surprised you haven't figured it out by now."

She extended the bag, holding it open so I could see the colorful boxes inside. "*No*," I gasped, turning my big eyes from the multitude of pregnancy tests back to her. "No. I can't be. That's not possible. No. No, no, no, no, no."

I couldn't get enough air in my lungs. It felt like the walls were closing in on me. Fiona quickly dumped the boxes into the sink and pressed the paper bag into my hands. "Here, breathe into this. I'll get rid of Caleb, and then you and I are going to have a nice long chat."

The paper crinkled with each inhale and exhale into the bag. I offered a jerky nod and closed the door behind her, and a minute later I could hear the two of them talking in the living room. It sounded like Caleb was standing his ground, but thankfully, after a long muffled argument I couldn't quite make out, Caleb's voice sounded from the other side of the door.

"Daph? Sweetheart, I'm going to leave you with Fee, but I'll check on you first thing Monday, okay?"

I nodded again, my panic attack having rendered me temporarily stupid. When I realized he couldn't see me I pulled the bag from my face. "Okay."

The sound of the front door opening and closing eventually penetrated my senses, and Fiona reappeared a moment later.

"Okay, honey. Let's get this done."

I PACED the length of my bedroom floor, wringing my fingers together. "That can't be right. It has to be like one of those false positive things, you know?"

Fiona looked at me from where she sat on the end of my

bed. "I think I read somewhere that a false negative is much more common with these things, not a false positive."

I stopped mid-pace and glared at her. "You're not helping!"

She blew out a sigh. "Seven tests, Daph. *Seven*. And they all said the exact same thing. Not to mention the one you forced me to take that was negative. I think it's safe to say you're preggers, babe."

Unable to accept what she was saying, I stomped over to my dresser and ripped open another box. After the first several tests came back positive, I'd demanded Fiona go back to the pharmacy and buy more. I pulled out a stick and shoved it at her. "Pee on this."

With a roll of her eyes, she pushed my hand away and got to her feet, taking me by the shoulders.

"Daphne, you're pregnant," she said in a tone that one would typically use on a misbehaving child. "Stop with all this craziness. You're going to be a mom. This is a good thing."

I slumped onto my mattress in defeat. "I'm pregnant," I finally admitted.

Fee sat down beside me, slinging an arm over my shoulder. "It's his, isn't it? Caleb's?"

I sniffled, wiping my nose with the back of my hand as I nodded. "It wasn't supposed to be like this, Fee. We weren't even in a relationship. It was just a fling."

"Honey. I know Caleb McMannus. Known him all my life, and he'd *never* go ungloved with a woman he considered *just a fling*."

I shot her a spiteful look. "Trust me, that's all it was to him. I'm on the pill, that's the only reason he ditched the condoms. I don't know how this happened. I mean, I might have forgotten to take them once or twice, but..." Then a horrible thought dawned on me. "Oh god. He's going to think I did this on purpose to trap him!" Then something even worse hit me. "*Oh my god!* My mom did that exact thing! She got herself knocked up with me to trap my dad!"

I collapsed onto my back and started sobbing. "I've turned into my mother, Fee! And she's just *the worst!*"

She grabbed my hands and forced me back up. "Stop that. He's not going to think you did this on purpose to trap him."

"Yes, he is."

"No, he's not."

"Is too!" I continued, because clearly being pregnant reverted me back to a teenaged maturity level.

"Good Lord," Fiona said to the heavens. "Will you just stop? Think about it. The guy I saw downstairs was *not* someone only interested in a fling. You should have seen his face, Daph. He was seriously worried about you. I had to swear I'd text him hourly updates before he finally agreed to leave."

I felt the panic building again. "You can't tell him about this."

The look she gave me was full of chastisement. "I'm not going to. But *you* have to. This isn't something you can keep from him. It wouldn't be right."

I chewed on my lips, feeling like the world's biggest coward. "I know. And I will. I just... I'm scared that he's going to hate me. We never talked about anything like this. I don't even know if he *wants* to be a dad. And he's a total playboy, Fee. What if... what if he decides it's not worth the stress?"

By the look on her face, I got the distinct impression that I'd gone too far. That was confirmed when she finally spoke. "Look, you know I love you. But I love Caleb too. And I've known him for a lot longer. You aren't giving him enough credit. He might come off a certain way in the media—hell, he even likes to feed that persona because he doesn't think he's any better than that—but I know that's not true. You do too, that's why you're in love with him."

I nearly swallowed my tongue. "I'm not... that isn't—"

"Oh, please. Don't bother denying it. You two might have been good at hiding it all this time, but I saw how you guys were together last night."

I narrowed my eyes in a ferocious glare. "I don't like you very much right now."

She smiled in a way that showed my words had zero effect. "Only because you know I'm right. But you'll come around."

We both lapsed into silence for what felt like an eternity. Hesitantly, I placed my palm on my still-flat belly. "I can't believe it," I whispered, wonder filling my voice. "I'm going to have a baby. I'm going to be a *mom*." Then, for an altogether different reason, I started crying again. That time it was because of the overwhelming happiness I felt at the thought of holding my little guy or girl in my arms.

"You are," Fiona whispered, wrapping me in a hug. "And everything is going to be just fine. You'll see."

I didn't know if she was referring to the situation with Caleb or not, but right then, I knew her words to be the stone-cold truth. Because even if things with Caleb *didn't* work out, I was still going to have my little one. And that would be just fine.

CHAPTER TWENTY-FOUR

CALEB

I'D SPENT the rest of the weekend worried sick over Daphne. True to her word, Fiona had texted me updates, but they consisted of menial information like "all is well" and "no need to worry," or my least favorite, "she's going to be just fine".

No offense to Fee, but I'd rather hear that from a doctor. Her zero years of medical training didn't provide me with confidence in her opinion.

Monday morning finally rolled around, and I found myself awake long before my alarm clock sounded. I rushed through my morning routine and made my way to the office, only stopping long enough to grab myself and Daphne a coffee from the Starbucks on the corner. Once in our building, I took the elevator to her floor, her friends be damned. I wanted answers and I wanted them *now*.

Luckily when I reached their office Daphne was already there, blessedly alone. "Thank god," I said on a relieved breath at the sight of her. She spun around in her chair, surprised to see me.

"Caleb. You're here early."

"Couldn't sleep," I replied, moving into the office. "I've been worried out of my mind, and *you* haven't bothered to return any of my texts all weekend." I pointed an accusatory finger in her direction. At least she had the good grace to look apologetic.

"Sorry. I slept a lot. But everything is fine. Just a bug. It should pass..." She got a strange look on her face that I couldn't read and finished on a mutter, "...eventually."

"Well here." I handed her the coffee. "I got this for you. Hope your stomach can handle it."

She took the cup and set it on her desk. "Oh, um... thank you."

I gave her a curious look. "Aren't you going to drink it? I thought you couldn't function before coffee."

"Oh, yeah! Totally," she chirped a little too brightly. "I'm just... I'm letting it cool, is all."

Something was definitely up with her, but I couldn't figure out what.

"Are you sure you're okay?"

Her smile didn't come near her eyes. "Yep. Completely fine. Promise. I just have to get prepared for this morning's show, so...." She looked from me to the door and back again, her meaning crystal clear. She wanted me gone. *What the ever-loving fuck?*

"Okay. Yeah. Well, I'll just...." Christ, what was happening to me? I was getting the brush-off from a woman, and it was driving me fucking crazy. I threw my thumb over my shoulder and started backing away. "I've got a lot of work too. Better get to it."

"Okay, bye," she blurted, spinning around in her chair, giving me her back. It was obvious she was trying to rush me out even faster. I didn't think my pride could survive another hit, so I turned and headed back to the elevators, taking one to my floor.

I didn't know what the hell was going on with her. One

second she burned hot, and the next she was so cold I got fucking frostbite. I needed answers. And if she wasn't going to give them to me, then I'd find someone who would.

And who better to grill on all things Daphne King than someone who'd practically grown up beside her.

I stormed into Dominic's office, ready to demand some inside information on what made that damn woman tick. He was sitting at his desk with a sickening smile on his face as he pecked away at his keyboard.

"Why the hell do you look so happy?" I grumbled, envious that his morning was evidently going better than mine.

He cocked an eyebrow and smirked. "I think the better question is why do you look so fucking miserable?"

Collapsing into one of the chairs in front of his desk, I ran my hands through my hair and admitted, "It's Daphne, man. That chick's got my shit all twisted up."

The asshole didn't bother to hide his laughter as he leaned back in his chair. "Still immune to your limited charms?"

I tried my best not to resort to violence, especially in the workplace, but the dude was pushing it. "Fuck off," I grumbled. "And yes. What the fuck's that all about?" I paused, realizing that my confession might make him start to question whether or not something was going on between us. The last thing I needed was for Dominic to get suspicious. It would just give Daphne another thing to hold over my head. I quickly backpedaled, amending my words to make it seem like I was just in it for the chase.

"I can't remember the last time I had to chase a piece of tail like this. I'm losing my goddamn mind. I mean, I get the whole thrill of a challenge thing, but this is ridiculous."

Dominic gave me a pitying look that I wanted to smack right off his face. "Look, man, let me give you some advice. I've known those girls for a long time. Daph's not the kind of woman who gets off on the chase. This isn't a game for her, that's not what this is about."

"Then what is it?" Desperation poured from my words as I rested my elbows on my knees, because this was so much more than just a chase. Not that I could admit that out loud. I didn't have a goddamn clue *what* it was between the two of us, but I could no longer deny the fact that it was more than just a simple fling. "Help me out, 'cause I can't wrap my head around this."

The look on his face told me he knew more than he was willing to admit. "It's not my story to give. But I will tell you this, that girl's been burned in a bad way. She's not putting up a challenge for you. And when I say that, what I mean is it's never going to happen. You have a reputation known to the whole country and most of the world. She's not going to get near you with a ten-foot pole."

I fell back into the chair. For the first time in my life, I loathed the fact that I'd done what I could to live up to the media's opinion of me. It had started as a way to stick it to my old man, and just became second nature. Now it was coming back to bite me in the ass. And I fucking hated it. "Jesus, dude. Way to break it to a person gently."

Dom held his hands up in surrender. "Hey, just trying to be honest. I think you should cut your losses and move on to the next one. Daphne King is in a whole other league."

If only the jackass knew the truth. He might believe she was out of my league, but I'd had the woman panting for it once. I could make her want me again.

I stood from the chair, a sense of determination heating my blood. I was going to entice the hell out of that woman if it was the last fucking thing I did. "Yeah, well we'll just see about that."

DAPHNE

IT HAD BEEN JUST over a week since I found out I was knocked up with Caleb McMannus's offspring, and so much had gone down that I'd barely had time to process just how significantly my life was going to change.

First, by sheer coincidence Sophia had been trapped into doing a radio contest where she'd end up picking one of five men at the end to take as her date to Lola's wedding.

I felt a little bad for the role I played in cornering her into that one. But on the bright side, it kept me and my kidney bean–sized secret out of the spotlight for a little while longer.

Second, Lola was in full-on bridal mode. We'd spent the entire afternoon at a chic bridal boutique. The plus side on that one was that we managed to find Lola's gown *and* we picked out beautiful bridesmaid dresses that looked *amazing* and had the added benefit of hiding what would be a four-month-pregnant belly by the time the wedding day rolled around.

I had to find the silver lining wherever I could, seeing as I was a woman in her early thirties who got pregnant out of wedlock by her steady booty call. I was a walking, talking cliché.

The downside of the day was when Lola, Sophia, and Fiona had decided we'd hit up one of my favorite Mexican restaurants when we were finished. They had *the best* margaritas, and there I was, with child, unable to imbibe.

God bless Fiona, though. When Lo and Soph weren't looking, she'd sneak sips of my margarita so it looked like I was drinking along with everyone else. Unfortunately, that meant she'd been doubling up, drinking hers *and* mine, so I was pretty sure she'd be on the floor by the end of the night.

Sophia eventually stood and announced that she was calling it a night. I breathed a sigh of relief, more than ready to get home since my little bean was making it to where I was exhausted twenty-four hours a day.

However, Lola had other plans. "But it's only nine," she whined. "And it's Saturday." *Shut it, you cow!* I screamed in my head. Then the bitch smiled a shit-eating grin and pointed in the direction of the door. "Oh look! The guys just walked in. Now you have to stay, Soph!"

Sure enough, Grayson was walking into the restaurant, but it wasn't him, *or* Deacon, *or* Dominic that I had eyes for. Oh no, I only had eyes for my baby daddy. And damn it, he looked just as sexy as always. I groaned and lifted my margarita glass, momentarily forgetting my current state.

The salty sweetness of the drink hit my closed lips just before Fiona pinched my leg under the table. I flinched at the sharp pain *and* my temporary lapse in sanity and set the glass back down, grateful none of the alcohol had actually made it into my mouth.

I didn't want to be *that* woman. I might have only been pregnant for a minute, but the instant I accepted Mommyhood the only thing that mattered to me was my baby's welfare.

"I need to go to the bathroom," Sophia mumbled, then took off like a bat out of hell. I watched with fascination as Dominic stopped by the table only long enough to mutter something to the waitress before taking off after Sophia.

I wondered what was going on there when the chair next to me scraped across the floor, pulling me from my musings.

"Hey there, sweetheart."

I made the mistake of turning and looking directly into Caleb's eyes, seeing that they held a desire so potent it was more intoxicating than any liquor.

Sweet baby Christ on a cracker.

I was in serious trouble.

CHAPTER TWENTY-FIVE

CALEB

WHEN GRAYSON HAD CALLED and invited me out with him and the guys for an impromptu dinner, I'd been geared up to shoot him down. It had been days since I'd last seen Daphne and I'd finally had enough. The plan was to show up at her house unannounced and tell her... well, I really didn't have the first fucking clue what I was going to tell her other than the current situation where one of us avoided the other wasn't working for me anymore.

But before I could shoot him down, he'd mentioned that the girls were already there. Deciding that Fate was smiling down on me for the first time in a really long fucking time, I agreed.

The instant I walked in and locked eyes with her, I saw it—the longing. It was clear as day. She still wanted me, and I was going to take full advantage of it. I'd rushed to the table, pulling a chair up next to hers, and started on Operation Entice the Hell out of Daphne.

We'd spent the evening tiptoeing around each other while our friends sat around us none the wiser.

When it was finally time for everyone to leave, I made my

move. Leaning in close, I rested my arm on the back of her chair and whispered in her ear. "Did you drive here?"

"Uh... no." Her pupils were dilated, goose bumps had broken out across her arms, and she chewed that bottom lip of hers in a very telling way. "I was going to take an Uber home."

"No need," I said, standing and pulling several bills from my wallet. I tossed them on the table, then grabbed her hand and pulled her to standing. "I'll give you a lift."

"You don't have—"

I started walking, not bothering to listen to the rest of what she was saying. She stumbled behind me as I pulled her toward the exit. I guided her to my car, opening the passenger door and depositing her in the seat. "Buckle up," I commanded before closing her in and quickly rounding the hood. I didn't speak again until we were out of the parking lot and on the road. "You know, I've been with my fair share of women—"

Before I could continue my thought, she cut me off with a disapproving, sarcastic tone. "Wow. Careful, Caleb. Your ego is showing."

I took my eyes off the road just long enough to shoot her a playful smile. "Would you let me finish?"

She crossed her arms over her chest and glared out the windshield. "By all means, please continue telling me about *all* the women you been with."

I cleared my throat and continued. "As I was saying, I've been with my fair share of women, but not a single one of them has gotten under my skin the way you have." I saw her straighten her spine and begin to fidget from the corner of my eye. "When we started this, I didn't have any expectations. I just planned to ride it out for as long as it lasted, but then I started counting down the hours until I got to see you again."

She inhaled sharply but I kept going, knowing that if I didn't get it all out fast, it was more than likely I'd lose my nerve. "It was only about sex with all of them. I didn't care about getting to know them or seeing what the future would hold. But it was different with you. The sex is...." I couldn't possibly put into words how unbelievable it was with her. "It's fucking phenomenal, Daph. You have to know that. But it's so much more. I like just being with you. Telling you stupid jokes just so I can hear your laugh. It's the best sound I've ever heard."

Silence enveloped the inside of the car for so long I feared I'd somehow screwed up. I flipped on my blinker and was turning into her driveway when she finally spoke. "Why are you telling me all of this?"

I pulled to a stop outside her house, throwing the car into Park before giving her my full attention. "Because I can't stand the way it's been between us lately. I think about you all the fucking time, Daph. You're all that's on my mind, and I hate that there's a distance between us now." She opened her mouth to speak, but I held up my hand to stop her. "I know it's my fault. I got weird and started pulling back. I'll take the blame for that. But I couldn't go another day without telling you how I really feel. I'll understand if you're not in the same place. I just had to get it out."

My palms grew sweaty, and I clenched the steering wheel tightly to prevent from reaching out for her. If she was going to shoot me down, I didn't want to make it even more awkward than it already was.

She remained quiet for several seconds, and I'd just started to come to terms with the fact that what we had was good and done when she spoke again. "Stay the night with me."

"What?"

She smiled, reaching over to place her palm against my cheek. "I feel the exact same way. And I want you to stay the night with me."

I had her unbuckled and across the center console in a blink.

I fused my mouth to hers, needing the kiss like I needed oxygen. We clawed at each other like animals. It hadn't been long, but it felt like an eternity since I'd last been with her that I couldn't wait any longer. With her still wrapped around me, I threw the car door open and climbed out, navigating my way up to the front door by feel alone.

Unable to stop touching Daphne the length of time it took for her to unlock her front door, I latched onto her neck, kissing my way across that sensitive spot I knew made her shiver and moan.

The deadbolt unlatched and she shoved the door open. I couldn't remember ever climbing stairs so fast in all my life. The taste of her mouth, the way she whimpered and pressed deeper into my touch and kiss drove me wild. I tore at her clothes and she returned the favor until we were both completely naked.

I pushed her onto the bed, letting out a feral growl when she spread her legs wide, opening herself up to me. "Caleb," she panted desperately as I came down on top of her.

"Are you ready for me, baby?" I asked as I ran my hard cock along her entrance. Her wetness coated every inch of me.

"So ready," she gasped, arching her back off the mattress. "Now, Caleb. I need you inside—" Her words morphed into a cry of pleasure as I buried myself to the hilt.

"Fuck," I grunted, pulling out and plunging back in. "Fucking missed this, Daphne. Missed you."

She wrapped one arm around my neck while bracing herself against the headboard with the other. Her hips came up to meet mine with every thrust, taking me harder than she ever had before. "Me too," she breathed, her face awash with desire.

But it wasn't enough for me. I needed to claim her, mark her. I needed every inch of her gorgeous body to feel me. Daphne whimpered when I pulled all the way out. "What are you—?" I silenced her question by flipping her onto her stomach and hiking her hips up. I rammed back in, causing her head to fly back as she pushed up onto all fours. "*Yes!*"

She shoved herself backward, riding my cock as I fucked her from behind. At one point she turned to look at me over her shoulder, biting down on that plump bottom lip. It was so goddamn hot I nearly blew my load right then and there.

"I'm close, honey." The endearment on her lips was my undoing. Reaching around her tiny waist, I zeroed in on her clit, circling it fast and hard with my fingertips as my cock swelled painfully. "God, Caleb! I'm coming!"

I followed right after, grunting and growling as I poured myself inside her tight, hot channel.

It had been rough and frantic—I couldn't remember the last time I'd come so quickly—but was still the best sex of my fucking life.

I collapsed onto my side, turning Daphne so she was facing me as I laid us down against the pillows. "Mmm," she moaned happily. "That was so good," she mumbled, an exhausted, dreamy look on her face.

I smiled as I lifted an arm, sifting my fingers through her soft golden hair. "Always is when it's with you."

Her smile lit up her whole face, and I couldn't help but lean in to kiss her red, swollen lips. I'd done that to her, and it felt amazing. "Feeling's mutual," she giggled. Pulling back, she looked into my eyes. "About what you said earlier in the car. I wanted to tell you something—"

I placed a finger over her lips to stop her before I spoke. She needed to know I wasn't going to push her further than she was willing to go. "Look, I think I know what you're going to say."

Cocking her head in confusion, she asked, "You do?"

"Yeah. And I want you to know there's no pressure, okay? I want more than what we had before, but that doesn't mean I'm thinking marriage or kids or anything insane like that."

For a second it looked like she stopped breathing. "You don't...?" Daphne's throat bobbed with a thick swallow. "You don't want kids?"

I rolled to my back, taking her with me. Propping one arm behind my head, I wrapped the other around her back, holding her warm, naked body against my chest as I stared up at the ceiling in thought. "I guess I've never really given it much thought. Growing up with my parents kind of put a damper on the thought of having children of my own. If I'm being honest, I don't even know if I'd be a good dad. I didn't exactly have the best role model, you know?"

Her breath hitched. I assumed it was in relief, but when I looked down I couldn't see her face to be certain.

"Hey." I tightened my arm. "You okay?"

"Yeah. Just tired." Her voice was husky with sleep, and I felt bad for keeping her up when she was still on the mend.

Placing a kiss on her head, I gently rolled her to the side and sat up. "Okay, sweetheart. You get comfortable and I'll get the lights."

I shut the house down for the night and crawled back into the comfort of Daphne's fantastic bed. Curling into her back, I held her tightly to me, my chest feeling light for the first time in weeks. I finally had her back where she belonged, in my arms.

I fell asleep with a relief I hadn't thought possible.

Unfortunately, a phone call late into the night ruined that sense of peacefulness.

THE RINGING of my cell phone jolted me awake. I checked the clock, seeing it was after two in the morning before reaching for my discarded pants on the floor. Pulling my phone from my pocket, my entire body tightened at the sight of my mother's name on the caller ID.

"Mom?" I answered on a whisper. "Is everything all right? It's the middle of the night."

"Did you know?" she asked, her voice horribly slurred. *Fucking wonderful.* I was getting a late-night phone call from her when she was sloshed out of her mind."

"What?"

"Did. You. Know?" she repeated slowly. From the sound of it, she'd already gone through a whole bottle of vodka. "Did you know about your father and that slut?" she hissed.

"Fuck. Mom, now's not really—"

"I can't believe you, Caleb! You've broken my heart!"

I carefully stood from the bed, starting for my clothes. "Look, Mom. Just calm down. I'm on my way to you right now, okay? I'll be there as soon as I can."

I ended the call and finished dressing. Daphne was sleeping like the dead, sprawled out on her stomach along the mattress. I didn't have the heart to wake her, knowing she needed her sleep, so I bent down and placed a gentle kiss on her forehead before rushing out to my car. I'd call her later and explain why I took off.

But right then I needed to take care of my mother, since it was clear she couldn't take care of herself.

CHAPTER TWENTY-SIX

CALEB

THE HOUSE WAS LIT up like a goddamn airport when I pulled up, in spite of the hour. With every mile that passed between Daphne's house and here, my anger boiled until it reached a full-blown fury.

I was pissed as fuck. She was the parent; I was her child. I shouldn't have had to climb from the warm confines of my woman's bed in the middle of the night to take care of this shit. But once again, there I was.

I used my key to unlock the door and stomped in. "Mom!" I barked, not giving a damn if my tone upset her further. She needed a goddamn wakeup call. She came stumbling from the back of the house where the kitchen was, the tumbler full of vodka in her hand sloshing precariously.

"Oh, look," she slurred, still managing to show her sarcasm even in her drunken state. "It's my loving, considerate son. The same son who left his father to the wolves when he came to him for help."

I jerked to a stop, staring at her in disbelief. "I'm sorry, *what*?"

She shuffle-stepped past me into the family room, heading

directly to the crystal decanters of alcohol on the table by one of the windows. She chugged the remains of her glass and quickly refilled it. "Your dad told me everything."

"Everything what? Because by what you're saying, I think you're still pretty fucking clueless."

"He told me about that evil bitch and how she's blackmailing him. He told me he came to you for help and you sent him away. How could you! Did you even take my feelings into consideration?" Mom let out a sarcastic snort. "Or course you didn't. Because you're selfish and don't care about anyone but yourself!"

My jaw dropped to the floor in bewilderment and disgust. "Are you... are you fucking kidding me?" I shouted. "Selfish? *You're* calling *me* selfish? That's unbelievable! I've spent my entire life putting your feelings over mine!"

"He's leaving me, Caleb! This is my marriage. My *life*."

"Your life?" I asked on an incredulous whisper. "That's funny, considering most mothers would consider their own child their life. But I don't know why I'm surprised that you'd blame me." I took a step back, reaching up to rub the back of my neck. "You know what? I'm not doing this. I'm done. I finally have a chance at something good in my life, something that makes *me* happy. And I left her in the middle of the fucking night to come here. Never again. I'm done trying to take care of you."

I turned and walked out of the house. The euphoria from only hours earlier had shriveled and died a miserable death.

DAPHNE

WHEN CALEB LEFT my room to turn off all my lights and lock up for the night, I'd taken the time to wipe at my damp eyes. He didn't want kids. He hadn't even thought he'd make a good father. My heart had crumbled to dust in my chest at hearing that. I thought we were finally starting something real, something worth keeping, but with that bombshell I knew I would lose him as soon as he found out.

It hurt in a way I never thought possible, and that hole in my chest expanded, blacking out everything inside me. As I lay wrapped in his arms, I had been convinced that sleep was going to be impossible, but my little bean wasn't having it. It amazed me how something so small could drain so much out of a person, but I somehow managed to conk out in just a handful of minutes, my sleep plagued with horrible dreams, each ending in Caleb disappearing in front of my very eyes.

I woke up with a start hours later when my front door banged from downstairs. I shot up, unable to see a thing through the darkness blanketing my room. "Caleb," I whispered, reaching across the bed. "Caleb, wake up."

My hand hit nothing but cold sheets.

I looked in the direction of my bathroom, hoping to see a light beneath the door, but as my eyes adjusted to the blackness, terror turned my blood to ice at the realization that I was alone.

And that someone was in my house.

A loud crash came from downstairs, but I was too scared to think about what had just been broken.

My limbs shook with fear as I silently climbed from the bed, shuffling across the floor as quietly as possible. I reached my bedroom door, feeling along the wall for the tennis racket I kept propped up so it looked like I at least attempted *some* form of exercise. I held it over my head like it was a baseball bat while silently wishing it *was* a baseball bat. That would have hurt a potential robber so much worse than a stupid tennis racket.

A glass shattered from the vicinity of my kitchen, and I clamped a hand over my mouth to keep my yelp silent. "Omigod, omigod, omigod," I whispered to myself as I slowly crept down the hallway, berating myself for not having my phone. Of course the one time I really needed it I couldn't remember where the hell I'd left it.

It was all Caleb's fault. If he hadn't been sucking on that sensitive part of my neck that made all rational thought fly out of my head, I would have remembered to take it up to my room. *And maybe if he hadn't snuck out on me in the middle of the freaking night I wouldn't be dealing with an intruder all on my own!*

I took the stairs two at a time, mindful of the creaky one in the middle of the staircase. Rounding the landing, I noticed the light from my refrigerator illuminating my kitchen. What kind of robber raided the fridge first—or at all?

The good thing about renovating your own house was that you knew every single piece of wood, every floorboard, by heart. I knew exactly where to step in order not to make a single sound.

The intruder's back was to me as he sucked down *my* orange juice right out of the carton. *The bastard.* Knowing it was now or never, I gripped the handle of the tennis racket as tightly as I could, ready to throw all my momentum into the first swing. With a battle cry that would have put any warrior to shame, I attacked.

"YOU SON OF A BITCH! GET OUT OF MY HOUSE!" *Whack!* "You picked the wrong woman to rob, asshole!" *Whack!* "I'm a goddamn ninja!" *Whack!*

"Ow! Ow! Son of a—Daphne! What the hell are you doing? Stop hitting me!"

"*Caleb?*" I squeaked, stopping midswing.

He stood from his cowering position, dropping the arms he

was holding protectively over his head. I moved to the light switch and flicked it on, bathing the room in brightness. "Jesus Christ, Daphne." He rubbed at his head where I'd used it as my own personal tennis ball. "Did you seriously think an intruder would go for the refrigerator first?"

I propped my hands on my hips, complete with tennis racket and all. "I didn't know that the hell to think," I spit accusingly. "All I knew was that I woke up in the middle of the night to my front door banging closed and someone ransacking my kitchen. And *you* were nowhere to be found! I thought you bailed on me. I wasn't thinking about anything but getting the robber before he got me."

Caleb looked down at the floor guiltily. "Fuck, I'm sorry, sweetheart." When he lifted his head, I noticed the racket had nicked his forehead.

"Shit. You're bleeding." I started for him, and he quickly raised his hands to stop me.

"No. Baby, wait. There's—"

"Ouch! Motherfucker!" I started bouncing on one foot, burning pain slicing through the other.

"Glass," he finished. "Fuck. Hold on. Just stay right there."

I hobbled in place the best I could as he stepped over the shattered glass scattered around my kitchen floor. He lifted me in his arms and deposited me behind on the center island, raising my right foot that had a piece of jagged glass wedged in it. "Shit, it's pretty deep. You have a first aid kit anywhere?"

"Uh, no. But I think I have some Band-Aids and rubbing alcohol under the sink in my bathroom."

"Okay, just wait here. I'm going to grab that, then clean up this mess. Be right back." He placed a lingering kiss on my forehead before bolting from the kitchen up the stairs.

I rubbed at my belly, wondering when I'd finally begin to show. I was only about six weeks along, so other than the insane nausea, there really was no way to tell. How had I gotten myself into such a mess? I was the woman who didn't believe in fairy tales. Life had kicked me when I was down, destroying the hopeful, optimistic girl I'd once been. I told myself I was never going to give my heart to another man, but there I was, in love with America's ultimate playboy. And to make matters worse, I'd gotten myself knocked up in the process of falling for a man who had no desire to ever have children.

"You okay? Is your stomach still bothering you?"

My head shot up, my hand falling from my stomach at the sound of Caleb's voice. "Oh, uh, no. I mean, I'm fine. Just...." *Crap.* "My foot really hurts," I said, hoping to divert his attention away from the fact that I'd suspiciously been caressing my little bean.

Thankfully it worked. "All right. Let's get you cleaned up." Placing the rubbing alcohol and a box of bandages beside me on the counter, he sat on my stool, spreading his legs so mine fit between them. Then he pulled my injured foot up and started inspecting it. "I'm really sorry about this," he said in a hushed tone as he went about removing the shards of glass from the bottom of my foot.

"What happened?" I watched his expression closely as he worked, serious lines marring his forehead as he gently poked and prodded. "I woke up and you were gone."

Caleb blew out a breath in frustration as he wet a paper towel with the rubbing alcohol. "I was going to tell you. I didn't want to wake you up when you were sleeping so peacefully, but I got a call from my mom. She was in a bad way, so I left to go make sure she was okay."

I winced, hissing between my teeth at the sting from the alcohol. He quickly pulled the napkin away and blew across the cut soothingly. God, it was too much when he was being so sweet like this. I'd never really been taken care of by another person before. Experiencing Caleb's tender side made me want to cry all over again.

"Is she all right?"

The skin tightened around his eyes and mouth, unhappiness tarnishing his handsome face. "She's fine. But we got into a fight, so I left."

Ripping the box of Band-Aids open, he pulled one out and started peeling it from its wrapper.

"So you came back here?"

He offered me a brief look before averting his gaze to my foot. "Only place I wanted to be," he answered quietly, slowly covering the cut. "I didn't mean to scare you. I was trying not to wake you up, so I kept the lights off. That's how I dropped the glass. I couldn't see shit and ran into the counter."

I couldn't help but giggle. "I heard more than one crash," I said with mock seriousness. "What else did you break while trying to be stealthy?"

Caleb flinched, giving me an apologetic look. "That blue glass vase you had on the sideboard."

A sharp gasp passed my lips. "My Waterford?" I looked over at where my pretty vase once sat. Now it lay shattered into a million pieces on my floor. "That cost over three hundred bucks!"

"You spent more than three hundred dollars on a vase?" he asked like I'd just lost my mind.

I snorted indelicately. "Hell no. I got it at a yard sale for five bucks. People didn't have a clue what they had on their hands. Suckers."

His deep chuckle resonated through me, warming from the inside out. "Well then I don't feel so bad." He finished tending to my injury, then did something that made me shiver in all the good places: he pressed a sweet kiss to my foot before lowering it. "There. All better. Why don't you head back up to bed? I'm just going to clean all this up really quick."

"You don't have—"

"I want to," he interrupted. "I had a shit night, and taking care of you makes me feel a little better. Just let me do this, okay?"

"O-okay," I whispered, unsure if I'd be able to walk now that his words had turned my bones into jelly.

I needed him to stop being so damn nice or there'd be no way of ever putting my broken heart back together when he eventually found out the truth and I lost him for good.

CHAPTER TWENTY-SEVEN

DAPHNE

"WHAT DO you mean you still haven't told him?"

I squeezed another slice of lemon into my water, giving it a good stir before taking a sip. By a happy coincidence, I'd discovered that citrus helped ease my stomach a little over a month ago. Lemon water had been a lifesaver. I was finally able to keep food down, and bonus, brushing my teeth no longer gagged me anymore.

I looked at Fiona from across the table, feeling like a thousand different kinds of shit. "I know. I'm a terrible person. But I am going to tell him. I swear." I just didn't know when. It had been a little more than two months since I'd gone all Venus Williams on Caleb's ass, and I *still* hadn't gotten the guts to tell him the truth.

"When?" Fiona demanded to know.

"I don't know. Soon."

Her face grew stern. "Daphne—"

"Soon, okay?" I interrupted. "It's just been going so well between us lately. And I know that's all going to go away when he finally finds out."

She reached across the table, grabbing my hand and giving it a squeeze. "You don't know that."

I gave her a droll look. "He all but said it himself," I replied, reminding her of what he'd said the night of the Mexican restaurant.

"But finding out the truth could change his mind. A person can't really know how they'll handle a situation until they're actually in it."

I lifted a bite of salad to my mouth and chomped down. "You're right," I finally relented once I'd swallowed down my food.

"So you're going to tell him?" she asked, visibly brightening in her seat.

Narrowing my eyes across the table, I answered, "Yes. I'm going to tell him. He's still in New York for work, but I'll tell him the truth when he gets back."

"This is going to be good, babe. You'll see. You've been so stressed, keeping this from everyone this whole time. It can't be good for you. And it *really* can't be good for the baby."

Looking back down at my lunch, I shifted the pieces of lettuce around on my plate. "I know. And I hope you're right."

She cut into her grilled chicken, a self-satisfied look on her face. "I am. And the good thing is you can at least use that whole thing about wanting to be out of the first trimester as an excuse for keeping it from Lola and Soph. They'll totally buy that."

"As long as you don't spill the beans that you've known this whole time." I pointed my fork at her in warning.

"Scout's honor," she said, holding up three fingers. "I'll pretend to be just as shocked as they are."

I breathed a sigh of relief, and the two of us went back to our lunch without further talk of my impending discussion with Caleb.

As I walked along the crowded sidewalks back to Hart Tower, I thought about the past two months with Caleb and how amazing they'd been. With the exception of his most recent business trip, he'd spent practically every night with me, coming over as soon as he got off work. He'd been living out of an overnight bag for so long that I'd finally shifted some of my things around to make room in a drawer and my closet for his stuff. There was a toothbrush for him next to mine on my bathroom sink, and a pair of his tennis shoes by my front door for easy access when he went for a morning run, something I discovered he did every single morning, rain or shine. It was just one of a million tiny little things I'd discovered about Caleb McMannus that I hadn't known before. The dude was serious about his fitness, leaving me in bed alone most mornings to get in a routine before starting his day.

I appreciated all his work as the woman who got to use his impeccable body on a daily basis, but if he ever tried to force me up to join him, I might just have to kill him.

It wasn't until he'd had to go to New York to the Bandwidth location there that I got to experience firsthand how much I would miss him when he was gone. I really hoped Fiona was right, because this already sucked enough. There was no way I'd be able to hack it if he left me for good when he found out about the baby.

My phone vibrated in my purse, and I smiled as I pulled it out and spotted the name.

Caleb: *Missing you like fucking crazy, sweetheart.*

That made me all kinds of melty inside.

Me: *Aw, that's so sweet.*

Caleb: *Pretty sure my dick's gonna get a blister if I have to jack off for one more freaking day.*

I burst into laughter in the middle of the street.

Me: *And then you go and ruin it. Perv.*

He responded immediately.

Caleb: *You love my perverted side.*

Sighing at how right he was, I messaged back.

Me: *I hate to admit when you're right. So when are you getting back to Seattle?*

Caleb: *Just a few more days, baby. Miss me already?*

I grinned at my screen as I typed.

Me: *Not you. Just your perverted side.*

He replied, calling me a tease, to which I responded with an emoji of an eggplant and a set of kissy lips before stuffing my phone back into my purse. I'd just cleared the revolving doors into the lobby of Hart Tower when I heard a man's voice.

All the breath left my lungs when I spotted the person who'd just said my name. "Shit. Stefan? What are you doing here?"

He closed the five feet between us, stopping way too close for comfort. "I need to talk to you. Please, Ducky."

Not wanting to risk being seen by Lola or Sophia with my ex-fiancé, I grabbed him by the arm and pulled him toward the alcove behind the elevators. "God, do you have any clue how badly I want to punch you when you call me that?"

His face pinched with hurt. "You used to love it when I called you that."

"No," I hissed. "I used to love *you*, so I tolerated the stupid-as-hell nickname because it made you happy. Now that I don't give a shit about your happiness, I can tell you the truth." I leaned in closer. "I *hate* that name. *Despise* it. Along with a million other things about you."

I could have sworn he was about to cry. "Don't say that, Daph. I still love you. I want you back. Please, just give me another chance."

Batting his hand away as he reached for me, I took a step back. "You're delusional," I hissed. "How many ways do I have to spell it out for you? Do I need to play you a Taylor Swift song to get it through your head?" I don't know what possessed me, maybe it was my bean controlling my body from the inside, but I opened my mouth and spit out, "I wouldn't take you back *ever*, but especially not now that I'm pregnant with another man's child."

What. The. Fuck! Did I just say that out loud?

"You're...." His face paled to a worrisome shade of gray, and his eyes darted down to my left hand as if searching for an engagement ring. "Are you marrying the guy?"

I fisted my hand and moved it behind my back as insecurity washed over me. "It's... complicated." *Jeez! Talk about uncontrollable word vomit!* "It's also none of your damn business."

"But Daphne, don't you see?" Stefan looked positively manic as he moved on me again. "If he doesn't want you, we can raise this baby together. This is perfect! This little baby can be what finally brings us back together. And I'd never hold it against you that it isn't mine."

Oh my god. He was certifiable! Stefan's hand came toward my stomach. I took two steps back, wishing I carried a pocket knife, or Taser, or something, because if his hand came anywhere *near* my belly, I was going to forcibly remove it from his body.

A throat cleared from behind us and I spun around, slumping in relief at the sight of Bob, the sweet old man who worked the security desk in the lobby.

"'Scuse me, Ms. King. Is this man bothering you?"

"Of course I'm not," Stefan snapped. "I'm her fiancé."

Bob's eyes got big, so I quickly amended, "*Ex*-fiancé. And yes, he actually is bothering me."

If you had told me the man who always had a bright smile

and kind word for everyone who walked through that lobby could look so menacing it'd make you want to pee your pants, I probably would have laughed in your face. The man was a bunny rabbit. But I would have been wrong, because right then even *I* was a little frightened of the kindly senior citizen.

"Time to go. You either walk out of here on your own or be carried out on a stretcher."

Gulp.

"*Pfft.* Please. Like you'd—"

Bob cut him off. "I fought in two wars, boxed professionally for twenty years, and still find an hour at the bag every single day. You don't want to test me, boy."

Huh. Well there you go, then. Guess Bob isn't a bunny rabbit after all.

Stefan swallowed audibly, seeing the seriousness in the old man's eyes. "Fine," he started, tugging nervously at his ear. "I'll go." Then he turned and pointed at me. "But we aren't finished here."

"Oh, you're finished," Bob chimed in.

"No, we aren't."

"You're finished, or you'll be eating your meals through a straw for the rest of your life."

If Bob hadn't been happily married for almost as long as I'd been alive, I would have proposed right then and there. Stefan quickly scuttled away, leaving me alone with my knight in security blues.

"You okay, Ms. King?" he asked once Stefan was out of the building.

I smiled at my new favorite person in the world. "I'm fine, Bob. But I think I might be a little in love with you now."

He winked, his aged face wrinkling with a brilliant smile. "Happens all the time. Has Loretta in fits," he replied, speaking of his wife.

I placed a kiss on his cheek and thanked him for saving the day. Then I took the elevator up to KTSW, ready to put my icky run-in with Stefan behind me.

CHAPTER TWENTY-EIGHT

CALEB

I COULDN'T GET out of that god-forsaken airport fast enough. I needed a scotch and a shower to wash the stale, sickeningly floral perfume of the woman in the seat beside mine off me. Flying didn't typically bother me that badly, but I'd been so desperate to see Daphne after a week and a half away that I'd switched my flight when my final meeting ended ahead of schedule, foregoing the comforts of first class for coach, all because I wanted to get back to her half a day early.

It was supposed to have just been a simple business trip, but knowing that Daphne had originally grown up in New York, I took the opportunity to hook up with the private investigator I kept on retainer to try and dig up any dirt on Connie King I could find to use against her. I couldn't stand the fact that I was once again trying to clean up after my parents, but this time was different. I wasn't doing it for them. I was doing it for Daphne, because she didn't need any of this bullshit blowing back on her.

I wanted to fix it before she got dragged into the situation, and had been hopeful when I first landed in the Big Apple. But Connie was just too damn clean. Other than being a shitty mother who had more failed relationships than Jennifer fucking Lopez, there wasn't anything to find on the bitch.

It was exhausting and frustrating, and there was only one person who could make me feel better about my failed mission.

I didn't even bother stopping by my place to get clean clothes; I'd wash what I took on my trip and just live with that. After spending nearly every free moment with Daphne at her house, my apartment felt cold and sterile in comparison. Even with a few of the upstairs rooms still under construction, her house was more warm and inviting, more homey than any place I'd ever lived.

I knew I couldn't broach the subject, at least not right now, but my goal was to eventually engrain myself into her life to the point where she wouldn't want me to leave.

Pulling into her driveway was like coming home. A weight was lifted off my chest.

Music echoed from upstairs. I dropped my bag by the door and took the stairs at a near run. She was in what I referred to as the bookshelf room, wearing those adorable overalls with a tank top that showed off a delicious amount of cleavage.

Christ, I missed her. It felt like it had been forever. I could have sworn her tits looked even rounder, fuller. My mouth watered.

She reached above her head, pulling at a piece of the old, outdated wood paneling on the wall, making my cock thicken behind my fly. I snuck up behind her as quietly as I could. Reaching out, I grabbed her hips and started tickling like crazy.

"*Argh!*" she screamed, spinning around with her hands flat like she was about to karate chop my ass. "Caleb!" I laughed, leaning back so she couldn't punch me in the throat. "God, you scared the crap out of me! How are you here right now? You weren't supposed to be back until later tonight."

I pulled her into me, clasping my hands at the small of her

back. When I held her against me, I felt like everything was right in my world. "My last meeting ended ahead of schedule and I couldn't wait. A week and a half away from you is too damn long."

Her face got soft as her whole body sank into me. "Caleb," she whispered, reaching up and wrapping her hands around the sides of my neck. "I missed you too, honey."

She used that word so rarely that when she called me 'honey' I felt ten feet fucking tall. "So what are you working on in here?"

She turned in my arms, inspecting her work with a heavy sigh. "Honestly, I don't know."

Resting my chin on her shoulder, I looked at the wall she'd been tearing apart before I walked in. "I thought you said you were keeping the paneling, that you were just going to sand and paint it white."

She glared at me over her shoulder. "It wasn't white. It was eggshell. You know that, I showed you the swatch."

I grinned down at her, placing a kiss on her nose. "Looked white to me."

"Whatever," Daphne grumbled with an eye roll as she turned back to the wall. "I woke up this morning and stupidly decided that I'd changed my mind. I saw this awesome textured wallpaper with a really pretty fleur-de-lis pattern that I thought would look amazing in here. But apparently the previous owners were in love with this paneling, because they nailed *and* glued it to the damn walls. It's taking forever to rip off."

"Well, I'm not sure about fleur-de-lis textured walls, but if that's what you want, then how about I go change my clothes so I can give you a hand?"

Warmth infused her expression. "Have I told you yet that I really missed you?"

"You did, but I'm a big fan of hearing it, so feel free to say it over and over."

She smiled up at me, but there was something deeper there, something more meaningful, though I couldn't quite put my finger on what it was. "I missed you. And I'd really love your help. And maybe when we're done we can order in some dinner? There's something I've been meaning to talk to you about. It's kind of important."

A knock sounded on her front door, interrupting the moment. "Hold that thought. I'll get the door, then get changed and be right back."

She blew out a breath like there was something heavy weighing on her mind. "Okay."

The knocking came again, that time more insistent. I pulled at the door, ready to send whoever it was away so I could get back to my girl. "Listen, whatever you're selling, we aren't buy —" The douche who'd tried outbidding me at the auction was standing on the other side. "What the fuck? What are you doing here?"

"What are *you* doing here?" the jackass countered. "I'm here because this is my fiancée's house."

"Your *what*?"

"Caleb?" Daphne called from upstairs. "Who was it at the door?"

Like the sneaky little fucker he was, the asshole darted past me and headed up the stairs. I took the stairs two at a time, reaching him at the same time he hit the room Daphne was in.

She jerked around at the sound of our rapid footsteps, ripping a piece of paneling off as she turned. "Stefan?" she screeched in shock. "What the fuck are you doing here?"

I spoke before he had a chance to answer. "Better question is why did this asshole just call you his *fiancée*?"

"His *what*?"

"Fiancée," Stefan answered. "I called you my fiancée, because that's what you are."

"I most certainly am not!" she yelled. "Omigod! What is wrong with you, you psycho? We haven't been together in *years*!"

I grabbed him by the collar and started yanking him out of the room. "Ducky, just give me a second! Please. I just want to talk to you, honey." He struggled against me, shouting for Daphne the whole time. There was something seriously unhinged about this guy.

"Get the hell out before I throw you out. I swear I'll take her to the courthouse to get a restraining order my-fucking-self."

"Get your hands off me!" He continued to fight against my hold. "I swear to god I'll sue you."

I was about to shove my fist through his fucking face when Daphne let out a pained cry that consumed all my attention. She held her arm to her chest, blood trickling down her forearm from her wrist. "Shit. Fuck, baby. Are you okay?" I released my hold on Stefan's shirt and rushed to her. I gently pulled her arm away from her body, finding a long, jagged cut that extended halfway to her elbow. "Jesus, sweetheart. What happened?"

"Oh god. That looks bad." I spun my head to find Stefan had come up to inspect Daphne's arm.

"Will you get the fuck out of here?"

"I cut myself on a nail sticking out of the paneling," Daphne said, tears pooling in her eyes.

I lifted the piece of wood lying on the ground to find a large rusted nail sticking out of it. "Fuck, okay. We need to get you to the emergency room, Daphne. I think you might need stiches."

"I'll take her in my car."

"Touch me and I'll rip your arm off," she snarled at Stefan, letting me guide her from the room.

Opening my passenger door, I got her settled in the seat and reached into the back, pulling a clean T-shirt from my gym bag and wrapping it around her forearm to try and staunch the blood. Then I drove as quickly as I could to the emergency room.

That bastard Stefan following us the entire way.

CHAPTER TWENTY-NINE

DAPHNE

"WILL YOU SHUT UP ALREADY?" Caleb hissed angrily.

"I'm not going to shut up," Stefan countered. "You shut up."

The two men currently standing inside the tiny curtained-off space that was supposed to be my room were going to drive me to murder.

I sided with Caleb, obviously. There was something seriously screwy with Stefan's head. But if the two of them didn't stop bickering like teenage girls I was going to lose my mind. My arm burned like a mother, and the stiches I had to get didn't make it any better.

I exhaled slowly through my nose, dropping my head back to look at the ceiling to silently ask God for patience.

"If you two can't stop arguing, I'm going to ask you to leave," the nurse said to Caleb and Stefan in a stern voice.

I could have kissed her right on the mouth. "Actually, feel free to kick out the one who looks like a PGA reject," I told her. "He's not welcome. The other one can stay." I shot Caleb a look. "If he promises to *be quiet*."

Just then the doctor threw the curtain back and stepped in. "What's going on here?"

The nurse pointed at Stefan and answered, "I was just about to call security to escort that one out. He's distressing the patient."

All eyes turned to an affronted Stefan as the doctor spoke. "Sir, I'm going to have to ask you to leave. I have to administer a tetanus shot for Ms. King, and if she doesn't wish for you to be present, then you'll have to step out into the waiting room."

"Or out of the hospital altogether," Caleb grumbled, crossing his arms over his chest. "Hell, while we're at it, why don't you just get the fuck out of Seattle completely?"

Oblivious to most everything that was just said, Stefan looked from me to the doctor. "A tetanus shot? Is that safe for the baby?"

Oh shit. Oh fuck, oh shit, oh damn.

Caleb's back went stiff. "Wait... baby? What baby?"

"I'm sorry, sir, who are you to Ms. King?" the doctor asked the bane of my existence.

"What baby?" Caleb repeated.

"I'm her fiancé," Stefan answered.

"*Ex*-fiancé!" I snapped. "And we've been apart for seven years. He's pretty much stalking me now." I was going to kill him. I was going to watch as I slowly choked the life from his stupid freaking body!

"*What. Baby?*" Caleb barked.

I looked to the man I'd fallen completely and madly in love with despite my best efforts not to. "Caleb, honey, please. If you'll just give me a minute to get him out of here, I promise I'll explain everything."

"Let me guess," Stefan snorted snidely. "You're the asshole who knocked her up. Well, you'll be happy to know that when she realizes you're not worth the dirt beneath her feet and comes back to me, I'll raise the child as my own and give it the kind of life a scumbag like you never could."

"Oh my god!" I shrieked. "Someone get him out of here!"

But it was too late. With a ferocious roar and a bellowed "I'm going to kill you!" Caleb lunged.

MY TEMPLES THROBBED beneath my fingers as I attempted to massage the massive pain in my skull.

"So you're saying that this man has been following you around, refusing to leave you alone even though you've asked him repeatedly?"

I looked up at the two police officers who'd been called by the hospital when the fight broke out between Caleb and Stefan.

"Yes," I answered the one who was holding the notepad, taking my statement.

"This is ridiculous!" Stefan exclaimed loudly, rattling the handcuffs that were holding his wrists behind his back. "I'm not *stalking* her! I'm just trying to help."

"By stalking her," the second officer deadpanned.

"I'm not—"

The nurse who had been witness to the entire debacle decided to wade in at that point. "Officer, I haven't been witness to all the encounters she described, but I will say that she demanded he leave countless times, and instead of doing as she asked, he instigated a fight with the gentleman who'd brought her in. He was defending his girlfriend from a man who was continuously harassing her."

That was it. I was kissing her as soon as this whole disaster was over. Unless that offended her. In that case, I'd write her a big fat check.

"Oh," she continued. "And she's also pregnant, so she doesn't need that kind of stress."

Right, could have done without that little reminder. Especially since Caleb had refused to look at me since several of the hospital staff pulled him off my ex.

"Okay, sir." The first officer slapped his notepad shut and glared at Stefan. "We're going to need you to come with us."

"This is ludicrous!" he declared as the cops pulled him from his chair. "Okay. Okay, I'll leave her alone. I promise. I'll leave her alone!"

"Too late," Officer Number Two stated. "When a woman tells you to leave her alone, it's time to get a clue, man." He looked to me as Officer Number One began pulling Stefan away. "And I'd suggest you come down to the station soon to file a restraining order against that guy. There's a couple screws loose with that one."

They left shortly after. With my arm stitched up and bandaged, and my tetanus shot administered, I'd been cleared to leave, but the whole police thing had kept us at the hospital longer than necessary.

"So...." I turned to Caleb once we were all alone. "I guess we should probably head out, huh?"

He barely looked at me as he stood up and started for the door. Even though he was so clearly pissed at me, he still made sure to open the doors and stay close to my side like he was waiting to see if I needed anything.

I couldn't take the silence filling the car during the drive. It was slowly crushing me. "Caleb—"

He cut me off. "No. You don't get to talk right now. I'm so fucking pissed at you I can't think straight."

I clamped my mouth shut for the rest of the ride. It wasn't until we were back at my house that I found the nerve to speak again.

"I was going to tell you. I was just looking for the right time."

"The right time?" he asked in a low, ominous voice, looking at me from the across the expanse of my living room. "The right time would have been when you found out you were *fucking pregnant*, Daphne!"

"I was going to," I cried, tears stinging my nose. "I wanted to, I swear. But when I was going to tell you, you made that comment about not wanting kids and thinking you'd be a bad father, and I just—"

"Wait. That was... Jesus, Daph! That was two months ago! You've known for that long and didn't say a goddamn thing?" He began pacing agitatedly. "Didn't you think I had a right to know you were having my baby? *Christ!*" he thundered so loud I jumped and lost my hold on my tears.

"I kn-know," I stuttered. "I know what I did was w-wrong. I'm so sorry. I just... I was so scared of how you'd take it when you found out, and I... I care about you so much. I was afraid you'd hate me when you found out."

"Do you realize how fucked up that sounds?" he asked in bewilderment. "You purposefully kept a massive, life-changing secret from me because you thought I'd hate you? What were you hoping for, Daphne? Were you thinking I just wouldn't fucking notice the further along you got?"

"I'm sorry," I whispered, moving closer. "There's nothing I can say to make what I did right. I can't excuse keeping it from you for so long. I was wrong, I know that, and you have every right to be angry. If you want to hold this against me, I wouldn't blame you, but you have to know that I wasn't going to keep this from you forever, Caleb. I was going to tell you tonight."

He stopped moving, turning his gaze to me, and what I saw in his eyes froze me to the core—pain, anger, but the worst of all was betrayal. "You know what hurts the most? That you would tell *that fucking guy* before me. Were you so sure that I'd be a deadbeat father to my own child that you'd set a backup plan in place before telling me?"

"God, no! No, Caleb. It wasn't like that." I rushed to him, grabbing hold of his face and forcing him to meet my eyes, praying he could see the sincerity in them. "He showed up at Hart Tower a few days ago. He wouldn't leave. I told him I was pregnant by someone else to try and make him see that I was never taking him back. I wasn't trying to find a backup plan. I would never do something like that to you. *Never*."

His fingers wrapped around my wrists, holding on to me while I held on to him, like we were the only lifeline the other had. "Why didn't you tell me you were engaged to that guy, Daphne?"

That was a story I would have been happy to keep to myself for the rest of my life, but I knew if I had any shot at getting him to trust me again, I was going to have to tell him everything. "Can we sit?"

He pulled my hands from his face and walked around the couch, taking a seat on the far left side. I followed suit, wanting to sit as close to him as possible but understanding that he needed that bit of distance.

"I was engaged to Stefan over seven years ago. We were only about a month away from the wedding when I walked into the apartment we shared together and found him and my mother having sex."

Caleb made a choking sound in the back of his throat while his eyes bugged out. "He... Holy shit. That douchebag and your *mother*."

I nodded. "And I haven't spoken to either of them since that day. Not until they both showed up in Seattle."

After several seconds of quiet, he finally scrubbed at his face and blew out a breath before asking, "Do you still have feelings for him?"

"God, no!" I declared. "No. Whatever I might have felt for him died the moment I saw them together." I knew where he was going with his line of questioning, and I wanted to cut him off at the pass. Scooting closer, I placed my hand on top on his. "But even if that hadn't happened, it still would have ended the same way."

"You can't know that."

"Yes, I can. Caleb, it took hindsight for me to realize the truth, but I didn't like who I was back when I was with him. I was this insecure girl desperate for someone to love me. The only parent I ever had growing up treated life with me like it was a competition. She had to be better than me in every way. I never felt like I was good enough because she made sure of it. When I met Stefan, all I wanted was for someone to take care of me the way my mother never did. I wanted someone who looked at me like I was everything, not just a runner-up to Connie King. But even he couldn't do that. I was just too blinded by my own desperation to see it."

Lacing his fingers with mine, I continued. "I'm not the same person I was back then. I'm so much stronger now. I can look back on my time with Stefan and admit that I never loved him the way a woman is supposed to love the man she's going to marry. I was more in love with the idea of him than anything else. If I could go back in time, I wouldn't change a single thing about how we ended. Please believe me when I say that I don't feel a single thing for him anymore. I haven't in a very long time. What I feel when I'm with you is so much stronger than anything I ever shared with Stefan. You make me happy in a way he never could. It never could have worked because I never loved him the way I love you."

His entire body went completely stiff at my admission of love, and I couldn't help but wonder if I'd just made everything worse.

The look he gave me was like a knife to the chest. "But it still wasn't enough to have faith that I'd do the right thing, was it?" His tone was cold, and even though I deserved every bit of his derision, it still hurt like hell.

He stood from the couch and headed for the front door. My stomach knotted in panic as I got to my feet. My knees trembled, threatening to give out. "Where are you going?"

"I need to think," Caleb answered, not bothering to turn around. "You gave yourself two whole months to come to terms with all of this. Now it's my turn."

Then he was gone. And I was left feeling like the lowest form of scum on the planet.

CHAPTER THIRTY

CALEB

DAPHNE WAS PREGNANT. With a baby. *My* baby. And she'd told me she loved me.

Christ.

No matter how hard I tried, I just couldn't seem to wrap my head around that fact, especially not with my anger toward her hanging around my neck like a goddamn albatross.

I wasn't sure where I was going or what I planned on doing when I left her house. I spent forever just driving around aimlessly before finally ending up at The Black Sheep.

The place was crowded, seeing as it was a Saturday night, but I still managed to find an empty stool at the bar.

"Hey," Deacon greeted, sliding a scotch in front of me. "I'm surprised to see you here. Didn't you just get back into town?"

I swirled the amber liquid around in the glass, unable to bring it to my lips and drink for some reason. "Yeah, earlier today."

"Figured you'd be shacked up with your secret girlfriend," he joked. "I mean, that's still going on, isn't it?"

I frowned into my drink. "Yeah. I think so. I don't know."

Finally looking up with a sigh, I admitted, "I'm not even sure anymore."

Deacon rested his forearms on the bar, giving me all his attention while his other bartenders continued scurrying around filling drink orders. "What makes you say that?"

I rubbed at the two-day growth of stubble that coated my cheeks. "She's pregnant, man."

He jerked back in shock. "Oh fuck. And you're...."

When he couldn't finish the sentence, I offered, "Yeah. It's mine."

His cheeks puffed out with a heavy breath. "Wow. I don't even know what to say."

"That makes two of us," I grumbled. "The real kick in the nuts is that she's known about it for two months now and never said a word."

"Wow," he repeated. "Just... *wow*."

I slammed the glass on the bar top with a roll of my eyes. "Think you could find something else to say than just 'wow'?"

Then he said something that hit me right in the stomach. "You're going to be a dad, brother."

I was going to be a dad. *Holy shit*. I was going to have a kid.

"How do you feel about that?"

How *did* I feel about that? No matter how many times I asked myself that very question, I couldn't seem to come up with an answer. It didn't feel real. It was like I was in some sort of parallel universe, living a life totally different from the one I imagined myself living.

"I don't even fucking know," I answered honestly. "I'm too hung up on the fact that she's known for two months and kept it from me because she was afraid I'd blame her or some shit." When Deacon didn't say a word in my defense, I looked from my untouched drink back to him. "What? What's that face about?"

"Well...." He hemmed and hawed for a bit. "Can you really blame her?"

"Unbelievable," I snapped. "You're defending her?"

Holding his hands up in surrender, he spoke quickly. "I'm not defending her, per se. Should she have told you about the surprise bun in her oven? Most fucking definitely. But put yourself in her shoes."

"What's that supposed to mean?"

Deacon didn't bother with gentle; he simply got straight to the point. "Look at your track record, man. You've practically lived the past decade in the gossip rags. It's not a stretch to think you wouldn't be thrilled at the idea of being tied to one woman for the next eighteen years."

"I wasn't that bad," I defended, even though I knew he was totally right about everything he'd just said. The look he gave me said that I wasn't fooling anyone.

"You were, Caleb. Look, I'm not saying your girl's not at fault here. I'm just suggesting that maybe you shoulder a bit of the burden as well. Have you two even discussed what you are to each other?"

My mouth opened and closed a few times before I was able to answer. "Well, no. Not exactly."

He took the untouched scotch and dumped it before pouring a glass of water and setting it in front of me. "What does 'not exactly' mean?"

"I told her I wanted to be more than a fling." Then I added that stupid shit about not wanting marriage or kids, all because *I* was afraid I was pushing for too much too fast.

What a clusterfuck.

"Are you kidding?" he asked with a sarcastic snort. "Oh, well then that changes everything! You want to be more than a fling. How the hell did she not see that as the declaration of love it was intended as?"

Flipping him off, I grunted under my breath. "Okay, I get your point. You don't have to be an asshole about it."

Deacon's face went hard, his tone serious as he spoke. "Listen, I'm not going to tell you whether or not you should forgive her. That's your call. But the fact is you're going to have a baby. It's time to let go of all the shit from your childhood and grow the fuck up. You were dealt a messed-up hand in the parent department, I'll give you that. You never got to see what a real, healthy relationship looked like. But only you can decide if you're going to let history repeat itself, or work your ass off to be better than them. And brother, just a word of warning. If I see history repeating itself, I'm going to personally kick your ass."

My blood heated at the accusation. "I'm nothing like them," I growled in warning. "I would never treat Daphne or our child that way." I couldn't even imagine being the type of father or husband my own dad was. In all the time Daphne and I had been together, never once did I think about going back to my old ways, a different woman warming my bed every night. She was all I needed, all I ever thought about.

If my father felt for my mom even an ounce of what I felt for Daphne, I couldn't imagine he'd ever turn his sights on another woman. It was unfathomable.

"Then stop moping around my bar and go figure out what the hell you want."

Figure out what I want.

The bastard made it sound so easy.

The life I'd always imagined for myself had been turned on its head in a second. I hadn't planned for Daphne to come in and shake up my carefree world, but I'd finally just started to accept the idea of settling down. Hell, I'd even grown to *like* the thought of having one woman to come home to as long as it was her.

Throwing a baby into the mix had rattled me all over again.

I felt like I was turning into a man I didn't recognize. It wasn't a bad thing, just a shock. I needed some time to adjust.

Daphne and I hadn't exactly started on the most stable foundation. You could barely call what we had a relationship. There were so many ways for us to ruin what we'd just started, and that thought terrified me.

But when she told me that she loved me, I could see it in her eyes that she really meant it. And fuck me, but I was starting to believe that maybe I felt the same. The problem was I didn't have the first goddamn clue what real love looked like. All I knew was that the thought of not having her in my life every single day from there on out was something I couldn't even bring myself to consider.

I had to tread carefully, because one wrong move and I'd lose her forever. And that just wasn't something I could live with.

CHAPTER THIRTY-ONE

DAPHNE

I HADN'T SLEPT for crap the night before. I kept picturing Caleb's face when he walked out my front door, and the pain I felt at that memory was just as acute as it had been the first time around.

I wanted to fall apart, wallow in a shitload of self-pity like I had when my engagement went belly-up, but I knew that wasn't an option this time around. It wasn't just me I had to take care of. I had my little bean. I had to pull up my big girl panties and carry on with my life for his or her sake.

That meant I was only allowing myself one day to binge on Ben & Jerry's while crying over sappy Hallmark movies where the woman overcame some clichéd adversity and got the man of her dreams in the end.

I started the moment the sun rose and was a good four hours into my sob-athon when my front door was thrown open. I was mid-lick on a spoonful of Chunky Monkey when Caleb came walking in, hauling two large suitcases behind him.

"You really shouldn't leave your door unlocked like that. Anyone could just walk—" He stopped the moment he set eyes on me. "Have you been crying?"

I pulled the spoon from my mouth, still in shock at the unexpected sight of him, and used it to point at the TV. "The guy in the movie grew up in a foster home," I said on a sniffle. "He never experienced love and believed he'd be alone forever. But then he hired a quirky book nerd as his assistant, and she broke through the walls he'd built around his heart to show him true love did exist." I let out a hiccupped sob as I finished with "It was very touching."

"Dear god," he muttered, looking at the TV in abject terror. "Do you watch shit like that all the time?"

"N-no," I stuttered. "Just when I'm having a pity party. But it's worse now that I have all these pregnancy hormones coursing through my system."

"I'll keep that in mind."

Wiping at my tearstained cheeks with the neck of my ratty sweatshirt, I asked, "What are you doing here? And what's with the luggage?"

"I'm moving in," he answered simply, like he was announcing the day's weather forecast.

"I... you... what?"

He left the bags by the door and moved to the couch where I was sitting, taking a seat on the cushion next to mine. "I'm moving in. I gave it a lot of thought last night, and decided that our baby needs to be raised with both its parents living under the same roof."

I could barely comprehend what he was saying, but the one thing that stood out the most was the way he said *our* baby. Hearing Caleb string those two little words together in his rich, velvety voice made my belly flutter. I gave my head a shake to try and stay on topic. "But what about your apartment?"

"I'll put it on the market," he said with a casual shrug. "I don't think it'll take long to unload it, especially since I'm selling it fully furnished—"

"Wait." I closed my eyes and held my hand up to stop him. I was struggling to keep up with everything he was saying. "Fully furnished? But that's all your stuff."

"It's not like I'll need it. Besides, my stuff would clash with everything you've got going on here. And I like your style better anyway."

"I... you...." Tears started leaking from my eyes again. "You're giving up all your stuff because it doesn't go with mine?"

"And I like yours better," he said softly.

"Oh god." I started blubbering uncontrollably. "Th-that's the sw-sweetest thing I've ever h-heard!"

"Fuck me," he mumbled, pulling me against his chest in a tight hug. "You really are a mess, aren't you?"

"I-it's the b-baby. It's t-taking over my b-body," I sobbed. "I c-can't control *a-anything*!" I finished on a loud wail.

Caleb rubbed soothing circles along my back while I used his T-shirt as my own personal tissue. I don't know how long we stayed like that, but he didn't let me go until I finally got ahold of myself.

Wiping under my eyes, I inhaled deeply, blowing the air out past my lips before looking at him again. "But I thought you hated me," I whispered.

"I don't hate you," he said softly, brushing at a stray tear with the pad of his thumb. "I'm pissed, but I don't hate you."

It took every ounce of courage I had to ask my next question, knowing there was a strong possibility I wouldn't like that answer. "So what does this mean for us?"

My anxiety doubled with each second that ticked by without his answer, until he finally said, "Well, that depends."

I chewed on my bottom lip until it became raw. "On what?"

"Did you mean what you said last night? Do you really love me?"

My head bobbed up and down in a frantic nod. "I do."

His shoulders slumped on a deep exhale, like me confirming my feelings for him had just lifted a weight off his chest. "I want to make this work," he said with such fierce determination that I could practically feel it radiating from him.

They were sweet words. What they weren't was a declaration of love. But that was okay. After all, I was the one who'd broken the trust between us; it was my responsibility to heal the breach I caused.

I could do that. And I could wait for him to finally love me the way I loved him, because for the first time in my life I finally felt like I had a man *worth* waiting for.

I only hoped I hadn't broken us so badly that I wouldn't be able to put us back together again.

CHAPTER THIRTY-TWO

THE PAST MONTH had been unbearable.

Caleb and I had been living together like two of the most considerate roommates to have ever existed.

I know that might not sound bad, but when you went from a passion that ignited in so many different ways that you had no choice but to fight or screw it out to constantly walking on eggshells around the other person, it was pure torture.

I'd have given anything for him to push my buttons the way he used to, even if it led to a fight, if it meant I'd get a glimpse at the Caleb I had fallen in love with.

Don't get me wrong, the way he tried to go about taking care of me—making me lemon water when my stomach was unsettled, or checking I was eating enough—only made me love him even more. But it felt like that fire that had initially brought us together had been snuffed out.

I missed it.

I missed *him*.

We might have shared a bed every night, but he hadn't touched me in an intimate way since moving in. I was afraid there was no going back to the us we used to be. And that realization made me unbelievably sad.

To make matters worse, I felt like the worst friend in the universe. I hadn't been there for Lola like she deserved during her wedding planning. And I'd completely dropped the ball with Sophia during her latest drama with Dominic.

The contest we were doing on our show had finally come to an end, and Sophia was all set to meet the man she'd chosen as the winner, who would be her date to Lola and Grayson's wedding. Turned out, the man who'd been known as BigSpoon for the past three months was none other than Dominic himself.

To say Sophia had lost her mind was putting it mildly. The entire segment had been streamed live for our audience to witness, and ended with Sophia going Ali on his ass, punching him right in the face for hundreds of thousands of people to witness. That ended in a hefty little fine we were responsible for paying and yet *another* reprimand from HR.

The three of us were quickly garnering a reputation around the station as the women who punched first and asked questions later.

Shortly after that shit storm, Lola and Dominic's estranged father passed away. I joined them in New York for the funeral to offer moral support, but other than being a shoulder to lean on, I'd been pretty useless. I'd been there in body, but my mind had been back in Seattle with Caleb.

The silver lining was that Sophia and Dominic seemed to be working through their issues, and Lola was only days away from walking down the aisle and giving herself over to a man who'd proven time and again that he was just crazy enough to handle her special brand of sass.

I was glad that my friends had found the loves of their lives, even if it was looking like I wasn't going to be so lucky.

I wasn't sure how much longer I could go on pretending like

everything was all sunshine and roses when it was so obvious there was a major disconnect between Caleb and me. Case in point: when I'd come downstairs after a midday nap the day before—something I seemed to be doing more and more—he'd been having a whispered conversation with someone on his cell phone. All I managed to hear was "I don't care how much time or money it takes. I want it done now" before he spotted me hovering at the base of the stairs.

The moment he saw me, he made a quick excuse to end the call, then pretended that everything was perfectly normal. I didn't feel I had the right to ask about it, so I'd brushed it under the rug, along with the billion other things that left me feeling unsettled.

A million questions ran through my mind. Was he talking to his lawyer? Was he going to try and take the baby from me once it was born? Was there already another woman in the picture?

Each question made that black hole in my chest grow bigger and bigger, and I'd silently cried myself to sleep that night, going up to bed well before he normally did so I could have that time to myself.

When I told him about the OB appointment I had scheduled for this morning and invited him to come along, I'd expected him to make some excuse. But he surprised me by not only accepting my invitation, but actually appearing excited about going.

"You ready for this?" Caleb asked, polite as ever as I looked from the monitor to him. The sanitary paper on the table crinkled beneath me as the doctor lifted my shirt and squirted a cold blue gel onto my stomach.

"Yep," I answered quietly as I watched the small TV screen in anticipation. The doctor spread the gel around with her wand, trying to get the best angle for a visual of my little bean. I was so engrossed in the screen that I gave a startled jump when

Caleb's hands came down on my shoulders. My gaze shot up to find him smiling down at me.

I felt the warmth of that smile all the way down to my toes. Then out of nowhere the room filled with the sound of rushing water.

"What's that?" I asked, looking back to the doctor.

She gave Caleb and me a knowing grin and announced, "That's your baby's heart. Listen carefully and you can hear the beating."

I focused on the sound and sure enough, a second later I could make out the faint *whom whom* beneath the whooshing. It was the most miraculous sound I'd ever heard.

"Oh my god," I whispered.

"And if you look right here," the doctor stated, pointing at a flickering light on the monitor, "you can actually see her heartbeat. It's nice and strong."

"Her?" Caleb asked, his tone full of amazement. "It's a girl?"

She grinned and pointed at something else on the screen that I couldn't make out through the glassy film of tears filling my eyes. "That's right, Daddy. You're having a little girl. She's cooperating perfectly today. Looks like she wants to put on a show for her parents." She rolled the little ball around, clicking it a few times to take some pictures. "All ten fingers and toes, and she's measuring at about eighteen weeks, which is right on schedule."

"A little girl," Caleb repeated, pulling my attention from my little bean, which wasn't so little anymore. I'd never seen his eyes so bright than when they met mine just then, and I couldn't help but smile at the joy radiating down at me. "We're having a little girl." His voice was rough and gravelly as he said it. And when he dropped his forehead to mine and pressed a kiss to the tip of my nose, a few happy tears trickled down my cheeks because I felt like I'd finally gotten a piece of *my* Caleb back.

"This is so amazing," he declared a while later when we were in his car on the way home. "I can't believe... Shit. Daphne. We're having a baby!"

I giggled, looking up from the ultrasound pictures in my hands. "Yeah, you've known that for a while now."

The smile hadn't left his face since we walked out of the doctor's office. "I know, but I guess it just didn't seem real to me until just now, you know? I mean, you get to feel everything since you're the one carrying her, but you're not even showing yet. Today was the first chance that *I've* gotten to experience anything."

I loved how he explained what seeing our daughter for the first time felt like. "I get it. I've been getting these little flutters in my belly that kind of feel like wings. I wasn't sure what it was at first, but then I figured out it was her flipping around in there. But it's so light that you couldn't feel it just by putting your hand on my belly. I'm glad you got a firsthand look at her today."

He reached across the console and took my hand in his, tangling our fingers together as he shot me an exuberant smile. "I am too. Although...."

"Although what?" I asked when he didn't finish.

"If she looks anything like you, I'm fucked when she becomes a teenager." I threw my head back in a fit of laughter even though he looked serious as could be. "And if she even *thinks* about bringing home a boy who's even the slightest bit like me, I'm boarding up her windows and locking her in her room until she hits menopause."

My laughter faded into a lingering giggle as I gave his hand a squeeze and looked out the window. "I don't know," I said quietly. "You're not so bad."

And he really wasn't.

As far as I was concerned, our little girl would be lucky to land a man like her father.

CHAPTER THIRTY-THREE

CALEB

"I'VE SAID it once and I'll say it a-fucking-gain, Henry. I don't care how much it costs. There's no way a bitch like that doesn't have *something* in her past that can be used against her. Go all the way back to her fucking birth if you have to."

Henry Danforth, my private investigator in New York, sighed through the line. "I'm telling you, McMannus, there's nothing *to find*. The only thing Connie King is better at than blackmailing people is covering up the fact that she's black-mailed people. If you'd just talk to the daughter—"

"Not going to happen," I told him for the hundredth time. "We aren't pulling Daphne into this. That woman made her life a living hell growing up, and I'm not adding to any of that. Besides, I'm not even sure that she's still *Daphne* anymore. I think what we thought was a baby is actually some sort of alien life form that's using her as a host and slowly taking control of her body."

Henry laughed heartily through the line. "Aw, yeah. I remember thinking something like that back when my Suzie was pregnant with our first. She was sweet as pie one minute, and the next she was waving a butter knife around in the air threatening to unman me for eating the last piece of banana bread. Good news is they snap out of it."

I blew out a puff of air and rubbed at the back of my neck. "I sure fucking hope you're right about that," I said. "She went off on me for a good thirty minutes the other night because I bought dryer sheets instead of liquid fabric softener. No freaking joke, man, she didn't take a single breath during that entire rant. Not one. Face turned all purple and everything. That can't be good for the baby. Ten minutes later she was sobbing on the kitchen floor because there was no mustard to dip her pickles in. Then she locked herself in the bathroom when I told her that particular food combination sounded disgusting."

There was more laughter. "Yeah, well you try growing another human being inside your belly, having it screw with every chemical makeup you got, and tell me you don't get a little touchy every now and then."

"There's a reason women are the ones in charge of populating the earth. If we were responsible, our species would be obsolete."

"Truer words have never been spoken, my friend. Anyway, I'll let you know if I manage to find anything."

I gave him my thanks and hung up, plopping down on one of the cement benches scattered around the garden. I gave my bow tie a tug, trying to loosen the stiff collar of my tux. Even with the cool temperatures outside my skin felt overheated.

I couldn't get comfortable no matter how hard I tried. I was happy for Grayson and all, but I was ready to get this day over with so I could get home and out of this uncomfortable-as-shit suit.

"There you are." I looked over my shoulder at the sound of Grayson's voice. He rounded the bench and took a seat next to me.

"What are you doing out here?" I asked. "Shouldn't you be

inside stalking your bride-to-be to ensure she doesn't make a run for it?"

"Real funny, dickhole," he deadpanned, a dry look on his face. "Like she'd try to make a run for it." His expression grew uncertain as he asked, "Do you really think she'd try to make a run for it?"

I laughed and smacked him on the back. "She's not going to do a runner, brother," I reassured him. "For reasons that will probably never be discovered, she seems to love your cranky, ugly ass."

He looked at the darkening sky. "Fuck me, I don't think I've ever been so nervous in my life."

"Not even the first time you handled a multimillion-dollar buyout on your own?" I teased.

His voice was dead serious as he answered, "Not even then."

My good humor faded as I studied my best friend closely. "You aren't having second thoughts, are you? 'Cause you know you'll never land another chick as hot as Lola, right?"

He smiled, chuckling softly. "Nope, no second thoughts. Never been so sure of anything in my life. I guess what I'm nervous about is not deserving her." He moved his attention from the sky to me. "Does that even make any sense?"

"Yeah, I think I know where you're coming from," I answered after giving it some thought. I understood because I pretty much felt like that on a daily basis when it came to Daphne. I was so fucking scared of screwing up somehow that I'd spent the past month on eggshells, careful not to do or say anything that could start a fight. My fear was that she'd wake up one day and realize I wasn't worth the hassle. Then she'd be gone.

I was so consumed with trying to be the perfect partner for her that I'd almost forgotten what it was like to just be myself. I got a piece of that back the other day when we went in for the ultrasound, but with her unexpected—and frighteningly violent —mood swings, the good feeling hadn't lasted long.

"Jesus," Grayson muttered, breaking through my miserable thoughts. "I don't think I've ever seen you think so damn hard."

Ignoring the dig, I looked at my best friend, the man who seemed to have his shit completely together, and asked, "How did you know you loved Lola?"

Seeming momentarily perplexed by my question, he hesitated before giving me an answer. "I guess I knew when I tried to picture a life without her in it."

"Were you able to?"

He watched me curiously. "What's brought all this on, man? Is there something going on with you that you haven't told me?"

Anxiety twisted my stomach into knots. "Just answer the question. Were you able to picture a life without her?"

"Yeah, I was," he replied like a punch to the throat. "But it wasn't an image I liked at all. In fact, I pretty much hated it. Then I tried to picture my life with another woman, marrying her, having kids with her. That was even worse. But it was when I pictured Lola having that with another man that I lost it. I knew that, even if I didn't deserve her, no man on this planet would try harder than me to come close enough. I knew I loved her when life with her was a hell of a lot brighter than one without her. Even when she pisses me off and drives me crazy— and she does that *a lot*—she lights everything up for me."

Christ. *Jesus Christ!* Fuck me, it was like he was speaking out loud every goddamn thing I'd been thinking for the past month. It felt like I'd been punched in the stomach. I struggled to breathe, to think.

I loved her. I fucking loved Daphne. In the back of my mind, I'd suspected that was what I was feeling, but I didn't trust that it was real until the guy I respected in every single way confirmed it.

I loved her. But what was more, she loved me too. She was the first woman to ever say that without using it as a way to manipulate me. My own freaking mother didn't tell me she loved me without attaching strings to it.

Daphne said it and didn't expect anything in return, and I'd been too busy turning myself inside out, worrying about a future I had absolutely no control over to really let it sink in.

I was a jackass.

"I love Daphne," I admitted out loud for the first time. "Pretty sure I have for a while, but I was too slow on the uptake to see it."

"Wait. What?"

No time like the present to tell the truth. "We've been seeing each other for a while. Longer than you and Lola, actually. But I was an asshole at first, so it took a while to get us to a good place. But now I love her."

"You...." He shook his head like he was trying to rattle something loose. "I'm sorry. You and Daphne have been together all this time? Why didn't you ever tell me?"

"It's a long, convoluted story, and we have to get you down the aisle pretty soon so we don't have time to dive into all that right now. But the short and sweet of it is that it started as a fling and we kept it a secret because our friends are all nosey bastards."

We stood from the bench and started for the door that led into the over-the-top venue Lola and Gray had chosen for their wedding.

He snorted loudly. "Can't even be mad at you for that one because it's the truth."

The frazzled wedding planner who'd been in charge of the

big day spotted us the minute we stepped inside and came running over. "Oh, and one more thing."

Gray looked at me over his shoulder as the hyperactive wedding planner started dragging him away. "Yeah? What's that?"

"I've moved into her house. My apartment's up for sale. And she's pregnant. We're having a little girl."

"*What?*"

Maybe it was wrong to drop that bomb on him when he couldn't pry for more information. But wrong or not, I sure as hell got a laugh out of it.

DAPHNE

MY LITTLE BEAN and I were going to have a serious talk soon. She was wreaking some serious havoc on my emotional well-being. First I was sobbing like a baby over cheesy Hallmark movies. Then I morphed into a raving banshee bitch from hell, snapping at Caleb over things I normally wouldn't give a shit about.

I mean, dryer sheets? Who the hell cared about dryer sheets? Psycho Pregnant Daphne, that's who.

Now it was taking everything in me not to throw myself at Lola and bawl my happiness for her out all over her immaculate dress. I barely made it through the ceremony without ruining the amazing job the makeup artist had done on my face.

Pregnancy was for the birds.

And I *really* wanted a glass of champagne... or a mojito. *Ooh, yeah. A mojito sounds good.*

Son of a bitch.

"May I have this dance?" My heart stuttered at the sound of Caleb's voice. Wedding party duties had been so consuming that other than spotting him during pictures—and maybe staring at him with a little too much longing during the vows—I'd barely said more than two words to him.

Without giving me a chance to answer, he took me by the hand and started pulling me toward the dance floor as the beginning threads of a slow ballad began to play. He stopped us at the center of the floor and spun me with surprising flourish before pulling me into his body. One arm wrapped around my waist while he kept my other hand firmly in his, and he started swaying us to the music.

"I haven't had a chance to tell you yet, but you look absolutely gorgeous tonight."

Goose bumps broke out along my arms at the same time my cheeks heated. "Thank you."

"How are you feeling? I know it's been a long day and you didn't have a chance to take one of your three daily naps."

He laughed when I smacked him in the arm. "Jerk," I mumbled without any ire. "To be honest I really just want to get home and get out of this dress. It's too tight around my boobs and my belly. I feel like if I bend over the wrong way I'm going to bust a seam. And these stupid shoes are pinching my toes."

His eyes traveled down my neck to the swell of my cleavage, and he let out an appreciative hum that had me biting down on my bottom lip. I hadn't seen that look directed at me in far too long.

We danced silently for a while, and I was a little amazed at how well he moved to the soft, melodic beat. "You're a pretty good dancer."

"I'm full of surprises," he said with a suspicious smirk.

"Oh yeah?"

"Yep. For instance, I'm about to say something that's really going to knock your socks off."

I giggled, sifting my fingers through the hair at the nape of his neck. "Knock my socks off, huh? Okay, well hit me with it."

"Okay. Here it goes." He paused for dramatic affect. "I think you and I should get married."

My jaw hit the floor. Then I screeched, *"Have you lost your mind?"*

CHAPTER THIRTY-FOUR

DAPHNE

CALEB'S EYES scanned the crowd around us nervously. "No, I haven't lost my mind, but if you keep shrieking like that, everyone around us is going to think *you* have."

I narrowed my eyes in a murderous glare. "Careful, Caleb. I haven't exactly been in control of my emotions lately. I'm liable to slap the shit out of you if you piss me off."

He pulled in air through his nose, making a face like he was searching for patience. "Will you just hear me out?"

"No, I won't. Because it's a terrible idea."

"It's perfectly reasonable," he grunted angrily.

"I'm not marrying you," I declared.

"Yes, you are."

"No, I'm not!"

"You're already having my baby. We're already living together. It's the next logical step."

"Oh, how romantic!" I exclaimed snottily. "Just the kind of proposal every woman dreams of."

It was his turn to glare. "Well maybe if you weren't such a sarcastic pain in my ass, I would have taken the time to put a little more effort into it."

That did it. My hand was flying through the air before I gave it a single thought. The crack of my palm against his cheek echoed through the ballroom like a gunshot.

I hadn't even planned to slap him. It just happened. What *was* it with my friends and me hitting people!

I was sure the look of shock on my face mirrored his perfectly, but I didn't hang around long enough to find out. Turning on my heels, I stormed off the floor and out of the ballroom.

"Holy shit. Holyshitholyshitholyshit. I can't believe I just did that," I muttered to myself as I speed-walked toward the nearest exit.

I let out a startled yelp when a hand clamped down on my arm and spun me around just feet from the door. Caleb looked ready to spit fire. "Oh no you don't. You aren't running out on me. Not after that."

"Look," I started quickly. "I'm sorry I hit you. I honestly didn't mean to. I don't know what came over me—"

"I don't give a shit about you hitting me. What I want to know is why the fuck you won't marry me."

"Don't you get it?" I cried, throwing my hands in the air. "I told you I love you, Caleb, and I meant it. But I can't marry you just because you feel obligated! That's something my mother would do. She'd get pregnant just to trap a man for his paycheck, and I swore I would never, *ever* turn into my mother. I already screwed the pooch on that one by getting pregnant. I'm not going to make it even worse by tying myself to a man who doesn't want to be tied to me!"

He stepped closer, crowding me. "Who says I don't want to be tied to you?"

Crap. I was going to cry again. "Oh please," I laughed humorlessly. "You haven't touched me in over a month. You treat me like I'm nothing more than a roommate to you. And I get it. I screwed up. I understand that you can't forgive me, but—"

"You think I don't *want you*?" he asked in bewilderment. "Have you lost your mind? I've walked around that goddamn house for the past month with a constant hard-on!"

"Then why won't you *touch me*?" I shouted.

"Because I've been so fucking scared of doing something that'll piss you off and make you realize that I'm not good enough for you!"

"That's the stupidest thing I've ever heard!"

We were officially yelling our argument at the top of our lungs, but neither of us seemed to care.

"It's not stupid! I know how much you hate it when we fight!"

"I miss our fighting, you idiot! I *want* you to fight with me! I can't stand walking around on eggshells for one more fucking second! I miss how we used to be, because at least then we were passionate about each other!"

"Oh, you want passion?"

"Yes!"

We clashed together just like we did in the past, biting and clawing, attacking each other like rabid animals. It was pure, unadulterated bliss.

"God, I've missed you," I panted as yanked at his bow tie.

"Fuck, baby. I've missed you too. So fucking much." He hiked my dress up and lifted me off the ground. Wrapping my legs around his waist, I held on for dear life, licking and nipping at his neck as he moved. The faint sound of a door clicking shut penetrated my senses just before my back hit a wall. I briefly opened my eyes and noticed that Caleb had somehow managed to locate the coat check room for a bit of privacy. *Bless him.*

"Let's promise each other that we'll always fight as long as we get to make up like this."

"Promise," I breathed as I pulled at the buttons of his shirt. I needed to feel his skin against mine. Sleeping in the same bed as him night after night and not being able to feel him had been a form of torture.

"And I want you to say you'll marry me." I tried pulling my head back, but he fisted my hair and held me in place as he feasted on the upper swells of my breasts. "And not just because you're having my baby but because you love me, and I love you."

That black hole in my chest shriveled and shrank until it disappeared altogether. I yanked his hair, pulling his head back until I could look into his eyes. "You love me?" I asked on a whisper, feeling the telltale sting of tears. *Goddamn pregnancy hormones.*

"I'm so in love with you I can't see straight, sweetheart. I can't imagine my life without you in it. I don't want a fling. I want so many strings attaching you to me that you'll never untangle them. I want you to marry me."

"Caleb, I—"

The door to the coat room came crashing open, and all our friends—*every single one of them*—crowded into the doorway.

"You're *pregnant?*" Lola screeched.

I turned bewildered eyes to Caleb. "You told her?"

"No!" Lola shouted. "I had to find out from Sophia!"

My accusatory gaze landed on Fiona. "You told them?"

Her hands went up in surrender. "I didn't tell anyone anything!"

"She knew before me?" Sophia yelled.

"Who told you?" Caleb asked.

"I found out from Dominic."

"And I heard from Grayson," Dominic chimed in.

Caleb skewered Gray with an evil look. "Jesus, man. Can you keep a secret for more than two seconds?"

"Hey." He shrugged nonchalantly. "You said it yourself,

we're all nosey bastards. Did you really expect anything less?"

Lola butted into the conversation, shoving her new husband out of the way. "So it's true? You're really having a baby?"

I nodded tentatively. "I'm sorry I didn't tell you guys sooner. I'm a terrible frie—"

She and Sophia let out ear-piercing shrieks of delight as they pulled me away from Caleb and wrapped me in a tight hug. Thank god we hadn't gotten to the stage where some very private parts had come out to play yet. "Oh, who cares that you didn't tell us sooner! We can give you shit about that later," Sophia chirped. "You're having a *baby*!"

Fiona joined our huddle and the four of us bounced up and down happily until all the movement caused my little bean to revolt.

"Oh. No. Nope. No more of that," I said, placing a hand on my belly. "She's not liking that."

"*She?*" Fiona cried.

I smiled a bright, beaming smile at my friends before moving to Caleb's side and wrapping an arm around his waist. He slung one over my shoulders and pulled me even closer. "Yeah," I answered, happier than I ever thought possible. "We're having a little girl. We just found out a few days ago."

I thought my girls were going to burst into tears as Grayson, Dominic, and Deacon offered Caleb pats on the back.

"Oh. And we're getting married," Caleb announced casually.

"We didn't agree to that!" I announced loudly, holding up my hands before the three women had a chance to lose their minds again.

Caleb's arm around me tightened, drawing my attention to his handsome, smiling face. "Maybe not, but I'll wear you down eventually."

I had a sneaking suspicion he was right about that.

CHAPTER THIRTY-FIVE

DAPHNE

I DON'T THINK I'd ever been as happy as I was at that very moment. Lying in bed, cuddling with Caleb after making love was the most content I'd ever been. His fingers played with my hair as I rested my head on his chest, listening to his heart beat in a smooth, soothing rhythm that was quickly putting me to sleep.

But there was still one last question I needed answered before I could allow myself to fully revel in my newfound bliss.

"Caleb?"

"Hmm?" he hummed sleepily.

"I know that we're finally in this really great place with each other, and the last thing I want to do is put a damper on that, but there's still one thing I need to know."

"What's that, baby?"

Propping my hands on his chest, I rested my chin on top of them so I could look into his eyes as I asked, "I know you've been sneaking off to have private conversations on the phone with someone. I can't help but feel like there's something important you aren't telling me."

He inhaled deeply, making his chest rise and fall with a

weighty sigh as he stared at the ceiling. Finally, his gaze returned to mine. "Before I tell you what's been going on, I need you to know that I haven't kept this from you because I didn't trust you. I just wanted to prevent any more added stress. You've been dealing with so much lately—"

"Just tell me," I pleaded, sitting up on the bed. I held the sheet around my naked breasts as worry lanced through my chest. "Dragging it out like you're doing is only making it worse. Rip the Band-Aid off."

Propping himself against the headboard, he took my hand and started slowly massaging it from the ball of my palm up to my fingertips. "It's your mom. She's, well...."

"A raging bitch who's having an affair with your father? Yeah, I already knew that."

"It's more than that. She's... fuck. Well, she's blackmailing my dad. Apparently, she recorded them... you know...." His face pinched in disgust.

It took a moment for what he said to register, and when it did I felt like I might be sick. "Ew! Oh god! Oh my *god*! That's so gross!" I waved my hands in front of my face frantically, trying to erase the mental picture he'd just drawn for me.

"Yeah. Tell me about it."

Once I was sure I wouldn't gag, I managed to ask, "How much is she asking for? I hate the thought of giving her money, but I can't help but feel like I'm responsible in some way. If it's a reasonable amount, I can pay—"

The fierce, serious scowl he gave me not only shut me up but sent a shiver down my spine. "First of all, you're not responsible for *any* of this, you hear me? Secondly, even if she were demanding money, you're crazy if you think I'd let you give her one goddamn cent of what you earned. The time for that woman to disrupt your life in any way is officially over. I won't allow it. I take care of what's mine, and you and our baby are just that. *Mine*."

I pushed down the warm fuzzies his declaration stirred in my belly and focused on something he said. "What do you mean, even if she were demanding money? That's what black-mailers typically ask for, isn't it?" He raked a hand through his hair and focused on a point over my shoulder, unable to meet my eyes. "Caleb? What aren't you telling me?"

It took way too long for him to answer me, and when he finally did my blood turned to ice. "She doesn't just want a payoff. If he doesn't divorce my mom and marry her, she's going to leak the video to the press."

If you listened closely enough, you could almost hear my brain explode. "That fucking *bitch*!" I shrieked. "That evil, manipulative *fucking bitch*!"

His hands shot out, wrapping around my waist and lifting me like I weighed nothing at all. Depositing me on his lap so my thighs straddled his, he banded his arms around me, making it impossible for me to move. "Calm down, baby. This is *exactly* why I didn't want to tell you. You can't get worked up over this. Not only because she's not worth it, but because it's not good for our baby. I'm taking care of it, baby. You can trust me. You've got nothing to worry about other than growing our little girl in here."

He placed his hand on my belly over the sheet. The gentle, sincere touch worked wonders in calming my fury. I closed my eyes, deep breathed, and counted to ten before speaking again. "I don't understand why you have to take care of this in the first place. I understand they're your parents, but this is your dad's mess. Why do you have to help clean it up?"

With a face like granite, he replied, "It's what I always do. He cheats and she calls me in a drunken stupor and expects that I can somehow convince him to stop."

I placed my hand on his cheek, hating the hurt and frustration I could see in his eyes. "You know it's not your place to take care of stuff like that, right? She should have been protecting you from it, not depending on you to fix her broken marriage."

He pulled my hand from his face and laced his fingers through mine, studied my small hand wrapped in his large one. "Logically, I know that. And when she called that night I left you, I told her I wasn't going to clean up his mess this time. She called me selfish, said I was ruining her life.

"Honey, I'm so sorry," I whispered, my heart breaking for him.

"Been that way my whole life," he said with a pained shrug.

I couldn't imagine Caleb as a little boy, having that kind of guilt piled on his shoulders. It wasn't fair, and I secretly hated his parents for doing that to him. I wanted to take away his sadness, but I didn't know how.

"So that's what you guys fought about before you came back here?"

His head bobbed in a short nod. "The funny thing is I meant it when I told her I wasn't going to fix it this time. I'd just gotten you back. I was finally happy, and I didn't want their bullshit tainting that. Then I thought about you finding out. I didn't want their shit to touch you, so I hired a private investigator to try and dig up some dirt on your mom that we could use as leverage to try and get her to back down. That's what all those calls were about."

Oh, you sweet, naïve man. "You aren't going to find anything," I informed him hesitantly. "My mom specializes in covering her tracks."

A snort burst past his lips. "Yeah, no shit. Tell me something I don't already know. Only thing he was able to find on her was that she's flat-ass broke. Obviously that's why she targeted my old man, but I can't exactly use her bad credit against her."

"The only reason I caught her and Stefan together was because she wanted me to. He was taking too long cutting me loose, so she decided to take the situation into her own hands."

"Jesus Christ," he hissed furiously. "No offense, baby, but your mother's a fucking piece of shit."

I took no offense to that. In fact, I couldn't help but laugh at his declaration. "Seems like we both got the short end of the stick when it comes to the people who brought us into this world, huh?"

With a look of pure love, he stroked my midsection again. "We're never going to make our girl feel even an ounce of what we felt when we were growing up."

God, I love this man. "Nope. She's not going to know anything but happiness and love. But in order to give her that, we need to cut this one last cancer out of our lives."

His brow furrowed in confusion and worry. "What are you talking about?"

I knew he was going to hate what I was about to say. He'd do everything he could to talk me out of it. But the truth was, there wasn't anyone on the face of the earth who knew my mom and her games better than me.

"Okay, I know you aren't going to like this, but I need you to trust me."

"What? No. Absolutely not. Whatever you're thinking, just forget it. My guy's on it. You aren't getting involved."

I placed a finger over his lips to silence his objection. "Honey." For some reason that one word took all the fight out of him and made his face go all soft and sexy. I'd have to remember that for later. "I don't really know much about how healthy relationships work. I'm basically just taking ours one day at a time, remembering everything I saw my mom do and doing the exact opposite. But the one thing I've learned by watching Lola and Grayson together is that when two people love each other the way we do, it's our job to take care of *each other*. You told me that you take care of what's yours. Well, so do I, and you're mine, Caleb.

"I love that you want to take care of me, but don't make me sit back and watch you suffer alone. I'm made of some pretty strong stuff, and if you let me, I can help. Please, let me help, honey."

That seemed to work, because he visibly softened before my very eyes. "Fine. We can try this your way. On one condition," he said quickly when he saw that I was building up to an excited dance. "Whatever crazy scheme you come up with, I have to be there."

"Deal." I held my hand out so we could shake on it.

Then I let him toss me onto my back so he could seal our deal in a much more energetic way.

CHAPTER THIRTY-SIX

DAPHNE

WHEN CALEB and I had finally gotten around to telling our friends the whole story of our relationship like they'd demanded, each and every one of them had been all too happy to throw their hat in the ring for what I was calling Operation Take the Bitch Down.

I'd been hesitant at first to bring them into our mess, but it was obvious that they wanted to help out of love. Caleb and I weren't used to having such a strong network of support, and it took us a while to fully trust it, but once we did and our plan was finally under way, I couldn't imagine pulling this off without them.

My phone chimed and I flipped it over to read the text.

Sophia: *We're in. Getting to work now.*

I exhaled in relief, placed the phone back on the table, and glanced out the window of the bistro I'd chosen when I called my mother to set up a meeting. Caleb's car sat parked at the curb just outside. I couldn't see him through the darkly tinted windows, but just knowing he was there, watching over me, gave me a sense of peace.

He wanted to be inside, but since Connie knew his face it

had been out of the question. He finally relented to waiting in his car outside as long as Grayson and Deacon were inside, close enough to intervene if need be. I knew it wouldn't come to that, but since it gave my overprotective man peace of mind, I allowed it.

Sophia was with Lola and Dominic at a different location, already carrying out phase one of the operation. All that was left was for me to wait until my mother decided to grace me with her presence.

I checked the time on my phone one last time, seeing that she was ten minutes late. Always wanting to make an entrance, my mother had never been on time for anything in her life.

Finally, five minutes later, she came waltzing into the bistro like she owned the place, decked out in an expensive winter-white pantsuit that had to have come from Christopher McMannus, seeing as she didn't even have two nickels to rub together.

Show time.

"Darling! So lovely to see you." I got to my feet, staying still as she placed air kisses on both cheeks. You never would have guessed by looking at her right then that she grew up in a trailer park in Poughkeepsie. Mommy Dearest was, for all intents and purposes, nothing more than trailer trash until she suckered her first unsuspecting victim at the age of seventeen.

She might have spent her entire adult life putting on airs, but as the saying went, you could take the girl out of the trailer park, but you couldn't take the trailer park out of the girl. You could see it in the way she conned and manipulated herself to the lifestyle she thought she deserved.

"Mother," I replied in a flat voice. "Please, have a seat. I got you an ice water while I was waiting."

She pulled out the chair across from me and sat down, placing her Louis Vuitton handbag on the table beside her. It wouldn't do to put such an expensive purse in a chair where other people couldn't see it. She was all about showing off her assumed wealth. Exactly what I'd been counting on.

"I have to say I was surprised to get your call."

I picked up my menu and pretended to look it over while I flipped my hair over my right shoulder. That was Fiona's cue.

A second later our table was jostled, tipping the water glass over right into Connie's lap.

Mom shot from her seat as Fiona apologized profusely, patting at the ridiculous white suit with a handful of napkins. "Oh, I'm so sorry! I'm such a klutz sometimes. I'd be happy to pay to have your outfit dry-cleaned—"

Taking advantage of the distraction, I reached into Mom's purse and pulled out her cell phone. I dropped my hands beneath the table and quickly entered my mother's security code to unlock it. As I'd hoped, it was the same code she used for everything—her own birthday. The woman was nothing if not consistent. Fiona's gaze met mine and I gave her an imperceptible nod. "Well, like I said, it was an accident. Again, I'm very sorry."

As Connie retook her seat, looking mad enough to spit nails, I discreetly slid the phone into Fiona's hand as she passed. From the corner of my eye, I watched her dart out of the bistro and climb into the passenger seat of Caleb's car.

Phase two was complete.

Now it was my turn.

"Some people just shouldn't be allowed in public," she grumbled, still dabbing at the damp spots on her jacket. "This suit probably costs more than that woman makes in a month."

If she only knew. Fiona probably had enough money in her wallet alone to buy out my mother's entire trailer park and level it to the ground to put in a high-rise.

"Mother," I spoke, pulling her attention back to me. "I

called you here because I know what you're up to, and I want you to stop."

She had the audacity to look innocent. "I don't know what you're talking about. You aren't making any sense, Daphne."

I propped my arms on the table and leaned in ominously. "Look, I don't know what happened between you and Stefan, and I really don't give a shit. What I *do* know is that you stupidly walked away from that relationship with nothing more than the clothes on your back and a few hundred dollars in the bank." She blanched, almost turning as white as her suit. "I know you've hitched yourself to Christopher, and I know you're blackmailing him to leave his wife. That was your first mistake. You should have gone for the cash, but you've always been too greedy for your own good. This is your last chance, Mom. I'm asking you, please, just stop this now."

Her sneer told me she hadn't heeded my warning. "I don't know what you *think* you know, but Christopher and I are in love, and we're going to get married. I'd hoped, as my daughter, you'd be happy for me, but I see you're still the selfish, bitter little girl you've always been."

I wanted to be thrilled that I was finally getting a chance to stick it to her for all the years of misery she caused me, but the truth was it just made me sad. She was still my mother, and deep down I'd hoped that there was a piece of her that wanted to try and fix our relationship.

The realization that she'd never be the mother I'd longed for stung, but knowing that, after today, I was going to get to move on and build a happy, loving family with a man who'd spend his life taking care of me made the hurt almost insignificant.

"And that was your second mistake," I said. "I gave you a chance. Unfortunately, you weren't smart enough to see it for what it was."

My phone chimed again, and I picked it up to read the message.

Sophia: *All done here. Heading out now. I have to say, I'm a little disappointed by how easy this whole thing was. I feel like I wore all black for nothing.*

I looked back up at the woman who'd given me life, unable to fathom ever treating my own child with the neglect and cold indifference my mom had shown me. I placed my hand on my belly and silently promised my little bean that I'd always love her, no matter what.

A flash of red from outside the window caught my eye, and I turned to find Fiona standing on the sidewalk, giving me the thumbs-up as Caleb started into the restaurant, my mother's phone in hand.

Once he reached the table, he took the chair next to me, dropping the cell in my lap before wrapping an arm around my shoulders in a show of support.

"What's going on here?" Mom asked, glancing suspiciously between Caleb and me.

I placed her phone on the table and slid it in her direction. "I took the liberty of unlocking your phone so Caleb could get in and erase the video you were using to blackmail his father."

"You...." Her eyes went wide. "You didn't."

"I did," I answered drily. "And when we called Christopher earlier today to let him in on our plan, he was all too happy to hand over the keys to that swanky new apartment he set you up in. Our friends are on their way back from there right now after wiping your laptop clean. You really shouldn't use the same password for everything, Mother. It's just not smart."

Connie's cheeks slowly grew a bright red as her fury boiled over. "You... you back-stabbing little bi—" she started, but Caleb quickly cut her off.

"I wouldn't if I were you," he said in a tone so threatening it sent a chill down my spine.

"The video's gone, Mom. All copies of it. You've got no leverage anymore. If you had just listened to me, we could have avoided all this ugliness, but you don't care about anyone but yourself."

"I regret the day I brought you into this world," she hissed spitefully. "You've caused me nothing but grief since the moment you were born."

"That's it. You're done," Caleb barked, climbing to his feet.

Seeing he was seconds from losing his mind, I touched his arm and tried to calm him down. "Caleb, honey. It's okay."

"It's not," he snapped. "I told you the other night that I take care of what's mine, and part of doing that is shutting this bitch down the second she starts insulting you. I'm not going to let you sit here and listen to her spew hateful bullshit. We're leaving. Now."

Grabbing my hand, he pulled me from my chair.

"Wait!" my mother cried, standing up. "You can't do this!"

Caleb spun around and skewered her with a glare. "We can, and we are. If you're too fucking stupid to see what an amazing, caring, wonderful daughter you were blessed with, that's your own damn fault. Unlike you, I know how special she is, and I'm not going to allow anyone to make her feel bad about herself. You're nothing but a cancer, scum on the bottom of her shoe, not even worthy of breathing the same air, and if I have my way, she'll never have to set eyes on you again."

As a parting shot, he pulled two twenties from his wallet and threw them on the table. "Here, treat yourself to lunch. And I recommend you buy something cheap, because that's the last dime you'll ever get from me or Daphne."

Then he dragged me out of the bistro toward his car.

"Have I mentioned that I'm totally, madly in love with you?"

Some of the thunder faded from his expression, a tiny semblance of a smile tilting his lips. "Once or twice," he answered, opening the passenger door. "But I don't think I'll ever get tired of hearing it."

Resting my hands on his chest, I stood on my tiptoes and pressed a kiss to his lips. "Well I do. And I promise I'll remember to tell you how much I love you every single day for the rest of our lives."

He hooked an arm around my waist, holding me close. "I love you too, sweetheart."

My belly flipped happily. I didn't think I'd ever get tired of hearing that either.

———

CALEB and I were one step closer to getting our happily ever after. There was just one last thing I needed to take care of.

I'd told a little white lie earlier when I said I needed to run a few quick errands, so he thought I was at the store at that very moment. And as I walked up to the front door, my hands began to tremble with nerves. There was so much riding on this one last task, and I hoped this meeting had a better outcome than the one with my mother had.

It took two knocks before the front door was thrown open and Caleb's mother came into view.

"What are you doing here?" she asked, her face muddled with confusion and a healthy dose of hostility. I'd wondered if she knew my connection to the woman trying to steal her husband. I guess I had my answer.

"I'm sorry to drop by unannounced like this. I won't take up too much of your time, but I felt that you should know that my mother won't be an issue any longer. She's out of the picture for good."

"That's... well... I don't know what to say."

"And there's something else you should know. You're going to be a grandmother." I placed my hand on my belly. "Caleb and I are having a little girl, and we'd love nothing more than for you to be a part of her life."

Her mouth dropped open, her eyes lighting with the kind of glee I imagined all grandmothers-to-be shared. However, I wasn't quite finished yet.

"But that isn't going to happen if things don't change. Caleb told me how he was always stuck in the middle of your problems with your husband, and I'm here to tell you that it stops today." She opened her mouth to argue, but I sallied on. "Your son loves you very much. I don't want him to lose you, but you've chosen a man who doesn't deserve you over Caleb time and time again. It hurts him, and I can't allow you to keep hurting the man I love."

I watched as tears filled her pretty eyes, and I knew that what I said had resonated. I held out the manila folder I'd been carrying.

"Wh-what's this?" she asked hesitantly.

"You deserve so much more than what you've settled for. I hope for your sake and for Caleb's that you realize that one day. In that folder is the information for Mary Weatherton, Seattle's top divorce attorney." Her mouth opened once more, but I held my hand up to stop her. "I'm not giving you this as an ultimatum. I'm doing it because the man you're married to isn't worth another minute of your time. Whether you choose to call her or not is your choice. I just wanted to give you the option. And if you decide this is something you want, I'll be more than happy to help you take that man to the cleaners. And trust me, I have the connections to do it."

She looked down at the folder for several seconds before finally lifting her head in my direction, a tentative smile stretching across her lips. "You're rather blunt, aren't you?"

I grinned and shrugged. "I am. He probably won't admit it, but I think it's one of the things Caleb secretly loves about me."

She let out a lovely, melodic laugh that transformed her entire face. Man, Christopher McMannus really was a freaking idiot. Caleb's mom was a knockout when her face wasn't weighed down with sadness. "I can see that. So... he's happy?"

I placed my hand on my belly and beamed. "He is. *We* are. And we'd love to share this happiness with you if you'll let us."

She glanced down at the folder one more time. "I may just have to take you up on that," she said softly.

"I hope you do," I returned. "And be sure to call your son soon. We'll have you over for dinner at our house."

"Your house," she whispered. Pain flashed through her eyes, and I could only assume it was because her son was building a life she'd had no clue about.

"Soon," I repeated, wanting to pull her from her dark thoughts. "It'll be great."

"Yes," she said in a strong, confident voice. "Yes, I do believe it will be."

My work there was done.

I felt light as a feather as I turned and started for my car. That went so much better than I'd imagined.

Now it was time for me to get back to my man.

EPILOGUE

CALEB

OUR NORMALLY PEACEFUL house had erupted into chaos. And it was all Daphne's fault.

The renovations of the sprawling Victorian had been put on hold the further along Daphne got in her pregnancy. And despite being more than capable of finishing the last remaining rooms myself, she wouldn't hear of it.

The house had been her baby. She'd brought it back to life with her own two hands, and she wasn't going to let anyone else finish the job she'd started.

But now it was done, and because she was so proud of the work we'd put into it, she wanted to show it off.

That was why she decided that it was a brilliant idea to host Thanksgiving for *everyone*. Lola and Grayson, Sophia and Dominic, Deacon and his date Leah, Fiona, and my mother. Hell, we even had Lola and Dom's crazy mother Elise, her husband Maury, and Grayson's parents and grandmother. I loved Nana like she was my own flesh and blood, but she was a menace with that goddamn cane of hers.

I walked past the living room where the men were gathered,

shouting over the football game playing on my new seventy-inch TV, and headed for kitchen.

My mother lunged the second she saw me. "There she is! There's my little angel. Come to Gammy, my precious." Mom snatched my daughter out of my arms and propped her on her hip. Evie shoved her fist in her mouth and started drooling all over it as her grandma showered her with attention.

"What?" I asked her. "No love for your own son?"

Mom rolled her eyes and placed a quick kiss on my cheek. "Oh, don't be so sensitive."

I chuckled as she moved back to the island with my daughter in tow. I'd never seen my mom so happy in all my life.

Ever since she—with Daphne's help—had raked my father over the coals during their divorce, taking more than half of everything and leaving him with a reputation that could never be salvaged, the shadows that plagued her eyes had completely disappeared. She hadn't touched a drop of alcohol in months. She was a better grandmother to my daughter than I ever could have asked for. And she and Daphne spent far too much time teaming up together against me.

It was bliss, seeing the three most important females in my life come together like that.

"Aw, honey. Is she ignoring you again?" Daphne teased from her place at the stove. "Come here. I'll give you a kiss and make you feel all better."

I made my way past the other women who filled my kitchen, always eager for a taste of Daphne.

Placing a kiss on her beautiful lips, I murmured, "Happy Thanksgiving, wife."

"Happy Thanksgiving, husband."

"Ew!" Sophia cried from the side of the island, waving a large plastic spoon at us. "Stop being all gross and mushy around the food."

Daphne giggled as Lola sniffled. "I think it's wonderful." Tears welled in the feisty Italian's eyes. "So much love in one room. It's beautiful." Then she burst into loud, ugly sobs.

"Grayson!" I shouted toward the living room. "Your woman's having a pregnancy meltdown again! Get your ass in here!"

That earned me a smack on the back of my head and a disapproving look from my mother. "Watch your language around the baby," she scolded.

"Christ, Mom," I said with an eye roll. "She's four months old."

"Still. I don't want my precious little angel's first word to be a curse." I didn't have the heart to tell her that Daphne cursed even worse than me, so the odds were stacked against her.

Grayson came rushing into the kitchen toward Lola. "Hey, honey. That Hallmark movie you like so much is on. Why don't I put it on in the den for you?"

"O-okay," she blubbered, allowing him to lead her from the kitchen.

"Good Lord," Sophia muttered a few seconds later, rubbing at the tiny bump in her midsection. "Is that what I'm in store for?"

"Probably not," Fiona answered, "Seeing as you have no soul."

Everyone laughed while Sophia threw a dinner roll at Fee's head.

"Okay, I need people to start setting the table," Daphne announced. "Dinner's almost ready."

The chick Deacon had brought to dinner hopped off her stool eagerly. "Is there anything I can help with?"

Fiona, Daphne, and Sophia gave the poor girl blank looks. "Nope. We're all good, Leah," Daphne answered before pasting a fake smile on her face.

She visibly deflated. "You sure?"

"Yep," Sophia chirped. "But you can go tell everyone else it's time to eat."

Leah headed out of the kitchen, everyone else following to start loading our table with the massive Thanksgiving feast Daphne and the others had been working tirelessly on.

"You know, it wouldn't kill you to be a little nicer to her," I mumbled once the kitchen had cleared out.

My wife stared daggers at me from over her shoulder. "Why should I? She's not one of us."

I rolled my eyes to the heavens, praying for patience. "Deacon's been dating her for three months. You guys took Fiona in after just a few hours."

Daphne looked back to the pot of potatoes and began mashing violently. "That was different."

Resting my chin on her shoulder, I spoke against that sensitive part of her neck, causing her to shiver and break out into goose bumps. All this time and I could still see the effect I had on my girl. I fucking loved it.

"Please? For me? Deacon can tell you guys don't like her, and it's starting to cause problems."

Her shoulders rose and fell on a deep breath. "Fine," she relented. "I'll make an effort." She spun in my arms and pointed the potato masher at my face. "But I want it on the record that I still think this is a huge mistake. Deacon and Fiona belong together."

"Consider it recorded. As long as you and the other two Misfit Musketeers don't go sticking your noses where they don't belong."

Her eyes darted away, a suspiciously innocent look on her face. "I don't know what you're talking about."

"Daphne," I warned. "I'm serious. Stay out of other people's business."

"Okay."

That was too easy. And when something with Daphne was too easy, I knew there was trouble ahead. "What have you guys done?"

Her response was to sling her arms around my shoulders and kiss me square on the lips. "Nothing, honey." I started to relax. Until... "Yet, anyway."

"Christ," I grunted, pulling her tighter against me. "You're lucky I love you so damn much, because you drive me crazy, sweetheart."

"I know." She smiled brilliantly. "And you drive me crazy too. It's why we're so perfect for each other."

She wasn't wrong about that. Being with Daphne meant I had a lifetime of crazy in store for me. And I wouldn't want it any other way.

The end

keep reading for a sneak peek of Charming Fiona, coming soon

CHARMING FIONA EXCERPT

PROLOGUE

AS CHILDREN we were taught that the sky was the limit, that when we reached adulthood we could become whatever we wanted. For a long time, I'd taken them far too literally, first deciding that I wanted to be a Barbie doll, then a princess, then a mermaid (that one was on you, Ariel).

By the time I finally got over the heartbreak of discovering that Disney princesses didn't actually exist in real life I'd decided I wanted to be the first woman president or an astronaut. That phase hadn't lasted long.

When I reached my teenage years, my father began grooming me to take over the family business. After all, I was Calvin and Evelyn Prentice's only child. So it came without saying that I'd one day carry on the legacy that had started as nothing more than a small, family run department store on the west coast and eventually grew into a worldwide fashion empire thanks to my father, and his father before him, and so on and so forth.

Most teenage girls would have dreamed of working in the high-end fashion industry, reveling in all the perks, the haute couture. But I wasn't one of those girls. I didn't dream of running an empire. I didn't care about notoriety or fame or any of that stuff.

I didn't care about being the next big *"it"* name or who walked down the red carpet in one of our designs.

Truth was, I hadn't earned any of that. It had just been handed down to me as the next Prentice generation. No, what I wanted more than anything in the world was to be a wonderful wife and mother. Yes, I was aware that my ambitions set feminism back by decades, but I didn't give a shit. I wanted a family. I'd grown up watching my father dote on my mother like she was the only woman on the planet. They kissed, they touched, they didn't care where they were or who saw their sometimes sickening—especially to a school-aged girl—displays of affection.

Most days my dad could barely keep his hands off of her. And I was sure had my mom been able to, our house would have been *full* of children.

Unfortunately, her body just wasn't built to carry a baby. Her pregnancy with me was difficult enough, and after nine months of living in constant fear of his wife's wellbeing, my father had decided that one was more than enough.

When I finally came into the world, I got all that adoration and love showered on me as well, so it had been engrained in me from day one to find a man who treated me like I walked on water and hold on tight to that.

Because of that, I'd grown up with a somewhat inflated sense of romance. Meaning I threw myself into every single relationship I ever entered and had my heart crushed when they eventually came to an end.

But the absolute worst heartbreak I'd ever encountered had come at the hands of a man I'd grown up with. A man who I'd idolized and placed on a pedestal for as long as I could remember.

Grayson Lockhart was absolutely *everything* a woman could want. He was kind and sweet, he was driven in success, smart, funny, and tying all of that up in a shiny, perfect bow was the fact that he looked like a Greek God.

The man was hot. I was talking take-your-breath-away, drench-your-panties *HOT*. He could give you a mini-orgasm just by walking into a room and smiling.

And he'd been all mine.

For a time.

After our relationship ended I'd been devastated. I threw myself into work, eventually jetting off to Prentice Fashion's Paris headquarters. I just couldn't take seeing him with other women. And since our families were such close friends it felt like every exploit since our breakup was being shoved down my throat.

It wasn't until years later when I'd finally managed to mend my broken heart that I realized Grayson was never supposed to be my everything.

No, that title belonged to the one boy who'd been a central figure in my life practically since day one. He was the one who held me when I cried, who I shared my deepest and darkest fears with, who knew each and every one of my hopes and dreams.

He had once been my everything, and I'd been too stupid to realize it, even though it had been right in front of my face all my life.

I'd been taught that I could be anything, do anything, that true, unflinching love really did exist.

But what I *hadn't* been taught was that it didn't wait forever.

Eventually true love got tired of sitting around, waiting for you to get your head out of your ass and realize you'd picked the wrong brother.

And that was exactly what had happened to me, because by the time I realized that Deacon Lockhart was the love of my life it was too late.

And I had no one to blame but myself.

Click here for more info

MORE FROM THE LADIES OF GIRL TALK

SEDUCING LOLA

I'VE HAD my fair share of bad relationships. I've dated liars, cheaters, shoe fetishists, and everything in between. Sure, these experiences would make any woman cynical when it comes to dipping her toe back into the dating pool, but I used my past for good and made a career out of helping other women avoid going down the same paths I had.

And I was damn good at it.

Until a random act of fate set my life on a course I'd been avoiding for years, and put me in the crosshairs of a man that made me feel things I swore to never feel again.

Now I'm in his sights and it seems like he'll stop at nothing to seduce the hell out of me. He might hold my career in the palm of his hands, but if Grayson Lockhart thinks he can blackmail me into submission with his sexy voice and sexy hands and sexy everything, then he's...probably right.

TEMPTING SOPHIA

HAVING my heart broken once was enough to make me give up on the idea of love all together. Instead of searching for The One I decided to embrace variety and turn my back on monogamy. I made a living convincing women they didn't need a man to feel complete.

And I totally rocked at it.

Until the man who shattered my happily ever after came waltzing back into my life, determined to make me fall for him all over again.

He claims that I'm the love of his life. He wants a second chance, and it seems like he'll stop at nothing to tempt the hell out of me. But if Dominic Abbatelli thinks he can win me back with his puppy dog eyes, heartfelt apologies, and declarations of love then he's...probably right.

DISCOVER OTHER BOOKS BY JESSICA

THE PICKING UP THE PIECES SERIES:

Picking up the Pieces

Rising from the Ashes

Pushing the Boundaries

Worth the Wait

THE COLORS NOVELS:

Scattered Colors

Shrinking Violet

Love Hate Relationship

Wildflower

THE LOCKLAINE BOYS (a LOVE HATE RELATIONSHIP spinoff):

Fire & Ice

Opposites Attract

Almost Perfect

THE PEMBROOKE SERIES (a WILDFLOWER spinoff):

Sweet Sunshine

Coming Full Circle

A Broken Soul

CIVIL CORRUPTION SERIES

Corrupt

Defile (Declan and Tatum's story – coming 2018)

GIRL TALK SERIES:

Seducing Lola

Tempting Sophia

Enticing Daphne

Charming Fiona

STANDALONE TITLES:

Chance Encounters

Nightmares from Within

DEADLY LOVE SERIES:

Destructive

Addictive

CO-WRITTEN BOOKS:

Hustler – with Meghan Quinn

ABOUT THE AUTHOR

Born and raised around Houston, Jessica is a self proclaimed caffeine addict, connoisseur of inexpensive wine, and the worst driver in the state of Texas. In addition to being all of these things, she's first and foremost a wife and mom.

Growing up, she shared her mom and grandmother's love of reading. But where they leaned toward murder mysteries, Jessica was obsessed with all things romance.

When she's not nose deep in her next manuscript, you can usually find her with her kindle in hand.

Connect with Jessica now
Website: www.authorjessicaprince.com
Jessica's Princesses Reader Group
Newsletter
Facebook
Twitter
Instagram
authorjessicaprince@gmail.com

www.authorjessicaprince.com
authorjessicaprince@gmail.com

CPSIA information can be obtained
at www.ICGtesting.com
Printed in the USA
LVHW111103200920
666576LV00001B/101

9 781982 049225